I0532774

PEOPLE ARE GONNA DIE

J.C. TANNELLI

FRESH WIND COMMUNICATIONS
Published by Fresh Wind Publishing
2774 N Cobb Pkwy Suite 109-254
Kennesaw, GA 30152, USA

PEOPLE ARE GONNA DIE

PRINTING HISTORY
Fresh Wind Publishing eBook / November 2013
Fresh Wind Publishing Paperback / April 2014

Copyright © 2013 by J.C. Tannelli
Cover art by itstockphoto.com
Cover design by Karen O'Neal, Fresh Wind Design

ISBN: 978-0-9911741-1-9

… for Jordyn and Marissa

ACKNOWLEDGMENTS

Our perceived understanding of the justice system usually, and unfortunately, differs depending on demographics and our involvement or exposure to the "system". While we may be biased independently, I think our society, as a whole, would like to believe that our justice system is fair and impartial. Even though some crimes go unpunished and others get over-sentenced, we feel that it fights for the greater good. In writing this, I have tried to be unbiased as well.

Thanks to my father who inspired parts of key characters in this book as well as friends and other family members. You have made a difference in my life and I thought it fitting to give some of my characters a mixture of your characteristics. To my children: you're more important to me than you know.

I'd like to give great thanks to all the people at Fresh Wind Publishing for taking a chance with me on this first novel. Without their help at every turn, this book would not have been possible. I look forward to all the other books to come.

Special thanks to my editor, Liam O'Neal, who put up with my constant questions, late-night hypotheticals, and keeping me on track while giving me valuable insight and the motivation I needed to keep writing.

CHAPTER 1

"You're Not Good Enough Miller!" screamed Jared's Commanding Officer. *"The Marine Corps does not need losers like you. All you ever do is screw up."* Breathing heavily, Jared sat up in his darkened bedroom.

His wife Debbie still lay asleep beside him with her arm shielding her eyes. He was still having nightmares after fifteen years.

Jared walked to the kitchen to get a glass of water and on the way back to the bedroom, he stopped and checked on both of his little girls. Chelsea, the oldest at ten, had just moved into her own room a couple weeks ago. They had spent forever painting and decorating; nothing ever being good enough, the story of his life. His youngest Isabella, Bella for short, didn't like being in a room by herself and, at four years old, she usually got what she wanted. Which is why every other night, she was propped up between Mommy and Daddy. Seeing that they were still tucked in, Jared made his way back to the bedroom. Looking at the bedside clock, he saw that it was only 5:03 a.m. *Shit!* Having to get up at six anyway, there was no reason trying to go back to sleep. Another night with only a few hours of sleep.

It had been happening a lot lately. The stress, deadlines at the office, the kids. What he needed was a vacation but of course that was not going to happen. Jared was normally a forgive-and-forget, happy-go-lucky kind of guy, but this new anger he'd been feeling lately was getting stronger. He noticed himself being short to his wife and kids and getting easily agitated at work. These damn dreams occurred almost every night now. He needed to get away. No kids, no wife, no job, just him doing what he wanted. He just needed to be patient, things were about to change.

Lately, he was trying to engage himself in his new hobby as much as possible. Doing things he enjoyed solely for the sake of himself was a rarity. It didn't seem to help with the dreams, but it wasn't stressing him out either.

It seemed like his entire adult life, all he had ever done was work, pay bills, and provide for others. Nobody did anything on their own. Almost as if they didn't have their own thoughts. At work or home, it seemed that he was the only decisive person. Everybody had problems, but no solutions.

Jared fixed himself an onion *Lender's* bagel while he waited on the coffee to percolate. He absolutely had to have coffee throughout the day. He used the caffeine as medicine, an anti-depressant, to keep his thoughts positive and out of the gutter.

Sipping the hot, dark liquid was instantly gratifying. He knew that it took about twenty minutes for the caffeine to have an effect, but just knowing it was coming was medicinal in itself. Looking out the window, he thought about his activities as of late. The plan was in motion. Yes, thought Jared, his life was about to change. A lot of people's were.

CHAPTER 2

Linda Hunt had been working for the Federal Government for ten years. She started out working kidnapping and logistics, but had now been working with the D.T.U. (Domestic Terrorism Unit) for the past seven years. Being Assistant Special Agent in Charge was often hectic but a gratifying assignment. It took Linda only five years in D.T.U. to have made it to a supervisory level. She was the youngest field supervisor in the whole agency. Not to mention being a woman in her position made it that much more of an achievement.

Moving from the DC area to Atlanta to head up the D.T.U. had taken place only six months ago. Though most of the other agents were cordial enough, you could still sense some of them were reluctant to have a female boss in an otherwise dominant male workforce.

Pulling her government-issued Crown Vic into the parking lot of the Atlanta FBI field office, she noticed that despite jogging an extra two miles over her normal five mile morning run, she still managed to be the first of their team to arrive at the office. Her office, one of the nicer ones in the building, was on the fourth floor and had a decent view, if you admired street traffic.

"Good morning, Lucy. Any messages from yesterday afternoon?" Linda took a couple hours to herself yesterday due to an appointment with a local real estate broker. Living in apartments and condos most of her life, she was finally using her brains in buying a home, or at least trying to. Everything the broker showed her was either out of her price range or just too big. It was just her and her cat, Baby. What was she going to do with a five bedroom house?

"Mr. Fletcher called and also Mr. Dalton," said her secretary. "Mr. Fletcher said he wanted those write-ups as soon as possible and Mr. Dalton didn't say, just left a number." Lucy was her personal secretary and had been with the Bureau for close to twenty years. She was in her early fifties and wore her graying hair in a bun. Her daily attire was unflattering, ankle-length dresses which could double as funeral home wallpaper. While she wasn't a joy to work with, she was a competent assistant who practiced punctuality in her tasks. Linda was glad to have her.

"Thanks, Lucy. Well, let me get my butt to work. Don't want to keep the big guy waiting." The "Big Guy", Jeffery Fletcher, was the S.A.C. (Special Agent in Charge) over the Atlanta office and also her immediate supervisor. Though a competent administrator, he sometimes let her know he thought a woman's place was at home with the kids. As she sat at her desk, she dialed her boss's extension.

"Fletcher," he answered in his all-knowing tenor. "Hey, Boss. I wanted to let you know that I am finishing up the case notes in the Lopez case as we speak and will have them on your desk within the hour"

"You know, Ms. Hunt, I thought I gave you ample time when I asked for the reports to be on my desk by the end of the day yesterday, but…" Here it comes she thought. "I guess some individuals need extra time." He didn't need to say **women**; it was all over his tone.

"Yes, sir. Will not happen again, Mr. Fletcher".

"It had better not," he said hanging up.

What a fucking jerk!

The Lopez case had finally been wrapped up about a week ago. It had taken over two months, but they finally locked up close to thirty people involved in the mostly S-13 gang operation. Everything from smuggling and manufacturing drugs to murder and extortion. Hector "Angel" Lopez, the number one guy of the north of the border manufacturing and distribution, was nothing special to look at. If it wasn't for the $500 crocodile shoes, Dolce and Gabana slacks, and *Gucci* sunglasses, he would have been indistinguishable to the hundreds of thousands of Hispanic immigrants. Though Hector had no formal education, he was highly intelligent and spoke English with only a faint accent.

S-13, the "S" standing for Sureno or Southern, the 13 standing for the thirteenth letter of the alphabet "M", standing for Mexico or Mexican. Their financial backing came from the notorious "El Golfo" cartel, which at the same time was going to war with the Mexican government. The almost 100% illegal immigrant gang was highly organized and let nothing get in their way of producing and selling drugs. Their operations were funneling tens of millions of dollars back to the cartel. Not to mention, thousands of weapons. S-13 is very widespread in the U.S., from LA to Atlanta. Hell, even in South Dakota. They had loyal members everywhere. Most of their manufacturing was done in Arizona and New Mexico. We're talking about Methamphetamines. Ice. Speed. Glass. The drug was taking the world by storm. Meth is to the 2000s as cocaine was to the 80s.

Linda and her agents were brought into the investigation when "Angel" himself was spotted having a dinner meeting at the restaurant *On the Border* off Mansell Rd. in Roswell, GA. Roswell being a suburb of Metro Atlanta, Agent Hunt and company were called into action. They set up major surveillance and eventually followed him and six other less than conservative Hispanics to an apartment complex in Gwinnett County. After weeks of surveillance, Hunt brought a plan to her boss that would not only confiscate 3000 pounds of Meth, but would bring down the man Hector Lopez himself.

The S-13 in and around Gwinnett County was flooded with Meth. They were taking in close to 5 million in cash every week. With so much activity and a lot of the newer and inexperienced members running around and spending money, Linda knew it was only a matter of time before something broke. S-13 member Julio "Magic" Hernandez after buying his second vehicle in as many weeks, refused to stop after a patrol car tried pulling him over. The chase lasted a little over five minutes before Magic took a turn too fast in his new Lincoln Navigator and ran directly into the front of a *Five Guys* burger joint on Sugarloaf Parkway. After a short stint at Northside Hospital, Hunt got him into an interrogation room. Of course, he had nothing to say but after six hours of psychological and emotional manipulation, he began to break. The promise that his mom, wife, and brothers would be going to federal prison and that his kids would be raised by an American foster home was all he needed to find his voice and he knew a lot.

Their leader, Hector Lopez, like most smart dealers, never traveled with dope or large sums of money. His one fault was waiting close-by while his drugs were delivered to local, high-level S-13 members. He always met with them afterwards. He wanted to personally look into their eyes as he promised them and their family death if they made him look like a fool. It was at one of these meetings that Hunt and her team chose to take him down. That had been a week ago and while she was satisfied with the job they did, she wanted another case and wanted to do even better. It was ingrained in her to constantly prove she was able as any man, if not better.

CHAPTER 3

Mark Glover was the only one in his family smart enough to move away from their miserably cold hometown of Altamont, NY. After graduating from *Guilderland High School* just outside the small village of Altamont at 18, Mark was ready for a change. Even as a kid he hated the frigid weather of upstate New York. Mark was going south, how far south he didn't know, but Mark didn't care. He was out of there.

With no girlfriend and just over $4500 in savings, he and his trusty 1976 Pacer hit the road. His mother and father thought it better to give it some more thought and try some colleges that were not so far away, but they knew it was no use. His mind was made up, so they wished him well. Mark ended up stopping in Atlanta, Georgia. He was mesmerized by all the tall skyscrapers and friendly people. Not to mention it being 80° in the middle of November. He found a small place right down the street from the prestigious college of Georgia Tech. He'd heard of the school before and their huge football program with the *Yellow Jackets*, but while Mark was very athletic at 6 foot 2 inches and 200 pounds he just wasn't into competitive sports.

What Mark was into was building and creating things; figuring out development to make current stuff better. That and his fast, agile mind fit right in the engineering program *Georgia Tech* was known for. The fact that Mark did not know anyone in Atlanta and that his only hobby was hunting, he put all of his time and effort into his studies. Getting his Bachelor's degree in mechanical engineering in just under four years, he felt confident he could give the time and effort needed for his Master's degree. He ended up loving to work with the mechanics of metal and majored in metallurgy.

After college, Mark found a job as a gunsmith's assistant and was immediately absorbed in the mechanics and design that went into making firearms. To this day he still worked in that store, though the old man he started with had been gone for close to six years. Through no fault of the old man, business had been declining and the store needed an influx of money to modernize. Mark, after working there for five years, made the man an offer he couldn't refuse. As the new owner, he renamed the place *Glover Guns*.

He was sitting on a perch in the woods off a country road in Dalton Georgia. He looked at his watch and knew he had to get going. He would have liked to sit and wait for the big buck he had been hunting, but he had clients to meet back at the store and it would take him a good hour to make it back.

His love for machines and automobiles were no exception. Rarely driving anywhere but from home to work and back or when he went out to his little hunting cabin where he kept his old pickup, he drove his prized possession. A 1970 Chevelle SSLS6 with 454 cubic inches of pure brilliance, he loved the car like it was his child. Pulling the old Chevy into his owner's parking spot in front of the store, he could see one of his customers already waiting. Mark had movie star good looks, with high cheekbones and a chiseled jaw line. His eyes were a pale blue and his hair a thick, dark brown. He would tell you his smile was his best feature with luscious lips and perfect, white teeth.

"Good afternoon, Mrs. Collins," Mark said in greeting, turning on the smile.

"Oh, I know I'm a bit early," the old woman said, "but I wanted to try out another gun tonight. I'm thinking of buying bigger."

"Are you tiring of the *Glock* 17 already, Mrs. Collins?"

"Oh, no. I love my gun. But after seeing a movie the other night about Freddie something-or-other, I'm thinking of getting more firepower."

Such a sweet lady thought Mark, though at 63 years old, he was not sure how many more years she was going to know which end of the gun to point at the bad guys.

"Well, I promise you Mrs. Collins, if you keep shooting as well as you have lately, you won't need a bigger gun."

"Awww, such a flatterer, this one."

After talking with one of his employees for a few minutes, he took Mrs. Collins into the back for her target practice.

Originally the gun store did not have a range. But after acquiring a couple of design patents and making some money investing, Mark decided to make his large, rear parking area into a 40 yard, six stall shooting range. Since he was a professional marksman himself, he started teaching sessions by appointment as well.

His life seemed to be right on track. Good business, nice house, and he was financially secure. Yep, everything was peaches and cream, except he had not shared his life, or his bed, with anyone in over five years.

CHAPTER 4

He picked up his phone and called his wife to let her know he would be late coming home.

"This is the second time this week, Jared," Debbie said in an annoyed but concerned voice.

"I know, Babe. It's this new account. I'm just trying to catch up."

"Fine, I'll leave your dinner in the oven. Please try to hurry so you can say good night to the girls."

"I'll try. Give them my love. Bye now," Jared said, hanging up the phone.

Jesus! "Hurry home, Jared." "The girls this, the girls that," he said aloud, mockingly. Jared wished they would all get in a nice, big car accident and stay in comas forever. He was tired of their shit! Why would they not just leave him alone?

Jared ran a small marketing firm called *Point Marketing Group*. He had 12 employees and most days he would be able to leave by four and let his assistant manager close up. He could always stay later if needed, but he never went straight home regardless of what time he left the office. Jared would rarely make it home before eight any night. He did a number of things with the extra "Jared time," but at least a couple times a week, he would go shooting. He used to go to a local shooting range but for the past couple of years, he was really into rifles and they couldn't be used at the range. Driving around after work one day he found a remote spot that had an abandoned construction site. It looked to be where a good-sized subdivision had been planned. It was perfect! Just him and a mostly cleared, wooded area with no one around for miles. Jared set up several targets at two to four hundred meters. He loved having to factor in the wind and other variables to make the shot. The farther a target was away, the more fun it was.

His wife and kids knew nothing about this little hobby, nor did they know about the 18 guns he kept in his home office/shed. On this particular day he was definitely going to shoot. Going out there to the old construction site helped him calm down and helped him decipher the nightmares. The nightmares were never the same. It seemed the dreams were only there to remind him of his past failures and mistakes. He couldn't pinpoint when the dreams started, but it was sometime during his years at the *University of Georgia*.

He was never the most popular kid in school, but he never thought of himself as the least popular either. Sure, he was bullied throughout his middle and high school years, but everybody was right? He never let these things get to him though, he was a tough kid and his dad often told him so. He was not overly small at 5'9" and 150 pounds, but he was not big by any means. He was handsome enough with a pleasant face, dark brown hair and a nice smile. But the reason he didn't hit it off with the ladies, his dad said, was because of the goofy glasses. He said they made him look like a dork. Jared tried to go to class without them a couple times, but he figured he looked even dorkier bumping into everything. Girls did not matter to him anyway; the only thing that mattered to him was becoming a Marine. Nothing else mattered.

Jared had the toy guns, camouflage paint, and over 100 military figurines. At 15 years old, he found some other guys that were into military stuff. They would hang out and plan make-believe wars and run around with walkie-talkies. Yeah, he was great friends with Joe and Paul; at least, he thought so. They were close all through their sophomore and junior years. Then, as they started their senior year, it was like everything changed. Joe never wanted to hang out because he was always with his girlfriend and Paul earned a spot on the varsity football team, which was like a full-time job. At the time, Jared felt abandoned. He didn't understand, but did he let it show? No way! Because he was tough, he was going to be a Marine.

He was tough, but he couldn't run fast. He was tough, but not very strong. He was tough, but he wasn't coordinated. And when he failed to graduate basic training, his drill instructors were not surprised. Jared was devastated. He didn't show it on the outside; on the inside he was crushed. The next day, acting as if nothing had happened with an expressionless face, he told his mother he was applying to the *University of Georgia*. Jared was a just-above-average student, but scored well on his SATs. Within a month, he had an acceptance letter.

The day after he received his acceptance letter, his father had a heart attack and died later that night at the hospital. The funeral was a week later and Jared did not cry. He was not sad, he was angry. He was angry that he was not able to prove to his father how tough he was. He was angry his father would not be around to see him be important, somebody to remember. But just you watch and see, people would remember him.

CHAPTER 5

Getting out of the car and closing his automatic garage door, Mark walked the length of his driveway to collect his mail. He noticed the perfectly edged grass at the tip of the concrete where it met his driveway. Not one usually to be caught stereotyping, but the Hispanics who handled his lawn care were excellent workers. He had used the same crew for the past two years and not once had he ever had a reason to complain. Being conscious of that, he tipped them generously every week. His house was not the greatest on the street, but that was not a put down in his neighborhood. Mount Vernon Hwy. in Sandy Springs is a street that plainly has money. With the two-acre lots, sprawling mansions, meticulously cut lawns, they were not trying to hide it. Mark really just liked the privacy afforded to him by not being so close to his neighbors. That plus the fact that this particular house had a four-car garage that a previous owner had added to the property.

He only used half of the garage for his cars, a Lexus LS430 and, of course, his baby, the Chevelle. The other half, he turned into kind of a dream workspace. To anyone who might see the room it looked as if he had every tool known to man. The back and side wall were filled with tools on appropriate hooks with their outline drawn in marker, behind them two huge, floor-to-ceiling, rolling toolboxes acted like a partition separating the cars from the work area. This was the place in the house were Mark felt most comfortable. He often worked into the early morning hours, lost in his projects.

After getting the mail, he unlocked his front door and immediately heard a chaos of nails scratching and feet thumping as his two mixed Labs fought to see who was at the door. "I'm gonna have to get you guys to the vet for a checkup on your ears if you didn't hear me pull up. How're my babies? I bet you're about to piss in your pants. Let's go. Out, out."

As he led the dogs into the fenced backyard, he could tell they were excited he was home by the way they didn't even finish pissing before running back toward him, sprinkling pee all over the deck. Running into the grass so they would follow, he couldn't help but laugh. He loved his dogs, Cherish and Slick, a girl and a boy respectively. He had rescued both dogs from the pound shortly after Jenny died. Puppies at the time, both had grown into beautiful, healthy, smart dogs.

Mark went back inside and began to prep his dinner. Tripping over dogs' legs as they seemed to be glued to his own, he went ahead and fed them as well. This had become routine for Mark. He would look through a book of recipes, pick out his dinners for the week, and go straight to the grocery store with his list. He rarely went out and, subconsciously, he knew why. Every time he went to a restaurant and saw other couples dining, he would get a pain in his chest. He and Jenny used to love to go out and experience a well-prepared meal from some of the nicer restaurants. "A perfectly prepared meal is second only to sex," Jenny used to say. They had been engaged for only a week when she died.

They had dated for over two years and been living together for less than six months when Mark asked her to marry him. She was amazing! She was of average height with long, blonde hair and had the cutest dimples in the world. Her breasts were small and firm but went with her athletic frame. She had big, brown eyes and a friendly smile. A cheerful and very caring person, anybody who met her could tell right off the bat that she had a good soul and would make you feel better just being around her. Mark fell in love with her very easily. They met at the gym where she was teaching aerobics class. Literally bumping into her going out the door one day, he made it a point to see her again. So, there he was sitting in her next class. He stuck out like a sore thumb in an almost all-female class. Throughout the session, their eyes met each other's and a smile always appeared on Jenny's face.

When the class ended, Mark was purposely being a straggler. Surprisingly, she walked straight up to him with a serious face and said, "I don't know what's going on, but I doubt this is a coincidence after the other day," referring to their bumping into each other. Mark tried to cut in, but she waved him off. "And now that you've paid for the class, I hope you can still afford to take me to dinner sometime." She walked out then and in the parking lot, she handed him a slip of paper with her name and number.

"Hey," Mark shouted after her, as she walked to her car, "don't you want to know my name?"

"I already know your name, Mark Glover."

Standing there in a daze with a goofy smile on his face, she pulled up beside him in her little Mazda Miata and rolled down the window.

"You signed in at the beginning of the class. Talk to you later, Mark. Bye."

After that, they were like peas and carrots. They went to parks, lakes, and mountains. They drove race cars and bungee jumped. They did everything together and they never tired of each other's company. They were most definitely soul mates.

Then during a high-speed car chase with police, armed

robbery suspects in a Chevy Suburban hit Jenny's Mazda head-on at 70 miles an hour. She died instantly. Both suspects of the armed robbery lived. Mark was in hell. He felt like his life had ended along with Jenny's. He went to every court hearing of the perpetrators to seek some sort of justice, but after each defendant took negotiated pleas and were sentenced to 10 years in prison, it did nothing to subdue his pain. He was depressed for what seemed like forever, even went to a shrink. But by immersing himself in his work and letting the grieving process do its thing, he was able to slowly return to normal.

There was not a day that went by that he did not think of Jenny. He had been out on a couple dates that friends had set up. They were nice, attractive women and he recognized he was a man and had needs, but there was just no chemistry.

As Mark finished his dinner, he had one hand patting each dog's head as he stared out the dining room window. He had to accept that nobody would ever replace Jenny, but he couldn't just sit here every day with only dogs as his company. It wasn't healthy. "No offense," he said aloud to the unknowing Labs.

CHAPTER 6

She finally did it! She bought her first house. Don't let anyone tell you buying a home is easy. Linda thought today had been one of the most tedious and stressful days of her life. They wanted your initials and signature a hundred different times and each time you flipped another page to sign, it looked like and said the same thing the last page said.

She bought a nice three-bedroom, ranch-style home that sat at the crest of a steep hill about 100 yards off Abernathy Road. The neighborhood was a little pricey, but she did some research and saw that the home values in this area have consistently rose 4% each year. So she paid a little more than she wanted, but she felt it was a good investment. She really liked the Sandy Springs area. The crime rate was one of the lowest in the Metro Atlanta area. Originally considered to be North Fulton County, Sandy Springs was incorporated in 2005. And the seven years since then, it had become a sought after place for small businesses and raising families.

Standing in the living room of her new home, she thought about her pitiful collection of furnishings and how empty the house would look once she lugged her belongings from her apartment. Thinking she would go look at furniture this weekend, she remembered she had her bi-annual accuracy assessment this Saturday. All agents that were assigned supervisorial jobs had to show that their marksman skills were not slipping. So twice a year, they would go to Quantico to shoot for qualifications. Shit! She had not been in the range in months. While she was a decent shot and had never come close to not qualifying, she had to get to a range to get some practice in.

Looking in the Yellow Pages using her iPhone app, she saw that there were two ranges within 20 miles of her. One place, Hotshots, she knew was a franchise operation and from prior experience knew how busy they got. The other place, with a name like Glover Guns, had to be more of a "mom and pop" outfit. Hopefully, that would allow her some privacy so she could concentrate. On top of that, it was right here in Sandy Springs, only 3 miles from her house. Seeing their hours listed as being open until nine p.m., she thought she could still make it for an hour or so.

Only going to a shooting range, she opted to skip the shower and just go. Grabbing her Glock and throwing her hair into a ponytail, she was out the door.

CHAPTER 7

Sitting in a shed behind his house that he converted to an office, Jared checked for the second time to make sure the door was locked. Usually, he would come in here to sit and clean his guns in peace, but today was different. Today, he would put into action the first part of "The Plan". The plan to prove himself, to show his importance. He knew he was ready, he could feel it in his bones. It was time. Jared had called his assistant manager this morning and told him he would have to make do without him today, that he wasn't feeling well. He told his wife that he would be working on something very important from home today and that he would be in a constant conference call. He was not to be disturbed.

After several hours of planning and researching he put on his best suit and, not wanting to hear his wife's bitching, quietly as possible made his way to the car and drove off. Living off Roberts Drive in Sandy Springs, it was only a short drive to the Mansell "Park and Ride" Station.

MARTA, Metropolitan Atlanta Rapid Transit Authority, had been around for decades. Their reaches on the rail system went from North Sandy Springs all the way

South of Atlanta to Hartsfield–Jackson Atlanta International Airport. It also had an East/West line that stretched from Hamilton E. Holmes on Bankhead Highway all the way to Indian Trail, practically Stone Mountain. And that was just the trains. Their bus service was very elaborate having some 800 buses in service every day. Yes, MARTA would definitely be smart today.

Locking his car door and straightening his sunglasses, he walked to a waiting number 85 bus. He rode the 85 to North Springs Train Station and as he walked toward the platform, his watch read 12:05 p.m. Perfect. Behind his shades, he noticed all the cameras as he made his way to the train platform. These days, it seemed that no matter where you were, you were being watched. He got aboard the Southbound train, then switched trains at Lindbergh Station and proceeded to lower Chamblee. Chamblee Station was off of Peachtree Industrial Blvd in the heart of what he called 'Carland'. Every car dealership known to man was out there, Lexus, Chevy, Porsche, Audi, etc. It was time to go shopping.

It was a brief walk before Jared made it to the side of the Toyota dealership. He walked onto the lot from the far side of the showroom. When the salesman saw the way he was dressed, he would assume Jared drove up and had started to look around. He looked to be browsing, but in fact he knew exactly which car he wanted. As he made it within 30 yards of the showroom building, a smiling, young man in a suit was walking toward him. He introduced himself as Corey. He was a blonde, thin, young man no more than 25 and asked if he could be of any assistance.

"Well Corey, I'll save you and me a bunch of time and cut to the chase being as I'm only on my lunch break." Cory did not even blink. "I'm interested in a silver Camry SE," Jared continued, "and I will be trading in a 07' Honda Accord with roughly 50,000 miles on it."

As he said this, Corey almost started drooling. He knew

for a fact they had two silver Camry SE in stock, just a row over. Sales were never this easy, today was his lucky day.

"I'd like to actually purchase tonight after work, but I thought I'd go ahead and get things started as I had some extra time".

Jared thought he had lost the salesman for a second. Corey just stood there smiling. He snapped out of it after a second and said, "Sir, you've come to the right place. If you could just follow me right over here." They walked directly to the silver Camrys. "Both of these," Corey said, pointing with his hands, "are the Sport Editions as you requested. If you give me just a second, I'll go get some keys." Corey left at a jog. Easy as pie thought Jared. He couldn't wait to see the look on the kid's face.

As Corey ran back, he used the key fob to unlock one of the Camry's doors. Jared got into the driver's seat as Corey came to the side of the car and handed him the key.

"You came on a great day, sir. Today is the last day of our mega sale, which will get you a $2500 rebate."

Paying absolutely no attention to Corey, Jared started the car and started messing with the knobs, trying to find a radio station. AC/DC's "Highway to Hell" came through the car's speakers. Perfect, thought Jared. He closed the driver's door in Corey's face in the middle of him explaining how he was sure he would get him the greatest deal on Jared's trade-in. Whatever.

He put the car in gear and swiftly backed out of the parking space. Corey was saying something, trying to get his attention, but Jared left the dealership, taking a left toward I-285. As he floored the accelerator, he thought he caught a glimpse of Ol' Corey in his rearview, standing there smiling and dumbfounded. Drumming his fingers along to the beat of the old rock classic, he took the 85 North ramp at Spaghetti Junction and knew he would be in Gwinnett and out of Dekalb County, in seconds.

Picking a Toyota Camry was not a random choice. It is one of the most widely sold cars in the U.S. and the less you stick out, the easier you go unnoticed. After getting a bite to eat off Jimmy Carter Blvd., Jared gassed up the Camry and drove to the nearest apartment complex. Finding another Camry wasn't gonna be hard, thought Jared already spotting two, but he wanted the same color and year as well. It took only a couple more minutes to find a replica of Jared's Camry. Pulling behind the car and kneeling between the two cars, he took the tag from the parked car and got back in his own with the tag in hand. He drove further down the road before attaching it to his car.

By this time, he was ready to head toward home. After depositing the Camry in an apartment complex close to the MARTA Park and Ride, he walked to the station and picked up his car. The plan was in motion. People are gonna die… lots of them.

CHAPTER 8

Man, was he tired! He had stayed up until almost 5 this morning trying to alter the design of the classic bullet. Mark already held a patent to a similar design that he called the "Fintip." Generally, the bullet's tip has its sides engraved with four meticulously measured fins or wings that help guide the bullets flight using less of its energy staying on course. Mark opened an hour earlier than his usual 11 a.m. He knew he had at least two regular customers coming in before lunch. On top of that, it was time to do inventory.

He was mildly peeved toward the end of the day when he saw Jimmy Merrit, his 7 p.m. appointment. Merrit, a 40-ish, cocky guy from Jersey, was also not the easiest guy to get along with. He wore these gaudy, gold chains and a hairstyle that showed he still thought he was in his 20s. He was one of those guys who knew absolutely everything, but somehow always needed your help. His choice of weapon matched his personality, a .50 caliber Desert Eagle. A beautiful work of art, but with bullets at a buck and a quarter apiece and a kick like a mule, it wasn't a great choice for target practice. As Jimmy walked up to the counter with some remark about the weather, a gorgeous redheaded woman walked through the front door. She was tall and trim with shoulder length, wavy hair pulled back into a ponytail. She was new to the store, no way Mark would have forgotten this woman. As Jimmy went on and on about nothing at all, Mark bobbed his head feigning his attention, while watching the redhead. Her walk was that of a runner, coming down onto the heel and rolling off the ball of her foot. Her eyes look to be Hazel and her mouth was a thing of beauty. She had those big, pouty lips that begged to be kissed.

There was nothing overly attention-grabbing about her, but she radiated a certain confidence that it seems she deserved. She wore nothing suggestive of her body's shape either. She had on jogging sweats and her hair was pulled back into a smart ponytail. Her face, in a word, was 'cute'. Very tomboyish, but there was also something seductive hidden in there. Shaking him from his daze, Jimmy was excited to get started. Uncomfortable with the power just seeing this woman had on him, he walked to the back giving Mr. Merrit the usual safety instructions. A woman hasn't had that kind of effect on him since…

About two clips into Merrit's practice the mystery woman came into the back and, shooting Mark a quick smile, stepped into the stall next to them. Giving Merrit instruction on stance and firing technique for the next clip, he saw the woman had already donned her safety gear and began firing a midsized Glock. Slowly at first, then pumping the last six rounds out quickly. As she called her target back to assess it, Mark saw his opening.

"That's some pretty nice shooting," Mark said turning a smile all the way up. When she didn't reply right away, his smile plunged and he quickly switched gears. "I'm sorry, I didn't mean for that come out like some kind of pickup line. My name is Mark Glover," he half screamed over the gunfire. "I own the place." Shaking his outstretched hand and yelling, she gave her name as Linda Hunt and they both signaled to each other that they would talk in the store afterwards.

That went great, thought Mark. Real smooth, trying to have a conversation in middle of what sounded like World War II. Linda Hunt, was it Ms. or Mrs. Hunt? He didn't see any ring. Thinking himself crazy for even wondering that, having just met the woman, he concentrated on his client. He was probably missing the whole target with his goliath pistol.

After ten clips and over $100 in ammo, he escorted Jimmy out the back so they could talk about his session. Mark was trying to expedite things in case Linda came out before he finished. Listen to him, it was Linda already. He didn't even know this woman!

"Good shooting, Jimmy. You make shooting that huge gun look easy." Stroke the ego, stroke the ego.

"It's my arms, I've been doing a lot of curls in the gym." Can you believe this guy?, he thought. Out loud, he told them he would think about that himself and said goodnight.

He didn't have to wait long before Linda came out. To his surprise, walking over, she called his name.

"Mr. Glover?"

"Please, call me Mark."

"Okay, Mark. And it is Linda." They shook hands again for some reason or another. "Mark, could you sell me five boxes of Remington 40 Cal?"

"A woman after my own heart. Sure, hollowpoint?"

"Standard is fine. I'll only be using them for target practice."

"You'll be practicing here, I hope?"

"Actually, I'll be using them out of state at a work-related event."

"Work-related?" Mark said surprised. "What exactly do you do, if you don't mind my asking?"

"I'm in law enforcement." Her lack of the elaboration told him she did mind.

"Well, we can certainly do that for you. Are you new to

the area? I've never seen you in here before is why I ask."

"Actually, I found a home off Abernathy Road. I'm very excited. I moved not too long ago from the D.C. area."

"How do you like the area?" Mark asked.

"Sandy Springs seems great. Very friendly."

"That it is. I've been in town almost 12 years now and I absolutely love it." Go for it, Mark thought. "Hey, being that you're new in town, I'd love to show you around sometime when you aren't busy."

Stuttering, not expecting to be asked out, she came up with, "Oh,um, well I haven't even moved my stuff into my house yet and things at work are pretty hectic, maybe…" She didn't know why she was making excuses. It's not like she had anything going on in her personal life.

Taking the hint, Mark interrupted to soften the blow to his ego. "Hey, I know how it gets. Tell you what, here's my card. I'm sure I'll see you in here again and if you ever change your mind, let me know."

"Okay Mark, I will and thanks again for the ammo."

"My pleasure. Have a good night."

"You, too. Bye."

Mark was glad nobody was around to witness the exchange because he totally got shut down. Was it something he said? Did he have something in his teeth? She probably had a boyfriend, that was it. He felt like such a putz. He noticed she didn't have any makeup on and didn't wear any jewelry. Not that she needed any. She had this tomboy thing going on that for some reason, on some level, made her that much more attractive. Well, she was gone now. At least he would probably see her again knowing she only lived down the street. This was abnormal for Mark to be obsessing over a woman he just met, or any woman at all for that matter. Mark just needed some sleep. That's it, thought Mark, a good night's sleep.

CHAPTER 9

What the hell was the matter with her? There was this nice, good-looking guy asking her out and she freaks out and puts up a wall. He wasn't asking her to marry him, only to take her out and show her around. Man, she blew it big time. She hadn't dated anyone since she moved to Atlanta over six months ago. She had been so engulfed in her career she had not even thought of it. Now that she didn't have anything pressing on her plate, why shouldn't she go out? There had been a handful of relationships in Maryland, but all the guys seemed needy and couldn't deal with her commitment to the job. She remembered when she first started with the Bureau someone told her "good luck" with any relationship she might be in because "you just got married to the Federal Government." And up to this point it seemed to be true, too.

Just then her phone rang and she looked at the caller ID. It was her best friend, Beth. She felt guilty. She had been taking their friendship for granted. Being busy, she hadn't talked to Beth in a while.

Answering, she said, "Hey, Sweetie," in an exaggerated spunk trying to dodge what she knew was coming.

"Don't, 'hey sweetie, me! You haven't returned my calls

in two weeks. So, until you make it up to me, you're on my shitlist."

"I'm really sorry, Beth. I…"

"What am I saying? I can't stay mad at my sister. How are you girl?"

"Awww, I love you too," said Linda. "Actually, right this minute I'm sulking over freaking out on a perfectly decent guy who asked me out."

"Well, don't leave me in suspense, is he hot?"

"He's actually great looking."

"So what's wrong? Was he a cocky jerk?"

"No, he was very polite," said Linda. "He was confident, but not overly so. He was the owner of the gun store I was buying ammo at."

"So, let me get this straight. A hot, confident, gentlemen, who owns his own business no less, asks you out and you say no? What the hell is the matter with you? I'm going to have to catch a plane down there and see if he likes blondes."

Both of them were laughing.

"Yeah, I think I'm going to go back up there early next week and see if his offer still stands."

"There you go, girl! Go out there and get you some booty."

"Oh, stop, Beth! He does seem like a cool guy though."

"Don't take too long baby girl, because like I said, I can catch a plane. A good man is hard to find. I'm living proof."

Beth seemed to be with a new guy every month. She usually said the guy was too immature or too needy or even "sucks in the sack". Linda didn't know exactly what kind of man her friend needed, but she was sure that at the rate she was going through them, she had a good chance to find him. Their friendship was strange. They had next to nothing in common. A totally different view of how the world works. Yet for whatever reason, they just clicked. The whole "opposites attract" thing she guessed.

In high school it was the same way. Beth was a cheerleader and Linda was the jock. Barely acknowledging each other before, both of them went out with the same guy and later found out it was also at the same time. They became friends by publicly putting the guy in his place and sharing insults about the jerk. They ended up going to college at different schools. Linda graduating from U.V.A. and Beth dropped out at Virginia Tech. They stayed in touch though, getting together a couple times a year. They even roomed together right after Linda graduated. Then the FBI recruited her and she had been pretty much hit or miss to everybody since.

Remembering she would be up that way for qualifying, Beth and she made plans to meet up. They went on talking and catching up and Linda told her about closing the Lopez case and buying the new house. "That settles it," said Beth. "I'm coming down there. I need a vacation anyway. Since you'll be up here to see me this weekend, not next weekend but the weekend after, I'm flying down. You can pick me up from the airport and I'm not taking no for an answer."

No matter how brash and out-of-control Beth got, Linda could never get mad at her. She had a soft spot for her buddy.

"Okay, Beth. I'll pick you up."

"And you better hurry and make up with the hunk at the gun store, too because when I come down, I want to meet him." With that, they said their goodbyes.

After catching a 7 a.m. flight to D.C. and going through her qualifying, she had to summon all her strength for a night out with Beth. Christ, could that woman drink! On her flight back to Atlanta on the next morning her body was telling her that she couldn't drink. She felt like absolute shit! She only had two drinks and two shots in the course of the whole night. What a lightweight!

As the plane touched down and taxied to the terminal, Linda was already planning a night of relaxation and recovery. A nice, long, hot, bubble bath and about 10 hours of sleep should do the trick. For what it's worth, the trip was a success. She had a great night out dancing with Beth and she shot a little better than usual with an advanced grade marksman rating.

After retrieving her dirty Honda out of airport parking, she made her way to her old apartment. She still had not moved anything to the new place yet, but the utilities would be turned on tomorrow morning. There wasn't enough stuff to hire movers so she would just move stuff gradually for the next couple days, prioritizing as she went. Anything that she was keeping that was too heavy for her to move would either get broke down or left there. The mattress and box spring were old enough to trash. This was her new beginning. A new city, a new house, and if she played her cards right, maybe even a new boyfriend.

After packing a couple boxes, she did as she planned and took a long bath. Putting on panties and a T-shirt after brushing her teeth, she set her alarm and flipped on the TV. After settling in, she channel-surfed to the evening news. Something was happening. At the bottom of the screen it read "shooting in Sandy Springs." Shootings? As in plural, thought Linda. She turned up the volume and caught the reporter saying "is not clear at this time Bob, but what we do know is that there are two victims at two different locations that were shot. I'm getting information now that both victims did indeed die from their injuries." Holy shit, two people shot to death in Sandy Springs? She moved here because it was safe! As the newscast went on, they were interviewing someone. The name on the bottom of the screen read Detective Brennan of the Sandy Springs Police Department. He was saying, "At this time, early in the investigation, we have little info to give. A male and a female victim have been shot and killed at different locations on Roswell Road. They took place half-mile apart from one another and at this time, we are unaware of any connection. The names of the deceased will remain confidential until we notify the next of kin. We will have more as information becomes available. Thank you."

Which translates to Sandy Springs PD doesn't have a clue what's going on. Even though the homicides were Sandy Springs PD's jurisdiction, she would get all kinds of reports on the shootings the minute she set foot in the office. Tomorrow would definitely be eventful with two people dead in the affluent Sandy Springs. Getting up to check the locks on the doors and windows of her apartment, she also took her .40 caliber Glock out of the nightstand and slipped in under her pillow. You could never be too safe.

CHAPTER 10

At 6 p.m., in the middle of rush hour, Officer Santiago was in the vicinity of a 'shots fired' call at a local supermarket. Immediately after that, another "shots fired' report came through his radio at a different supermarket but very close to the first. He radioed back en route to the closest store to make sure he heard correct and it was confirmed to be two separate calls. Arriving at the closer of the two grocery stores in less than two minutes, he was the first unit on scene. There was a huge gathering of people around the entrance to the store. What the hell was going on? The people heard the siren as he pulled up and they started to disperse.

As he got out of his cruiser, he saw a body lying in a pool of blood just outside the entrance/exit doors. Backing the crowd away while looking for possible perps, he called in the situation and asked for the EMTs. Moments after replacing his mike, he saw an ambulance and another patrol car coming his way. He tried to find a pulse on the victim, though by the amount of blood and a huge hole in the otherwise attractive woman's head, he knew she was gone. Letting the EMTs at it, he went to his fellow officer and told him what he found. They both then taped off the area with crime scene tape.

Meanwhile, exactly 800 meters away at the entrance of a rival grocery store, Officer Mears of the Sandy Springs PD was looking down at the body of a middle-aged male. This victim was apparently coming out of the store, seeing that there were bags of groceries on either side of the body. When he had first pulled up, he too checked for a pulse, even with the huge pool of blood around his head. He gave up when upon closer inspection he noticed almost half his head was missing.

Homicide Detective Thomas Brennan had spent his career investigating gruesome murders all around the city of Atlanta. After 10 years of shaking his head, he wanted to try something a little more watered down. He started working homicide for the Sandy Springs PD a little over two years ago. This was more his speed, in two years' time they had only three homicides. Due to that statistic, he found himself working all types of crimes. He liked the fact of not having to notify people that their father, daughter, or brother was just murdered. Now it looks like he was back in that business.

Brennan pulled into the Kroger parking lot at the 4000 block of Roswell Road. It was a high traffic area that was pretty much the center of Sandy Springs. The ramps for Interstate 285 were a block down and there wasn't an inch of empty street frontage. This part of Roswell Road was packed with plazas and freestanding businesses. You could get a taco here and pay your cell phone bill next door. You could get your nails done and pick up your dry cleaning without moving your car. It was free enterprise at its best.

The crime scene was completely taped off and the officers had directed all the customers parked in the lot out a side exit. There were a few cars left in the lot, but not many. He ducked under the yellow tape and walked over to where the victim lay. The crime scene people were there in full force taking pictures and collecting evidence. As Brennan bent down to get a closer look at the body, an officer walked over with a grim face.

"What do you got for me Santiago?" Brennan said.

"Her name is Jamie Cantrell and according to her ID, she was 38 years of age. I've been talking to a couple people that were near her when it happened and nobody saw or heard anything except her just falling over."

Brennan stood up as the officer was called away. He looked around and thought about how it could have played out. Someone walking behind her with a silenced weapon? Surely someone would have seen that. Nobody heard a shot. So, there was a silenced weapon involved some kind of way. He took out his notepad and scribbled, "Professional hit? Why? Where does she work?". Just then his phone vibrated. Looking at the screen he saw it with his fellow Detective Jenkins.

"What's up?"

"Are you at the first shots fired call?"

"Sure am and it's a homicide."

"Well, I'm a half a mile down Roswell Road at the Publix and I've also got a homicide."

"Stay there, I'm on my way," Brennan said sprinting to his car.

Two homicides this close on the same night had to be connected. He drove the half-mile and was greeted with an almost identical scene like the one he just left. He walked over near a male shooting victim where Jenkins was standing and looked at the victim.

"Some mess huh?" Said Jenkins "I've talked to everybody and…"

"Let me guess. No one heard or saw anything. He just collapsed with a hole in his head."

"How the hell…"

"I've got the same thing at the Kroger."

"Same shooter?" asked Jenkins.

"Couldn't be. The calls came in second apart, remember?"

"Two shooters?"

"That's what we're gonna find out."

CHAPTER 11

Look at the idiots! Jared was watching a previously recorded newscast from the security of his office. Sandy Springs PD didn't know squat, he thought laughing. They would never figure it out, at least not in time for the next "lucky" victims.

Next time would be a real masterpiece, too. He had gone over the plans in his head a thousand times. People would always remember this one. It would go down in history books. Jared felt so good he was going to go inside. Entering the side door into the living room, he saw both his little girls propped up in front of the TV watching some cartoon.

"Daddy!" both little girls screamed as he came in. Chelsea, his oldest, was pulling his arm trying to show him something.

"Dad, Dad, come look at my report card."

His wife was smiling at him as he allowed himself to be steered into his daughter's bedroom.

"Look Dad, all A's and one B."

"Let me see that," he said with a non-believing face. "I don't know. This looks like a forgery."

"No, it's not Dad. No, it's not." Chelsea playfully

whined.

Still carrying on, Jared called for his wife.

"Debbie, have you seen this? I think I see some erase marks here."

Coming into the room his wife said that she was very proud of Chelsea and believed they were real.

"OK. If you say so. Mom." Rubbing Chelsea's head he told her he was very proud of her. Not to be outdone by her sister, Bella, his youngest, started tugging him toward her room.

"Daddy, Daddy, rook what I did."

Upon entering her room she ran to her coloring station and held up this huge 2' x 3' color drawing of their family standing out in front of what he supposed was their house.

"See, Daddy. Isn't it great?"

"That's nice, Bella. It's big, too. How long did it take?"

"A rong time, Daddy."

She pronounced it 'wrong', that meant 'long'. Isabella had a slight speech impediment for all her L's came out sounding like R's.

"I bet it did take a long time, Baby. It's beautiful. Do you want to hang it up on your corkboard?"

"No, not yet. It isn't finished."

Just then Debbie announced dinner was ready. Leaving their Dad and running to the dining room like he was never there, he followed and sat down at the prepared table.

After dinner, his little girls took baths and he tucked both of them in their beds. Coming back to the living room, his wife was smiling and reaching out for a hug. As he went to her, she said, "I don't know what happened, but I'm glad your back to the old you." Looking at her quizzically, she continued saying, "You look happy again and relieved."

"Really?" Jared said. "Well, I did finish with that new account and finally have the numbers where I want them at the office."

"Whatever it is, Jared. I'm happy for you. Sometimes you walk around the house like you're mad at the world. I just want to remind you of how much the girls and I love you. You are a good father."

"Thank you, honey. That means a lot to me. I know I've been in a funk lately but that's over now. You know, Debbie. Maybe we can find a babysitter tomorrow night and you and I can have a date night."

"Aww, that sounds wonderful, Jared! I can't wait! I know just the person who can watch the girls."

"It's settled then. Tomorrow, 7 p.m. It's a date."

Coming out of their embrace, Jared sat down in his recliner and started flipping through the channels on the TV.

"Oh, honey," she said walking back in the room from the kitchen, "did you hear about the two people that were shot today?"

"What?" Jared said, sounding surprised.

"Yeah, they said it was just random violence."

"Well, I'll be. That's just terrible."

CHAPTER 12

Brennan was tired, angry, and stumped. It was exactly what people figured from watching the news. He didn't know what was going on. As far as he could tell, neither victim knew each other nor did they interact through employment or have any of the same friends. They didn't look to be connected in any way. He interviewed over 30 so-called witnesses through both scenes combined. The witnesses' statements varied but pretty much concurred that each victim was just walking along and wham, they keeled over. A couple of witnesses that were standing close to the victims were sprayed with blood and hit with brain and skull fragments. They were detained until evidence could be recovered. There was also a video camera that was recording above an ATM, close to one of the entrances. Viewing the video earlier, the recording gave no indication of new evidence besides having a partial shot of one on the bodies falling.

At this point, Brennan could only come to the conclusion that (A) the shootings were connected, (B) there were at least two suspects, one at each scene, and (C) the shots look to have come from the parking lot. He was on his way now to the Crime Scene Investigation Unit, hoping they had some leads. At 11 a.m. the day after the shootings, the Sandy Springs CSI was a beehive of activity.

Walking up to a friend of his in the unit, investigator Maria Flemez gave him a sympathizing look.

"Please Maria, tell me you got something."

"Well, the truth is between pathology and us; we can tell you a lot but I don't know what we have to say will lead you to who's responsible."

"I'll settle for anything," Brennan said. "Give it to me."

"Okay. First, I can tell you by the splatter pattern that the bullet was shot from an elevated position."

"Elevated? You mean like shooting over the top of their car or from the top of the grocery store?"

"No, depending on the distance of the shot, I'd say like shooting from a three- or four-story building."

"Are you saying this was a long distance shot? Like with a rifle?"

"Definitely. Look at this," Flemez said, walking over to a lab work station. "This is a fragment we got from the Cantrell scene. We dug it out of the trunk of a small Dogwood that caught the ricochet off the store wall. It's a special bullet made of a lead titanium mixture." She showed him the small, deformed piece of metal.

"Special. Like I can track its origin, special?"

"It's a possibility, but I doubt it. They're sold commercially to the public. The titanium rounds are specifically designed for rifles, that I can tell you."

This just wasn't making any sense he thought.

"The rifle that took that shot," Maria continued, "was high powered. As for the caliber, I'd say big, but you'd have to check with T.J. to be accurate."

"I'm going to do that now. Thanks again, Maria. You're a lifesaver. This is a huge help."

"Any time, Brennan."

A rifle? Long-distance shot? Now, he was totally confused. T.J. Barber was 61 years old and had been a medical examiner for close to 25 of those years. 15 of those years he spent in Lancaster, California. He and his wife, Donella moved there soon after he graduated Med school at UCLA. He was offered a job there as an Assistant Medical Examiner and Pathology being his course of study, he jumped at the opportunity. His wife, Donella died of an aneurysm at the young age of 41. There were too many memory triggers left in Lancaster after that, so T.J. just decided to up and move one day. For no particular reason, T.J. chose Alpharetta, Georgia.

For three years, he had no will to work. But, shortly after Sandy Springs became a city in 2005, he saw that Fulton County had an opening for an Assistant M. E. With his savings dwindling, he applied for the position and began working at Northside Hospital serving North Fulton County. Six months after he started, he met a sweet Southern Belle named Faith and she immediately brought T.J. out of his depression. There was an instant connection and they wasted no time tying the knot. After five years, she gave him reason to smile. T.J., a tall thin man with heavy, graying, dark hair walked around with what seemed like a perpetual smile and seemed pleased with his occupation. Brennan didn't know how. No stranger to dead bodies, he still got queasy every time he came to the morgue.

Getting off the elevator on the basement level of Northside, he strode to the left until he came to the door that read Timothy Joseph Barber, Assistant Medical Examiner. Soon after his knock, T.J.'s thin figure appeared with a smile as if he had just won the lottery.

"Detective Brennan," T.J. said offering his hand. "I guess it's a good thing I haven't seen you in a while. Having said that, how are you?"

"Well, right now, T.J., I hate my job. But later, when I catch the guys responsible for this, I'll be doing great."

"I can appreciate that. I was actually just on the phone with investigator Flemez. Such a nice person, by the way. Comparing our notes, we've established that in all probability, at least for the Cantrell woman, the caliber of the bullet was a .308. In the case of Mr. Driver, the wound pattern is almost identical. But, if it wasn't also a .308 caliber gun, it was something very similar. Without a fragmentation, I can't be positive. As you know," T.J. continued, "in gunshot cases, we pathologists are not able to gather too much information. I wish there was more I could give you, but with these victims it's pretty clear-cut. One minute they were here with us. The next, they were not. It's very sad, Detective. I hope you catch those responsible."

CHAPTER 13

Linda had been on the phone all morning, still wrapping up loose ends with the Lopez case. Now that Lopez and company had lawyered up, they were filing all kinds of preliminary motions trying to get their client off. Linda was talking to an array of organization commanders whose units were involved in the case, making sure all their ducks were in a row. The two killings in Sandy Springs, dubbed "The Supermarket Slayings", were getting a ton of publicity. The pressure would come down the bureaucratic ladder if the locals didn't figure something out soon. If they didn't make some progress, she knew the Feds would be involved soon and it would be her unit.

Driving to her old apartment to complete packing some stuff, she was racking her brain at how she was going to approach Mark Glover. She felt like an idiot. Maybe she should just go up to him and say, "You know, I'm sorry I was such a prude bitch last time, but I'd like to date you now." Mark was a really good- looking guy. He reminded you of one of those Ralph Lauren Polo ads that seem to always be set on some beach. Those piercing, blue eyes with that chiseled jaw line and high cheekbones. He was well over 6 feet tall and looked to be in pretty good shape by the way his muscles pressed against the fabric of his shirt. Damn! She was getting turned on just thinking of the guy. How could she be this attracted to the guy and at the same time turn him down flat like he was some kind of begging bum? Is she so involved in her career that she just tunes everything out? Even hot guys? She thought about his offer to show her around. Maybe she would just call him to ask his opinion about a place and he would take the hint. Yeah, right. He would probably tell her to Google it.

After bringing over a couple boxes to the new place, she showered then took over an hour figuring out what to wear. She decided she would just try her luck with going back to his store for some pretend target practice. Dressed in her best, not to mention tightest, designer jeans and a clingy sleeveless blouse, she made the short trip to Glover Guns. This was crazy! She didn't even know if he was there. That thought quickly left as soon as she pulled up to the store and saw Mark's handsome face through the window. Breathe, Linda. As if she wasn't nervous enough already, she walked through the door and a loud chime announced her arrival. Hey everybody, look at me! Mark looked over and their eyes met. She tried to pull off a 'Hi, nice to see you' smile, but she was sure it looked more like an 'I'm embarrassed and trying to look normal' smile.

Walking over, Mark said, "Nice to see you again, you look absolutely incredible, by the way. Are you on your way somewhere?"

Now she was embarrassed. What was she thinking? Who puts on makeup to shoot a gun? Recovering, she said, "Oh, I met up with a friend earlier and…" His face showed nothing, but she knew he wasn't buying it. Dropping her voice she continued, "you know what, that's a lie." Mark looked unfazed, but there was a smile at the corners of his mouth. Biting her lip, she said, "I actually drove up here to ask if your offer is still on the table."

Stone faced, Mark said, "What offer?" Oh my God, thought Linda! Cheeks at full flush she started to stutter a reply when Mark interrupted. "I'm absolutely joking,

Linda. I would love to show you around." Linda's exhalation was audible.

"That was for not taking me up on my initial offer," Mark said, offering the most seductive smile she had ever seen. "I'll tell you what. It's a nice night out, how about we put the top down and I take you to the greatest steakhouse this side of Texas."

"That sounds great, I've been eating salads and TV dinners for what seems like forever."

"Give me just a minute," Mark said as he walked over to one of his employees.

Breathing somewhat normal now, Linda watched as Mark was obviously relaying some instructions. Linda had butterflies in her stomach. It had been six months since she had been out with a guy and she was nervous. Even so, when Mark looked at her, it had an uncanny calming effect. It was his eyes, she decided. Eyes and mouth. The way he looked right into her while his lips were fixed as if he knew something she didn't.

A couple minutes later, they were walking outside and getting into a beautiful, old, muscle car. She didn't know much about cars but she knew nice when she saw it. The car was fire engine red with white stripes running the length of the car over the hood and trunk. The convertible top was white and Mark was lowering it.

"This is my baby," Mark said. "I know it's very stereotypical, the whole guys and cars thing, but some people like art on canvas, some like art etched in stone, and I like art in mechanics." Looking into her eyes he hit her with another one of those million-watt smiles.

"It's beautiful," Linda said.

"Thank you, but she is no competition with you here."

With Linda blushing, he started the big motor and pulled out onto Roswell Road. Mark then took his phone out and excused himself for a moment. He spoke briefly and tucked the phone away.

"Sorry about that. Just making sure we had some seats.

I'm a semi-regular at the place were going to and while they're not by reservation only, they do get packed pretty early. So, Linda, how do you like your new place? Is Sandy Springs any different from back home?"

"Well, back home is a suburb of DC and the first thing that comes to mind is the people down here. To offer another stereotype with Southern hospitality, it seems to be true. People here not only seem nicer, but as a whole, they seem happier and more content. Sandy Springs seems to hold a higher standard than where I grew up. Brookridge, outside of DC, while about the same demographically, it seems less couth in comparison. Does that make sense?"

"Absolutely," Mark said. "I'm originally from upstate New York and while I've been in Georgia the better part of 20 years now, I remember being unarmed by people's generosity here. I didn't make it up to Sandy Springs until after college. I couldn't afford it. When I started making some money at the store and moved up from the city, I knew I'd found home." Pulling into the parking lot of the restaurant Mark said, "You're gonna love this place." At the valet station Linda and Mark's doors were open for them. Grabbing a ticket, they made their way inside.

"The name doesn't fit the establishment, does it?" asked Mark.

"Not at all."

And it truly didn't. The big red and white sign outside read 'Ruth's Chris Steakhouse' and conjured up visions of cowboy hats and rodeos. Inside though, it was the absolute opposite. Everything seemed to be dark mahogany and shiny brass. Glazed glass separated seating areas and elaborate, crystal chandeliers hung from high ceilings.

A host walked them to a long, heavily lacquered, mahogany bar with leather stools. "Please have a refreshment," said their host, "while your table is prepared."

Sitting side-by-side on the stools, Linda ordered a

CHAPTER 14

Brennan was on his way to the crime scenes. After leaving T.J.'s office, he spoke with Flemez and asked some questions that would give the direction from which each shot was taken. The investigator thought the shots had come from a pretty high elevation and Brennan knew the area. There were only a couple options.

Arriving at the Cantrell scene, he sat in his car more or less right in front of where the body had laid. She was shot in the back of her head with the slug exiting around her cheekbone area, or what was left of it, a third of her face was missing. Looking in the direction of where the shot would have come from, there were only two places the shot could have been made within 500 yards. The first was a cell phone tower which was around 150 yards away. He looked up at the 300 foot tower and decided it was definitely a possibility. The only security was an 8 foot, chain-link fence surrounding the base with a No Trespassing sign. Even though it would be awkward to set up for the shot, there were plenty of valid places once up the ladder.

The other structure was much farther away. It was around 400 yards from the entrance of the grocery store.

He didn't know too much about shooting rifles, but it seemed like a "long shot" to him. The structure was a six-story parking deck that serviced two sprawling office complexes that sat on the same road as the grocery stores. Driving to the entrance ramp, he saw a sign showing the hours of operation. Beyond the sign was a Plexiglas and metal booth which held an attendant with tollbooth-like swinging arms on either side. Brennan parked his unmarked Crown Vic and walked to the booth.

"Good afternoon."

"Same to you. What can I do you for?" said a middle-aged, black man in a polo shirt.

"Name's Detective Brennan." Showing the guy his badge, he told him he was investigating the shooting that happened yesterday.

"Well, I don't see how I can help you. Being as you can tell by the sign here – I wasn't here."

"Right, my question was, kind sir, if you're closed, could a car still get onto the parking deck?"

"Sure they could. The only time these arms are down is when I'm here. Which for your benefit, I'll add, is during the hours displayed on the sign, kind sir."

Feisty old bastard, wasn't he? Of course, anyone could have just walked into the parking deck regardless, but he was betting if someone was planning a sniper shot, they might want to have a ride nearby.

"I see a camera there above the booth. Is it on all the time?" Brennan asked.

"I reckon it is, but I don't have access to it. The company that owns the place keeps the video equipment in a locked closet around the corner there. And I don't have a key, if that's your next question."

"I see, and I'm guessing that R.R.C., Inc. is that company, being as it's also on your sign there. I'm also guessing that they will have the key."

"With you as a detective, criminals don't stand a chance."

He was starting to like the old man. Shaking his hand, he thanked him and told him he was going to take a look around. There was no elevator, so Brennan took the stairs and figured he would start from the top. He didn't know what he was looking for but he wanted to see what taking the shot would look like from there. The building was built in a square with a typical, elevated parking design. The corners of the parking deck were like points on a compass. Each corner pointed North, South, East, or West. The South corner pointed toward the Cantrell crime scene about 400 yards away and the North corner pointed toward the second crime scene, also around 400 yards away. The East corner pointed toward Roswell Road and gave a perfect view of both supermarkets. If he were to have to make the shot of both victims, this would be the optimal spot. He didn't even know if it was possible to make the shot from this far away. But if it was, this had to be the spot.

Still thinking the guy would have had a car nearby, he called information and got R.R.C., Inc.'s number. He got a machine which in turn gave him another number in case of emergency. Dialing that number, a female voice answered after two rings.

"R.R.C."

He gave his name and asked to speak to someone in charge. A deep, gravelly voice, reminding him of Barry White came on the line a minute later.

"Detective Brennan, is it? What can I do for you?"

"I'm sorry. I didn't catch your name."

"The name is Dunningham, Frank Dunningham."

"Well Frank, I'm trying to look at security footage from one of your cameras located at a parking garage at 4500 Roswell Rd."

"Right, our Sandy Springs space. I'm sure we can make that happen as long as what you're looking for happened in the last 72 hours. Our cameras work off a 72 hour loop."

"That will work," said Brennan, "I'm investigating the shootings from yesterday."

"I'm lost as to how our cameras can help, but I can send someone out to meet you if that's alright. Shouldn't take them longer than 20 minutes." Thanking Frank, Brennan hung up.

Twenty minutes later on the dot, waiting inside his air-conditioned Crown Vic, he saw a young, white guy with a tie pull up in a nondescript Ford Taurus and approach the booth. The booth worker pointed Brennan's way. The man introduced himself as Todd Stoker, Mr. Dunningham's assistant, and asked Brennan to follow him. They walked a short distance to an unmarked, steel door. Using his keys, the man opened the door and walked in flipping on a light. The room was small, maybe 5' x 10' with some rolling metal shelves. On two of the shelves set files of some sort and on one set a neat stack of electronics along with a 15 inch LCD monitor. The picture on the monitors showed the exit and entrance of the ticketing booth and on into the connecting lot about 20 yards to Roswell Road.

"I need to look back to around 6 p.m. yesterday, if that's possible." Brennan said.

"No problem."

Todd manipulated what looked to be a rewind track button you might find on a regular DVD player. Each time he pressed the button, the video footage jumped back an hour. There was absolutely no movement in the footage once it went past 6:30 that morning all the way until 5:30 p.m. the previous night. The night of the shootings. Brennan had the man stop at 4:30 p.m. He told Todd that he could handle it from here.

"All right, then. Just press resume when you're done and let the door closed behind you, it locks automatically.

Brennan thanked the guy then turned back to the paused video. He watched for the next hour and there was nothing except a car pulling in just to turn around. At exactly 5:32 p.m., a silver, midsized sedan pulled in and drove into the parking deck. The video quality wasn't that good, probably an old camera. All he could tell was that there were no passengers in the car, only the driver. Whether they were male or female, he didn't have a clue. Maybe CSI could make it clearer for him. Continuing to watch, he saw nothing until three minutes after six. The same silver car pulled out and turned north on Roswell Road.

The shootings seemed to happen almost simultaneously at exactly 6 p.m. Calls started coming in to dispatch as early as 6:00 and 42 seconds. Could this silver car be the shooter? If not, what was this car doing at a parking deck for 30 minutes on a Saturday evening? Calling Mr. Dunningham at R.R.C., he explained he would need the video for further analysis.

"Is there evidence of a crime on the video?"

"I can't discuss an ongoing investigation," Brennan said, "but I promise you our findings will not be made public without realizing the integrity of any businesses or properties involved."

He knew the guy was just concerned that his company's name would be linked to bad publicity.

"I'm going to contact the firm's attorney," said Dunningham.

"You do that. Meanwhile, I'm confiscating this video. Good day."

CHAPTER 15

Knowing the killings would be tied together by numerous different consistencies, Jared still saw no reason to use a different car. He liked the Camry's inconspicuousness while he was driving it and if later they linked it to the crimes, so be it. Of course, none of that mattered now. He had parked it in a nice, gated apartment complex not far from the MARTA park-and-ride. The new Camry fit right in, he had beaten the entrance gate by tailgating someone.

This morning, parking his car in a similar but ungated complex a quarter-mile away, he walked and was dumbfounded to find the Camry gone. Not letting his presence at the apartment complex call attention, he pretended to be a potential renter and looked at a couple floor plans. Utterly frustrated, he made the trek back to his own car. What happened to the Camry? Did the cops somehow trace it there? Regardless, Jared had to find another means of transportation. He knew by now it was a possibility that with all the media coverage, other car dealerships might be hip to his game by now.

There had always been something he wanted to exploit, anyway. It would make things more risky, but that was part of the fun, right? He always went to this hand carwash near his office. You know the one, they're everywhere. You pull in behind another car that's in the line of cars shaped into a circle. You get out while leaving your car running, so when one station of Mexicans are finished they pull it around to the next station. One station does the windows, one the vacuuming, etc., etc. When the car is done, they call your number on an intercom and you come out of the air-conditioned building to find your car all nice and clean. Ten minutes from beginning to end, not bad for 12 bucks. But what Jared always wondered, was what kept a thief from just getting in the car at the end of the circle and hauling ass? There is absolutely no security, just some kid running around calling ticket numbers and saying, "Have a nice day." He doesn't even know if the car you're getting into is yours. It's nuts.

Now, those nuts are going to pay off. Once again taking MARTA, Jared got off the train at Lindbergh Center and caught the 27 bus which cruised down Monroe Drive and continued to North Avenue Station. While efficient, public transportation had the smell that reminded you of that gas station bathroom that forced you to hover. Getting off at Monroe and Armor Drive, he looked up an extremely steep driveway at Atlanta Costumes. This place had been here for what seemed like forever. He remembered being a kid and seeing their neon sign whip by as he and his Dad took I-85 North. This place had everything from latex skin to police uniforms. Atlanta Costumes was the place to come to. Jared knew that numerous people would see him at the car wash. He may even be recorded on some security camera. It was risky, downright brazen, but Jared also thought he might use being seen, but looking different, to throw investigators off. He knew sooner or later they would link this car theft to the shootings. Why not leave a little misidentification behind in the process? He wanted to have a drastic effect, but he wanted to do it subtly. He couldn't change the fact that he was white, well he could, but that wasn't subtle, or easy for that matter. He was thinking of changing the size of his nose, getting a nice wig, and maybe a fake mole or something.

The guy sitting behind the counter looked extremely bored and without closer inspection, his face looked to be one-third stainless steel. He introduced himself as 'Cipher' just as Jared figured out that the guy had no ears. I mean the guy had ears, but none you could see through all the earrings and bars. Cipher took Jared's staring in stride, no doubt used to it. He told the guy what he wanted to accomplish and without so much as a question, Cipher gave Jared exactly what he was looking for with plenty of advice for application.

Two-hundred and fifty dollars later; Jared walked back to the MARTA stop. Getting off the bus close to the carwash, Jared went inside a nearby Target store to find a bathroom. This was going to take a while. He had bought a very realistic, blondish-brown wig of medium length, much longer and lighter than his own almost black hair. He ended up getting the latex nose, as well. The nose definitely changed the appearance of his face. It wasn't anything weird, no Owen Wilson shit, but it was much broader and a good deal longer with a small hump. Instead of the mole, Cipher sold him on a John Travolta-'ESQUE' cleft chin that was also done using latex. After using makeup to blend the latex, Jared took off his usual glasses and inserted contacts. Looking at himself in the mirror after almost an hour, he was astonished. He didn't look freakish or crazy; he just looked like a different guy. An ugly guy no less, but different. It was perfect. To complete the transformation he had bought some black sneakers and chunked his loafers in the trash. He took his watch and wedding band off and put them into a small, nylon, drawstring bag which he secured around his belt, then stuck it in his pocket. Glancing at himself in a storefront window, he was elated.

Avril's Car Wash sat at the corner of West Wieuca

Road and Roswell Road. Across Wieuca was a Sun Trust Bank and across Roswell was a Sean's Liquor Store. The carwash sat just outside the city limits of Atlanta and just inside Sandy Springs. The actual 'washing circle' was in Avril's big parking lot directly in front of a small building with a large sitting patio. This is where most of the patrons were sitting, reading papers, or surfing the net on their smartphones.

The lot was pretty full. There were around 12 cars in the lot at some stage in the wash line. He went inside feigning his purchase of a wash ticket. This act was more for the customers seated on the patio than anything else. Upon entering though, he just asked where the restroom was. An elderly, fat, white man pointed in the direction of an unmarked door. He went in and immediately started applying clear superglue to his palms and fingerprints. Superglue was the way to go. That way, he wouldn't leave behind any identifying prints, and he also wouldn't be seen wearing gloves. He let the glue dry for about 60 seconds then went back out. He thanked the fat guy and walked out toward the wash line.

He immediately saw that two cars were at the last station in near completion. One was a white convertible BMW, the other a black Volvo S60. While the Beamer would be fun, the Volvo was much more practical for his purposes. He saw no customers looking or rising to prepare for either car. Walking toward the running Volvo, he saw two Mexican workers drying the wheels with yellow shammies. Perfect. He walked straight to the driver's door and got in. He calmly shifted into drive and besides the young kid shaking a ticket as he pulled out, there was nothing to cause undue attention. Taking a right on Wieuca, he floored it knowing they would immediately call the cops upon noticing the theft. The problem they had was that they were located in Sandy Springs and he would be in Atlanta in 30 seconds. Police departments rarely alerted other agencies in such big metro areas over a vehicle theft. He had known this would be easy. He had run it through his head 100 times.

Now, he had to go set the stage for the next victims.

CHAPTER 16

"…ello," Brennan said, heavy with sleep.

"Are you still sleeping?" asked Flemez. "I know it's officially your day off, but it's close to noon!"

"Good, that means I have 19 more hours until I have to go back to my nightmare." He had been without sleep, investigating the shootings for close to four days straight. He had been back and forth over what they knew and nothing made sense. After drowning his sorrows with half a bottle of Kettle One, he had slept for 13 hours.

"Our IT guys finished enhancing your video, so get your butt in gear and make your way down here, pronto."

After Flemez hung up, Brennan was still clearing the cobwebs out of his head. What had they found? Did he miss something? Fixing a cup of coffee, these were the thoughts that kept running through his head. He rushed through a shower and threw on some clothes. He always felt as if he was forgetting something when he was leaving the house.

It was still strange to not have Samantha around. It had been three years since the divorce, but it still hadn't completely set in. He met Sam at a bar in Buckhead right after his promotion to Detective for the Atlanta Police.

She was waiting tables while also going to Law School at Georgia State. There had been instant chemistry and mind blowing sex. They moved in together after only a month of dating. A little because it made sense financially, but a lot of it was because of the sex. They had trouble communicating sometimes, but they shared roughly the same goals and did he mention the sex was awesome? Sam graduated about six months later and around the same time, Brennan solved a big double homicide. With euphoria on wholesale and the love bug working overtime, Brennan popped the big question. The next spring, they were married.

For the next three years, they were living the dream. Samantha graduated in the top 10% of her class and had offers from two law firms. They would talk into the night about plans for their future. They would have a house built in the suburbs and do all the decorating themselves. They would buy a dog for their fenced backyard and they would always talk about having their 2.5 kids and what their names might be. Then she met Matthew.

They had met through a friend that invited her to a yoga class. Brennan couldn't really pinpoint exactly when, but soon after meeting Ol' Matt, his wife changed. She talked only of cleansing her body of all the negative energy and how everything they ate should be organic. It was always, Matthew this and Matthew believes that. After six months of what seemed like the "yoga era", they sat down and Sam told Brennan she needed her space. That they had grown apart and wanted different things out of life. Three days later, he was living by himself. They were separated for almost 2 years before she filed for divorce. Of course, he always knew it was just a matter of time. Brennan, while wishing it could have been different, took it in stride and tried to start over.

Driving to the Sandy Springs Police Department and parking in front, he made his way to the CSI unit. Upon seeing him, Flemez smiled and waved him over to her workstation. Investigator Flemez had been with the department going on four years. She was a confident and energetic addition to the Force. While petite at 5'2" and 100 pounds soaking wet, she was relentless and a very competent investigator. She was of Spanish descent, though Brennan hadn't a clue as to what origin.

"Afternoon, Detective," Flemez said, leaning on the word afternoon.

"Good afternoon, Maria."

"This is the video feed you gave us Monday. Enhanced of course."

Looking at the footage he saw that it was much clearer. He let it play through until the silver sedan was passing directly in front of the camera.

"Pause it," said Brennan.

Flemez stilled the video and said, "I know, I know, zoom in on the face." She did and while much clearer, it wasn't very distinguishing. Brennan took out his notepad and started scribbling. The face was that of a white male with dark hair, the age was anywhere from 30 to 50 and there were no distinguishing marks. A very average-looking guy.

"Okay, zoom back out." As she did, Brennan could make out the car. It was a Toyota Camry, a newer model. "Now, fast forward until the car is exiting." She manipulated the video as instructed.

"I know you'll make your own conclusions here, but I went ahead and helped you a bit." Pausing the video on a still of the car's rear end, Flemez zoomed in on a tag. "We ran the tag and it came back stolen. Not the car that goes to the tag, just the tag itself. Although, the tag does belong to a silver Camry." Brennan understood. The perp stole a car and switched tags with a similar car. Smart, very smart. "We then cross-referenced any reports for stolen Toyotas and we got a hit."

Jumping ahead of her, Brennan said, "Where was the tag stolen from?"

"The owner lives in Gwinnett County, Norcross to be exact, but they're not sure when or where the tag was taken. Now, the APB on the stolen Camry was put out on Friday the 18th, 24 hours before the shootings took place. The car was stolen from a Toyota dealership on Peachtree Industrial in Dekalb County and get this, the guy acted like he was interested in buying the car and then just drove off the lot in the middle of the guy's sales pitch."

"What's the salesman's name?" he asked.

"I called Nalley Toyota and the guy's name is Corey Oglesby.

"Did they get any video of him?"

"Negative, but I'll print you a still from this one to show your witness. This guy went above and beyond just to steal the car. I'm betting this is your shooter, Brennan."

"I have a feeling it is too, but let's let the evidence lead us. The evidence has to bring us to the conclusion. Trying to make the evidence meet our assumptions is like driving with only one eye open. I'm going to talk to the salesman. Don't know what I'd do without you, Maria." His eyes held hers and he had a sudden urge to kiss her.

"Like I said, Brennan. Any time," with that, she walked away.

What just happened here? Brennan asked himself. Did he have feelings for this woman? Did she just let on that the feeling was mutual? Walking out the door, he thanked one of the IT guys that he had worked with before. He called Nalley to make sure Mr. Oglesby would be working and made his way to Chamblee.

The dealership sat facing Peachtree Industrial between a dozen of other dealerships. They all sat no more than half a mile from the I-285 Junction, the getaway. He pulled his Crown Vic to a stop directly in front of the showroom. Through the big front windows, he could see maybe half a dozen salesmen looking at him, figuring their odds of selling him a car. He guessed he didn't give off the car buying vibe because no one came out to greet him. Or, maybe it was the gun on his hip. Who knows? Walking into the building, he approached a cheerful-looking blonde whose eyes showed she'd had way too much coffee that day.

"My name is Detective Brennan, I'm with the Sandy Springs Police Department," he said, showing his badge. "I need to speak to a Mr. Corey Oglesby."

"Gosh, you look just like the detectives on TV. I watch all y'all's shows. Law and Order, CSI. I even…"

"Miss, I'm sorry. I'm in a bit of a hurry. Is he available?"

"Oh, oh yeah, of course."

Mrs. Brains then got on the phone. "He'll be right out, Sarge," the blonde said smiling and winking like they were in on some big secret. And he thought he had no life.

Corey Oglesby was a slight built man of about 25 years. He had light-brown hair with pale, blue eyes and he was dressed very smartly in a suit that made him look more like a banker than a car salesman. Why did the powers that be think it important for their salesman to dress so uptight? Their business wasn't in front of a judge. They weren't on Wall Street. They're selling Toyotas, people!!

"Is there a place we can talk privately?" Brennan asked.

Corey led him to what looked to be a conference room and offered him a chair.

"Mr. Oglesby, I just need to ask you a few questions about the other day."

"Okay."

"What time did the theft occur?"

"It was around 1 p.m. I remember because it was right after my lunch break. Maybe 1:15."

"Okay, and in as much detail as possible tell me what happened?"

Corey stuttered through what he remembered, ending with, "Heck, I thought he was a serious buyer. All the signs were there y' know?" That's because the guy really was shopping for a car, he just wasn't paying for it, thought Brennan.

"I have a photo here I want you to look at," Brennan said. "I know it's of bad quality, but see if you recognize the guy, okay?"

Corey studied the picture. "To tell you the truth Detective, I just don't know. He had on these big sunglasses. I mean it could be, it sort of looks like him."

Brennan had hoped for more but the picture was pretty bad. Just then his phone chirped. "Excuse me a second." Walking to the doorway, he answered.

"We got the car," said Flemez. "One of our boys was combing the impound yards and it was towed from a gated apartment complex in Roswell. Somebody got mad about the car being in their regular spot. Go figure."

"I'm on my way."

CHAPTER 17

Mark went to the shop this morning and unlocked the door for his employees, then went back home. He felt like shit! Not physically, just depressed.

He was sitting in his living room with tears running down his face. He wanted Jenny back, it just wasn't fair. They were so deep in love, and then a couple of nobodies just took her away. No time to say "I love you" or "Goodbye." Just wham! Dead! Then, the stupid DA agrees to a 10 year sentence for the guys responsible. 10 years? They killed my soul mate, my wife, my everything! God damn them. They deserved to die! He had called the governor, the media, even the judge. They all had the same mantra, "Justice was served. Sometimes the system isn't fair." What did they know about fair? Let's see how they feel when someone they love is killed for no reason. In a fit of rage, Mark kicked the glass coffee table, toppling and shattering it. He sat and stared at the glass for almost an hour.

Out of the void Mark heard his phone ring. He looked at the caller ID, it was Linda. Taking a deep breath, he answered, "Hi, I was wondering when you were gonna call. I left a message for you yesterday. Did you get it?"

"I did," Linda said, "but I didn't check my voicemail until I was home and I thought it was too late to call. How do you feel about maybe catching a movie or something? There I said it."

Laughing, Mark said, "Of course. I'd love to. While I was waiting for you to call me back, I was practicing restraint not to call you again. Look at us, like a couple teenagers."

Sighing with relief, Linda said, "Is tonight good for you?"

"Definitely. I'll call the theaters and check showtimes. Let's shoot for around eight. How's that sound?"

"Perfect."

"It's a date then," Mark said. "Wait, I don't know where your place is." Linda gave him the address, "Nice Street. I know it. I guess I'll see you tonight, then."

"Sounds good. I'm looking forward to it, Mark. Bye."

Hanging up the phone, Mark sat, still staring at the glass. Maybe she was the one, he thought. Maybe Linda could take his pain away.

CHAPTER 18

The American company Arnold Arms, made a beautiful rifle. The example he held in his hands was called a Grand Alaskan. It was a .338 Magnum with a 26-inch barrel. The high-powered rifle could shoot a 160-grain bullet accurately to over a mile and a half. The scope was a Leica Ultravid Model. It was equally exclusive and also came with night vision, in case he wanted to kill people in the dark. He did. The whole package had cost a little over 7000 bucks. Of course, the shots that were about to be made weren't even half that of the gun's full capability. But, he liked knowing it could go further. He took pride in it. It was like knowing you had a big Johnson. He felt superior.

The gun was sitting between two big pine trees, propped up in its bipod on a nonslip mat. It was toward the end of rush hour and the cars on I-285 were all barreling along, clueless of what was about to transpire. The wooded areas that sat on both sides of the highway were slightly elevated and were the end of several property lines of huge mansions. The Riverside Drive exit ramp sat about 100 yards away, directly across both directions of traffic from where he laid. The place he was lying down at was actually Riverwood High School's property, which sits further away from the Interstate through the thickly wooded area. The stolen Volvo sat in the high school parking lot about 50 yards from him. He would easily walk back to it after he had his fun.

From his elevated position, he looked through the scope down over the Westbound lanes and into the oncoming traffic of the Eastbound lanes. The targets today would be specific, but at the same time random. He would be shooting in a definitive area, but it could affect any number of drivers.

At 800 yards, the shot was very difficult by itself. Add in the factor that the targets were all moving around 60 mph and it moved the difficulty into the extreme. What helped tremendously was the fact that the lanes of traffic were headed in a direct straight line toward him. If there was even a slight curve it would have made an accurate shot next to impossible. The scope was dialed into the required distance so he wouldn't have to elevate his shot. The bullet, at 800 yards, would drop some 14 inches. He would factor in the distance covered by the car from the time he pulled the trigger to the point of impact and aim 2 inches lower. It would take the high-powered round almost 2 seconds before savagely slamming into its target.

Looking through the scope, he studied several faces of possible targets through the windshields of their cars. It was time. This was it. He tried to control his breathing as he slipped his finger through the trigger guard.

CHAPTER 19

Emily Sprayberry didn't have a good day at school. A kid named Ralph wouldn't leave her alone. Ralph was big and fat and walked with a slump as if his head were too heavy. He had horrible breath and was constantly teasing Emily. Her mom said that Ralph more than likely teased her because he liked her and didn't know how to express himself. Emily didn't care, he was ugly and mean and she just wanted him to go away. Emily was nine years old and she was in the fourth grade this year. Her brother Mitchell was only six and he was only in the first grade. He was in the backseat playing his Nintendo DS as usual while she sat up front with her mom.

Her mother, Cindy was talking on her cell phone while driving them home from their afterschool program. Cindy had been working hard for the past three years trying to save up enough money to move her and her kids out of the sticky part of Marietta. As a single mother, it was no easy task. The person on the other end of the phone was a mortgage specialist with Wells Fargo. He was in the middle of explaining how her loan was approved and that the amount of money needed for the down payment was much lower than he had anticipated. With that good news, he gave her some more, "the offer you made on the Olsen property has been accepted. It looks like you're a new homeowner." Cindy was ecstatic! Closing her phone with a big smile, she started to tell the kids the good news, "Guess what, troopers? Mommy was just on the phone with…"

A strange noise cut her off. Emily first saw the window shatter; a small star pattern with a hole in the middle. Had a rock hit it? It scared Emily so much that she instinctively reached for her mother. As she did, she looked up to her for explanation. What she saw caused her to jump back and start screaming. Where her mother's delicate nose had been was now a bloody, gaping hole. Her mother's head was listed to one side leaning against her window and the headrest was covered in blood, hair, and skull fragments. Emily and Mitchell were screaming and crying as their car started swerving into the next lane.

* * *

Patrick Leary had been driving tractor trailers for 25 years. He hated having to drive through the city, too much traffic and too many bad drivers.

He was driving his rig back home to Snellville, after almost 14 hours at the wheel. His wife, Betsy, was awaiting him with some kind of special night planned. He hadn't been home in almost a week. She was such a patient person, never complaining and always understanding. They were each other's worlds.

He pulled out his phone to give her a heads-up that he would be home soon when he saw the car next to him start to veer into his lane. He hit the horn and started to hit the brakes when all of a sudden he couldn't breathe. Something wasn't right. It felt like hot, coppery liquid was dripping down his throat and there was a horrible burning sensation. He grasped at his neck only to find it slippery with blood. As his world started turning black, his only thought was that it looked like he had a crack in his windshield.

CHAPTER 20

Brennan sat at his desk in the detective's squad room going over, yet again, what he knew about this case. The lab had come back with nothing after going over the Camry. The car was stolen from Nalley Toyota in Dekalb County at approximately 1:00 p.m. on Friday, the 18th. Somewhere between then and 6 p.m. Saturday, the perp also stole the tag off another Camry which was in Gwinnett County. The guy then drives to the parking deck in Sandy Springs, sets up his shots, and within seconds of each other, shoots and murders two of what seems to be random people, the degree of difficulty in the shots were not as great as he previously thought. After talking with some guys from SWAT, it seemed an intermediately-skilled person could have made the shots, no problem. Which only made the suspect pool larger. He had absolutely no leads on the Camry getting to the apartment complex in Roswell and couldn't even come close to figuring a motive. Way to go, Big City Detective! As he rummaged through his desk for a pen his phone rang.

"Brennan here."

"Heads up, Captain wants all available units down at the accident site," said his fellow detective Lopez.

"What accident?"

"Jesus," said Lopez. "You don't know? Turn your damn radio on man. There is a huge pileup at 285 and Riverside, multiple fatalities."

"Holy shit! I'm on my way."

Brennan ran out to his car and floored it toward Riverside, lights flashing. He turned to WSB radio and the announcer was saying "police are on the scene and are working to move traffic around the wreck using the shoulder. Again, no idea at this time what started the 14 car pileup…" 14 cars?

Brennan quickly dialed his Captain. "It's Brennan. I'm on my way."

"Good, and get here quick. This is no regular car accident."

CHAPTER 21

The movie started at 8:55. Showing up a little early, Mark closed the door on the convertible and approached a beautifully done screened-in porch. There was no knocker or doorbell, so he called Linda on her cell to no avail. Hearing some music further in the house, he opened the screen door while calling out several 'hellos'. The music got louder and he noticed the interior front door was ajar. Putting his head through the doorway to call out for Linda once again, they almost head-butted each other as Linda was coming out. They both let out a short yelps before realizing what had happened and laughed.

"I thought I heard something out here," Linda said. "I'm sorry. I didn't realize the time."

Mark was unable to speak. Linda looked absolutely ravishing. Gone were those loose-fitting clothes and tomboy demeanor. She wore a simple, sleek black skirt with a red blouse that had spaghetti straps wrapped around her bare, muscled shoulders. She also wore a single strand of pearls to showcase her lovely neck.

"You'll have to excuse me. You look amazing."

Blushing, Linda said, "What, this old thing? Actually, I bought it on the way home," she said laughing. "As I said before, I haven't been on the dating circuit in a while."

"Well, I guess some things you never forget. Your taste is impeccable."

"Thank you," said Linda standing on her tiptoes to give him a peck on the cheek. "I'm almost ready. Give me just a minute."

"Take your time. We still have another 30 minutes before showtime."

The small TV in the living area was tuned into a shopping network. Using the remote sitting on top of a packing box, Mark changed the channel. He stopped on a local news station. The anchor was reporting live. "That's right, Bob. 14 cars were involved in the accident. Paramedics and Sandy Springs Police are on the scene and have already airlifted at least two people. At this point the numbers aren't certain, but I talked with a Captain Kirby and this is what he had to say…" The camera flipped to a 50-ish, large, white man in a trench coat. "The cause of the accident is still unknown, but we are investigating. At this time, four people have lost their lives and at least 15 were injured. We have…" Mark turned the set off as Linda walked into the room. Placing the remote back on the box, he said "I hope you don't mind, I was watching a little TV."

"Not at all, I've been meaning to finish unpacking and buy some new furniture, but with work and all it seems impossible."

"I'll tell you what," said Mark. "You pick a day in the week coming up and I'll take you to IKEA, or wherever you like, we'll come back and spend the day getting you settled in. How's that sound?"

"Oh, I couldn't ask that of you. I was going to have some stuff delivered and…" Interrupting her, Mark said, "I know how independent you are and I don't want to step on your toes, but I'd really like to help you with this. I have a truck we could use and it'll be fun. Come on, what do you say?"

God, he was so sincere. So genuinely nice, thought Linda. Walking over to him and putting her arms atop his shoulders, she looked into his eyes and said, "You are one of the sweetest men I've ever met. You know that?"

"I try," replied Mark. Pulling her closer so their lips met softly with their mouths opening simultaneously, their tongues slowly moved in rhythm together. Even with her eyes closed, Mark marveled at what a beautiful woman she was.

The theater they went to was one of the new 'Café Theaters'. Your seats are more comfortable, you can order food and beverage, not to mention, order alcohol from discreetly prancing waitresses. Nothing like getting totally hammered while watching a good action flick, y'know?

They saw the newest Seth Rogan comedy and it was a good one. Mark loved to see her laugh. She had a great smile that made her whole face light up. It was contagious too. Mark hadn't been this happy since…

Driving Linda home after the movie, he walked her to the door.

"Linda, I had a great time."

"So did I."

"Well I guess…"

Interrupting Mark she said, "Do you want to come in for a minute? I bought some wine on the way home…"

Before she could finish, Mark pulled her to him and kissed her deeply. Both breathing heavily, he pushed her against the door as she fumbled with the keys to get the door unlocked. Once inside, Mark closed the door with his foot. Picking Linda up by her butt, he easily carried her to a small sofa. As he started kissing her neck, Linda was panting and frantically unbuttoning Mark's shirt. Reaching behind her, he unzipped her skirt and standing up he took it off in one fluid motion. Mark then worked on his pants while Linda took her blouse off. Looking down at her he said, "God, you're beautiful." Smiling, she pulled him back on top of her.

On the small sofa, they laid awkwardly; both spent still trying to catch their breaths. Relishing the last hour of passionate lovemaking, neither wanted to move. If Mark could only stay this satisfied. For now, his pain was gone.

CHAPTER 22

Absolute pandemonium! That's what Brennan thought as he traveled the wrong way on I-285. Using the highway's shoulder, he crept toward the accident site. It looked like World War III. In all his years, he had never seen such a concentration of police activity. He saw the State Patrol, Sandy Springs PD, ambulances, fire trucks, and even the coroner's vans. Haven taken place during rush hour, traffic was backed up as far as the eye could see.

Parking out of the way, he hurriedly walked up to what looked to be the make-shift command center. A couple uniforms along with three detectives were in a semi-circle around his commanding officer, Captain Jacob Kirby. As he approached, the officers dispersed and Kirby called him over.

"Tom, I've never seen anything like this."

"Me either, Jake. This has to be the biggest accident site I've ever seen."

"This isn't just a pile-up." Brennan looked at his Captain and, in the two years he had worked for him, he had never seen so much fury and anguish in the man's face.

"Walk with me, Brennan."

They made their way to the back of one of the coroner's vans. Once there, Kirby opened the door and motioned Brennan inside. There were two bodies inside, zipped up in plastic bags. There was barely enough room to stand between the two.

"Go ahead," said Kirby.

Brennan unzipped the first body bag and had to take a second to gather himself. No stranger to dead bodies, he couldn't believe the carnage he was looking at. There were massive contusions and gashes all over what was once a woman in her late 30s. She was mangled. What held his attention though was unmistakably a gunshot wound in the center of her face. Looking back to his boss, he was nodding confirmation of his own thoughts. This was his shooter. He had struck again.

"The body of her nine-year-old daughter is next to her. She wasn't shot, but died of her injuries. The woman's six-year-old son was also in the car. He is in critical condition at Northside and not expected to make it."

Brennan shook his head. This was horrible. "Was she the only one shot?"

"No, let's go to the other van."

They walked a short distance through the massive accident. Tow trucks were doing their best to get the twisted cars and trucks loaded on their beds. There was a tractor-trailer truck turned over on its side with a small car partially trapped under the trailer. Several other cars waiting to get towed were smashed beyond recognition. There seemed to be wounded people everywhere. Some had already been air-lifted, but several others were still being treated and loaded into ambulances. Opening the doors to the second coroner's van, Brennan saw two more bodies.

"The one on the left was the driver of the big rig you see turned over out there."

He stepped into the van and unzipped the bag. The victim was a middle-aged black male and besides a couple cuts here and there he looked as if he should still be living – until he looked at his neck. His throat was completely covered in blood along with the front of his shirt. In the middle of the throat, where the Adam's apple should have been, was a neat hole.

"The slug went through his neck, missed his spine, traveled through the seat, and lodged in the truck's cab. Crime scene has your slug."

Brennan stared off, dazed.

"You there, Brennan?"

"Yeah, I'm here. Just trying to put it all together."

"Look, this is major. A sniper, serial killer loose in Sandy Springs. So far I've kept the fact that this is connected with the other shootings quiet, but it will get out soon and the media is gonna have a field day. The Commissioner and the Mayor are gonna come down on the department like a ton of bricks. It's gonna get national coverage and is only a matter of time before the Fed's stick their head in this. I want you to be lead in this case partly because you're heading up the first one, but mainly because you're the best detective I've got. Lopez and Jenkins will give you the help you need. This is priority one, Brennan. Get me some answers. Do you understand?"

"Yes, Captain. Thank you."

With that, he walked off and Brennan stood there surveying the carnage in front of him. He was going to get this sick fuck. If he had to work 24 hours a day, he would find him and when he did, he wouldn't hesitate to take his crazy ass out.

CHAPTER 23

Jared sat in his living room watching the news. There was coverage of the accident on almost every channel. All of them saying this had to be the worst pile-up in years. Five people had died now and 17 injured. It excited him to hear these numbers. He had hoped they would be higher of course, but beggars can't be choosers. Jared couldn't help but think of that old video game Mortal Combat. "Fatality Wins."

Laughing to himself, he wondered why he hadn't heard anything about the victims being shot. Surely the people had figured that out. If not, they would. Just as soon as they put their asses on the slab. Yes sir, they would put it together and still wouldn't be any closer to catching anybody. He was smarter than all of them. The detectives, the psychological profilers, the criminalists, all of them. All they could do is sit back, wait and clean up the messes. Jared loved it!

He heard his wife still cleaning something in the kitchen. That's all the woman did. Clean this, clean that and when she was done, she'd do it all over again. He took her out to dinner and a movie the other night and though he played the happy, interested husband, he was puking on the inside. She was so 'touchy-feely' and every time he looked at her, she seemed to have already been staring at him. That gave him the creeps. He truly couldn't remember why he had married this woman. Besides taking care of the brats and being his slave in the bedroom from time to time, she was worthless. That was okay though. She and the kids had only a number of weeks left anyway. Jared was going to fix them up in a nice, big, happy accident. He couldn't wait to be rid of them.

"I'll be in my office. Don't disturb me," he said, walking toward the door.

"But Jared, you only got home from work a couple hours ago. I was hoping we could talk."

"Well, I've got work to do so, it'll have to wait." What was her problem? Why did she constantly want to talk about things? She should see that he doesn't care. If she doesn't get it by now, she'll definitely get it later.

Laughing at his clever thoughts, he locked himself in his sanctuary and sat at his desk. He had a lot to think about, a lot to plan. While the highway shootings were successful, he felt somehow unfulfilled. He needed to affect more people. Sure people were going to remember the I-285 shootings, but it wouldn't be considered one of the greatest. It wouldn't make history. He had to think bigger. He had to prove himself.

He was online looking at rifles when a pop-up on a sidebar came to his attention. It was something about breast cancer awareness or some other crap. That wasn't important, but it reminded him of something he saw earlier in the week. Yes! He thought. It could be perfect. He was so excited he got an erection. He remembered seeing somewhere that a charity was hosting a walk for Down Syndrome or something similar in north Sandy Springs. It was almost too perfect. Jared returned to the net and Googled what he was looking for. Bingo! Saturday, May 1, multiple charities were hosting a walk for autism on Dunwoody Drive in Sandy Springs. That was in eight days.

He could see it in his head as if he were already there – looking through the scope as hundreds of retarded kids bunched together. It would be like shooting fish in a barrel. Of course, the shot would have to be taken from afar to ensure the getaway. He couldn't think of any elevated positions off the top of his head. He would have to make a drive over there to look around.

He would definitely be remembered for this. He was thinking of what nickname the media would give him as he dozed off.

CHAPTER 24

Linda felt great! Last night had been wonderful. She couldn't believe she actually did it! She hadn't planned on having sex on only the second date, but she was sure glad she did. She felt refreshed and ready to take on the world. Mark seemed too good to be true. He was a passionate lover. Gentle, yet powerful. Demanding, yet willing. It was as if he knew exactly what she wanted, even what she was thinking. He took her to a place she didn't even know existed.

She got up at her usual 5:30 a.m. and was preparing for her run. This would be the first time she ran in her new neighborhood and she walked outside and started stretching. It was still dark outside. She noticed the many streetlights lining her streets, thinking she had made a good choice on the neighborhood. Earlier in the week, she looked at the neighborhood from an aerial view using Google Maps, trying to find a new jogging route and found a nice 4.2 mile circle.

At the end of her street she took a right onto Abernathy Road. If she followed it up, it would cross over GA 400 and lead her to Perimeter Mall. Instead, she ran right at Barfield and followed it down to Hammond Drive.

At the intersection of those two roads sits the seven-year-old building of the Sandy Springs Police Department. It was a good size department with around 30 patrol cars. Sandy Springs didn't have their own jail so, depending on the severity of the offense, you either went to Doraville City Jail or Fulton County Jail, the County holding the more serious offenders.

She made a couple more turns admiring the dense vegetation of the area and made her way home. 4.2 miles in a little under 36 minutes. Oh yeah, she was feeling good and she continued to feel good all the way until she walked into her office. Lucy, her secretary looked distraught.

"Mr. Fletcher wanted to see you as soon as you got in." Hell, her boss was already in? He usually didn't get in for another hour or so. "He doesn't look happy either Ms. Hunt."

"Okay, thanks, Lucy."

She dropped her briefcase in her office and taking a legal pad with her, she headed to the "Big Guy's" office. The "Big Guy" really wasn't a 'Big Guy' at all. At 5'7", 150 pounds, it was more like 'The Small Guy', or maybe 'The Medium Guy' on a good day. His authoritative demeanor and slight God complex is where the nickname came from. Knocking on his already open door, she went in.

"You wanted to see me, sir?"

"Sit down, Agent Hunt." She did. "You probably already know that there was a huge pile-up on I-285 last night." She didn't, but she said nothing. "What you do not know is that the accident was caused by a sniper."

"I'm sorry, sir. Did you say sniper?"

"Yes, a sniper. As in a guy with a high-powered rifle with the scope. A sniper."

"It could be a woman," Linda said.

"What?"

"I said, a sniper could be a woman. You had said as in a guy with a rifle. It could be a woman with a rifle as well, sir."

He looked at her like she was some kind of bug he had never seen before.

"You know, Agent Hunt, your sarcasm is borderline insubordinate. Maybe you should pay more attention to the instructions of your assignments rather than the politically correct terminology of my speech."

"I'm sorry, sir." She wasn't.

"As I was saying, a sniper was the cause of the accident that took place at rush hour last night. Five people's lives were lost and over triple that injured." My God, she thought as she took notes. Five people dead. "Only two of the victims were actually shot," Fletcher went on. He gave her all the information they had so far.

"Sandy Springs PD also feels very strongly that this is in direct connection with the so called 'supermarket slayings' that happened last week, again in Sandy Springs." Linda knew about the murders that took place last Saturday, but Sandy Springs PD had been holding details of the investigation close to the vest. Locals never wanted to voluntarily share information on cases that were in their jurisdiction.

"It's been handed down from the director himself to take over the investigation while allowing Sandy Springs PD to continue in theirs. It's important to ruffle as few feathers as possible with the locals, but know that this is now our investigation. Use your judgement, but try to keep a certain level of camaraderie here. I'll expect daily reports and instant updates of any new findings. Do we understand each other, Agent Hunt?"

"Absolutely, Mr. Fletcher." This is what she had been waiting on. This was one of those cases that could make or break your career. She was confident that she was the one for the job. Walking out of Fletcher's office, he stopped her at the door calling her name. "Yes, Mr. Fletcher."

"I know we don't see eye-to-eye from time to time, but do us all a favor and go get this asshole."

"You got it, Sir."

She had a lot of work to do. She needed to know every piece of information available on both investigations backward and forward. Knowledge was power and research was the key. Like most prominent lawyers would tell you, you're only as good as your research department.

Lucy was standing outside the door to her office, notepad at the ready. Either secretaries were clairvoyant or they always got a heads-up from somewhere.

"Lucy, I need copies of anything this office has printed on both of the Sandy Springs shootings. Also, I want all agents on duty to report to the conference room in fifteen minutes and any agents currently in the field on regular assignment need to call me with their ETA"

"Is that all, Ms. Hunt?"

"No. Also, find me the strongest cup of coffee on earth."

Smiling, "Yes, Ma'am."

Linda went into her office and looked through her messages. Let's see. You can wait. So can you and, damn, mom is going to have to wait, too. She had been procrastinating talking to her mother for a couple weeks now. It was just that speaking to her always made her sad and put her in a state of agitation. Ever since her father died of cancer last year, she had more or less tried to avoid thinking about it and talking to her mother brought back all these suppressed emotions.

Her father had been her world. She had never been a prissy child coming up and that had suited her father just fine. He had been a track and field athlete all throughout Junior High and his freshman year of High School. His events had been the 400 meters and the high jump. To this day, he still held a record at Riverwood High outside of Baltimore in the 400 meters. Then in the summer of 1968, when he was 15, his life changed forever. He and some friends went out to a nearby lake where one of their fathers docked his fishing boat. They were taking turns trying to water ski. The group of boys found some left behind beer in a cooler in the boat and each had drunk their share of the hot suds. After her dad had taken a turn, the boys had the boat idling and he was resting at the left rear of the boat with his arms resting atop the side of the boat. Buzzing from the alcohol, the kids thought it would be fun to act like they were leaving him in the lake by just taking off in the boat. Going ahead with the joke, one of the boys floored the throttle without any warning. Forgetting that the prop was turned all the way to the right, the back end kicked to the left and over the top of her father. The propeller turning at full blast, cut through her dad as if he were warm butter. It cut him across his arm, chest and leg, all but severing his left leg. In a state of severe shock, her father swam toward the shore over 50 yards away. As he swam with the force of the water pulling at his mutilated leg, he felt it detach from his body. He woke up at the hospital three days later with his left leg missing just below his hip.

He had risen from his disability and found a passion working with automobiles. He started out changing oil and rotating tires at a station close to his neighborhood and within eight years, he was practically running the place. Her mother met him there after blowing a head gasket on her junkie El Camino. They went on a couple dates and after only two months, against her grandfather's wishes, she moved in with the man of her dreams. Her mother adored her father. He could do nothing wrong in her eyes. She became pregnant the next spring and they were married that summer. They were married 33 years until the cancer took him away. Coming back to the present, she dabbed at her eyes and reached for her phone.

"Is everyone assembled in the conference room?"

"Yes, Ms. Hunt. I was about to buzz you."

"Thanks, Lucy." Taking a deep breath, she headed for her team.

CHAPTER 25

Mark opened his store with zeal this morning. Last night had been amazing. He had no idea he could feel so good after losing Jenny.   Jenny…   How he missed her. While feeling the joy that accompanied a night of good sex, he somehow felt as if he did something wrong. Had he betrayed Jenny's memory? Should he not be happy? His love for Jenny was deep and he would never stop thinking of her until the day he died, but could he not find love again?

Making an effort to put Jenny out of his mind, he composed a text to Linda. YOU WERE GREAT LAST NIGHT. He paused mid-text thinking of what to say. He didn't want to come across as obsessive, but also wanted to sound meaningful. I LOOK FORWARD TO SEEING YOU AGAIN. Short and sweet was the saying, right?

"Yep, you had sex."

"Excuse me," he said to Tanya, one of his new sales employees.

"I can tell. You haven't stopped smiling since I got here," she said with a conspiratorial smile on her face. "It's okay boss, I won't let anyone know you're human."

Her saucy, upbeat demeanor was infectious. Mark kept

his expression passive, but he couldn't keep the smile out of the corner of his mouth. "That's none of your business, young lady. Besides, a gentleman never kisses and tells."

Tanya was a short, energetic woman of 25 that had a way of making you feel good about whatever she was talking about. That's why he hired her in sales. It helped to have a woman in the store. Buying a gun is intimidating to a lot of people and Tanya made it seem as if you were purchasing bread and milk. She was what today's youth would call thick, which was a nice way of saying, slightly overweight. Her perfect, white teeth and disarming smile were probably her best features. She was an asset to the store and he was glad to have her.

"Whatever you say, Mr. Glover. Did you want to assemble the new case today?"

"Definitely. Break down the old one and store it in the back. Even though the new case is a little longer, it should still fit in its place."

"Okay."

"Get Brian to help you. I'll be gone most of the day, but I'll be back for an evening appointment and check it out."

"All right then, Mr. Glover. See ya later."

"Later, Tanya."

He had bought a new display case for his Glocks. Glock had so many models of pistols that it took up one and a half of the old displays. This case would allow him to keep his Glocks separate from other gun manufacturers, making it more organized. It really shouldn't matter, but Mark liked everything in its place.

Walking out to his car, his phone alerted him that he had a text. It was Linda. It read, I HAD A WONDERFUL TIME TOO. WE SHOULD DEFINETLY MAKE PLANS TO GET TOGETHER AGAIN SOON. I'LL CALL YOU LATER.

She was probably at work. It wasn't crazy to picture her working for the FBI. The woman had passion, for that he could testify to. She was very intelligent and had an air of determination that surrounded her. No doubt, she was dedicated to her job and probably very good at whatever she did. She said she was little more than a glorified secretary, but he sensed she probably was more important than she led on. Linda was one of those women who most men felt intimidated by. That wasn't the case for Mark, but all the same he could imagine.

Mark headed for home with plans to do some work around the house. He still had work to do on his newest bullet design. Mark had a very quick mind and with intricate problems, he could usually find a solution. His new design involved multiple facets of complexity and he had been studying various fields of ballistics to accomplish his goal. This new idea wasn't mind blowing. In fact, it accomplished little more than his Fintip design. The difference this time around was, again, the shape of the slug itself. This was a special engraving that allowed wind to spin the slug, slowing it down while keeping it on course. The result was rate reduction, which multiplied impact force. The bullet didn't go through you so much as ran you over. This would be more useful in handguns, of course, as the Fintip was for rifles. It wouldn't cause as much damage as a hollow tip but it would stop the unlucky target with the same force. This would be useful to law enforcement agencies and those that were not trying to specifically kill their targets but, instead, put them out of the game until help arrived or some other liberal way of thinking.

He sat in his workspace surrounded by open ballistics reference books and sheaves of schematics. He couldn't concentrate. His mind kept going back to Linda Hunt. She really intrigued him. She was confident and ambitious, but she also had a softer side that was almost submissive. Her professional role was the opposite of her sexual desire. Her muscles were taunt and fit, yet she still was soft in all the right areas. She was also highly intelligent, but never came across the least bit arrogant. Mark dozed off while thinking of their lovemaking.

CHAPTER 26

All the information that Brennan had on the case was sitting in front of him. The complete murder books of the first shootings sat closed on the corner as he stared off into space. After going over everything, using logic and his investigative intuition, he knew he had a serial killer on his hands. Who would have thought? A mass-murdering sniper in Sandy Springs. Knowing what he was more or less dealing with now, he sat assembling a psychological profile of his killer in his head before writing it down. What did he know? He knew the victims were random. He ran the same checks through the backgrounds of his new victims as the old – and nada. They were not connected. He felt like Alex Cross in a James Patterson novel. The thing was, was he up to the task? He knew the killer was organized by the stealing of the cars. This took planning and it took brains. The trick with the tag, the locations of the thefts, the killer knew how to use jurisdictional boundaries to his advantage. The killer is also very confident. Brennan thought that could be because of a handful of different reasons though. It could be because he's done this before. It could be that he is a genius strategist. Or it could be because he's fucking crazy. Hell, it could be all three. Regardless, he felt the guy has some form of higher education as well as a high IQ, which is pretty much a textbook serial killer. They hadn't found the exact spot the shooter fired from but from projections and assumptions, the shot came from a wooded area on an elevated bank of the highway which was a public school's property. Nobody would be suspicious of anyone in that area. There was even a park on the other side of the school. Nobody had seen anything out of the ordinary. He started murder books on his new victims noting what he knew and taping in pictures. This was high profile and he had to double check that he did everything by the book.

"Brennan, in my office!" He heard from the general direction of the captain's office. Taking the murder books with him, he walked in and took a seat. Capt. Kirby sat opposite him behind a polished mahogany desk with the newest innovative desk lamp from somewhere like Sharper Image. There were three large windows behind him that gave a view of the famous 'King and Queen' buildings that sat at the corner of Hammond Drive and Peachtree Dunwoody Road. Brennan wasn't sure, but he thought the real name of the towers were the Concourse or Concorde. Whatever. There were your stereotypical pictures with VIPs and the certificates on the "ego-wall". He also had a state of the art computer workstation that looked like the cockpit of an F-22 Raptor in his office. It was clear Sandy Springs Police Department wasn't broke.

"You wanted to see me, Captain?"

Capt. Jacob Kirby looked as distraught as he felt. The years were definitely beginning to show in his face. Hell, they were creating a Broadway. He wasn't far from retirement and Brennan knew that the captain wanted a national, high-profile case like he wanted to manually blow up a bunch of kids' swimming pool toys.

"I know you've had less than 24 hours with this Tom, but it's out of our hands. The Feds are taking over."

"Hold on a second. Like you said, I just got to work on

this. Can't I at least get the customary 72 hours?" It was thought by the brains of the law enforcement that after 72 hours of not having a bead on your perpetrator, the odds of you solving the case more than tripled.

"I understand your frustration Brennan, but like I said, it's out of my hands. There is tremendous pressure from the top to wrap this up expeditiously. I am to instruct you to aid the local Feds with whatever they need."

"That's bullshit and you know it, Captain. We have jurisdiction on this and I'm not a Federal employee, so I won't be a tour guide."

"I'm your superior and you'll follow instructions!" Kirby yelled. "You think I like this? You think I like some wanna-be supercop with political ambitions breathing down my neck and tattle-telling everything to the Chief? You and I are in the same boat on this one, Brennan, and we have to make the best of it. Are we in agreement on this? Are we clear?"

"Yeah, we're clear, Captain. But I damn sure don't agree with it."

Brennan had to get the hell out of there. He went out to his car and rummaged through his glove box for his emergency pack of cigarettes. He had quit six months ago, but quitting really only meant slowing down when it came to cigarettes, right? He couldn't believe he was being taken off the case. Now he was going to have to listen to some patronizing Fed, who couldn't find tits in a strip joint, tell him how this investigation would go. Fuck that! He was going to find this sick bastard and if he had to kiss a little Fed ass to stay in the investigation, then so be it. Starting his car he heard his phone ring. He saw that it was Maria Flemez and answered on the third ring.

"I'm sorry, Brennan. I just heard. You okay?"

"Yeah, I'm all right. Just frustrated, y'know?"

"I do know. I feel the same way. What I also know is I get off in 15 minutes and I need someone to have a drink with. Anyone come to mind who may be interested?"

"Hmm, let me think for a minute. Nope can't think of a soul, Maria."

"Asshole."

"You know I'm just kidding."

"Just for that, you're buying, Brennan. You know where Mazzy's is on Alpharetta Highway?"

"Vaguely."

"It's on the right, about a quarter of a mile after you cross over Holcomb Bridge."

"How about I just follow you. I'll wait on you while I sit out here and finish my sulking.

"Suit yourself. See ya in 15."

"Bye"

A drink sounded good. It sounded real good. He followed Maria's small Lexus to Holcomb Bridge Road, which was only one of the many names of Georgia Highway 92. Why did they do that? Why call a road Jimmy Carter Blvd. here, and then call the same road Woodstock Street 10 miles down the road? All the while, every inch of the thoroughfare was Highway 92. Why not just call the damn road Highway 92? Are the city and county planners trying to cause confusion and therefore traffic? The world was full of geniuses.

It was only a 15 minute drive to their destination. From the outside, Mazzy's looked like about 10,000 other modern sports bars. Lots of parking. His thoughts were reinforced as they walked through the tinted glass doors. There were flat screens everywhere. At least 50 TVs. The smallest screen was a 42 inch and this was how stores like Best Buy made billions in profit. To the left, separated by a 5 foot, wood-paneled wall were about 10 pool tables. A couple tables were in use but that side was mostly deserted. In front of them was a big, highly lacquered, horseshoe-shaped bar. Almost every stool was taken. They walked to the right past an array of arcade machines. One being a golf game called 'Golden Tee'; which, by the way, was about the best arcade game on earth. You know the one. It's the game with the little white ball that you shoved forward to swing the club or even throw your bowling ball. No? Well, here is your warning: STAY AWAY. The game is addictive. They sat at a high table about 3 feet from a TV that was bigger than the pool tables.

"Nice place." Brennan said.

"Yeah, my girlfriends and I have been coming here since college. I even worked here for a while waiting tables."

A nice-looking, young woman dressed in all black approached their table. "Hi, I'm Doni. I'll be your server." Good thing she told them, because they might have thought she wanted to prepare their taxes. "Can I get you something to drink?" She said this putting menus in front of them.

"A vodka cranberry," Maria said.

"Give me a shot of Jaeger with a Bud Light chaser," said Brennan.

"Bottle or draft?"

"A glass is fine." With that, the waitress left.

"Of course, I saw it coming," Brennan said. Maria knew what he meant, but stayed quiet. "I won't even pretend that I didn't need the help. I mean, I know I could have got the guy on my own -- but at the rate he is killing people…" Their drinks were delivered. They both dove in.

"We can still be the one who puts the collar on this guy, Brennan. Notice how I said 'we', by the way. No matter if the Feds get the credit, we'll know the score and that's good enough for me." Brennan wore an 'I guess' facial expression.

They got away from the topic of work and shared some loaded nachos. After they ate their share, there was still enough left to feed a small country. They each had one more drink and Brennan started to notice how beautiful Maria really was. It wasn't just the alcohol, though Brennan was sure it helped. He had found himself thinking about her on other occasions as well. She wasn't so much as beautiful as she was sexy. In one word, she would be described as 'sultry'. Her complexion was closer to caramel than light brown. Her hair dark and thick and while slender, she had a great ass. She had almond-shaped, brown eyes, a slender nose, and lips so pouty and soft-looking you couldn't help but look at them as you spoke to her.

"Are you okay to drive?" she asked, breaking his reverie.

"Huh? Yeah. I'm okay." He was more than a social drinker. It would take more than two drinks to impair him.

"Could you give me a lift home? I'm a little bit tipsy, though I'm sure I could drive. I just don't wanna…"

"Say no more," interrupted Brennan. He paid the check and they walked out to his Crown Vic.

During the meal he found himself loosening up and even flirting a little with Maria. She was definitely responding and Brennan started to get a little nervous about what might happen next. I mean, they were both single adults who were obviously attracted to each other.

* * *

She lived in a nice apartment complex that sat on the bank of the Chattahoochee River. She explained that her unit actually took up the whole apartment building that they pulled in front of. It looked more like a house. As she opened the car door, Brennan got butterflies in his stomach. It had been a long time since he had been with a woman and this was the point where the woman usually asked the guy…

"Do you maybe want to come in and have one more drink?"

"Uh,… Yeah. I mean, yes. I'd love to." Mr. Smooth.

She locked the door behind them and slid off her shoes. "Will a beer be okay or maybe some wine?"

"A beer would be great."

"Go ahead and make yourself comfortable," she said pointing to the living room.

The living room was big and tastefully decorated. He sat in an overstuffed, sectional sofa and looked at some of the intricately-carved figurines that stood atop her fireplace mantel. These tiny statues sat in a line from smallest to largest, maybe eight of them. From the couch, they looked like big birds. Ostriches, maybe?

"They're emu," Maria said, coming into the room with his beer and a glass of wine for herself. "They are large birds closely related to the ostrich and dodo bird."

"I could've told you that." Brennan said. "I love emus. I had three of them when I was a kid."

Laughing, she sipped her wine. "You know, I really like being around you. You make me laugh."

"I enjoy your company as well." Take notes folks, a real Casanova.

She put down her glass then and moved closer to Brennan. He set down the beer and he didn't have to think anymore. He was on autopilot. He pulled her to him by her shoulders and kissed her deeply. Her mouth was open and her tongue exploring. She was more or less laying on top of him now and he could feel himself growing against her leg. She felt it too. She reached down then, stroking him through his pants. A small moan escaped his mouth. She sat up, and then easily removed her blouse. Their eyes met briefly as he took in the view. She was ridiculously sexy. She unclasped her bra and let it fall, then slung it across the room. Her breasts were exquisite. Full and round with dark-brown, perfectly-proportioned, erect nipples.

"I want you," she said looking into his eyes while cupping and squeezing her breasts. "Could you help me with these?" Didn't need to tell him twice. He flipped her on her back and started unbuttoning his shirt. Once off, he resumed kissing her and made his way down to her breasts, taking a nipple in his mouth. She pushed him up suddenly and got up. She undid her jeans and shucked them off standing there in a black thong. She turned and started to walk away giving him a view of the most edible-looking ass he had ever seen. He sat there dazed, hard as a rock.

"Your services are needed in here, Mr. Brennan," she said as she moved a couple steps and went through a doorway. Kicking his shoes off, he unbuttoned his jeans as he went. He went to the doorway and stepped in. She lay on her back with her legs spread atop a white goose down comforter. The thong was gone.

CHAPTER 27

Her whole team was updated and assigned to various tasks. She was just on the phone with the chief of Sandy Springs Police Department and he promised their full cooperation on every level. They were both to give a press conference in a few hours and she had called to make sure everybody was on the same page. Mr. Fletcher had already sent down a typed, official statement which she would give. She was on her own with the press's questions, though.

Already, they had a working sketch with several changed variables such as facial hair, glasses, etc. They would blast that during the press conference, hoping to create a lead. But from prior experience, she knew that broadcasting to the public opened up the dam for all sorts of crackpots and weirdos who happen to see the perp on a daily basis. They had two agents that would take the more promising leads handed off from a team of operators and delve further into them.

Linda felt confident they would get their man and she was gonna do it as quick as possible. She felt that the killer was organized but not excessively so. Just earlier, she'd gotten the report that a car was brazenly stolen from Avril's car wash right on the Sandy Springs/Atlanta city limit. They didn't have any video, but several witnesses gave roughly the same description of the perpetrator: white male, 5'10" to 6'0", 150 to 180 pounds. That matched the guy who stole the Camry, as well as half the population of Metro Atlanta. There was only one witness from the carwash who got a good look at him and that's where the similarities stopped. The clerk at the carwash said the guy came in and asked to use the restroom minutes before walking out and stealing an S60 Volvo right off the wash line. He said the guy had a dimple in his chin and had shaggy, blondish brown hair. The guy from the video of the Camry and from the description of the Toyota salesman both showed the guy with short, dark hair and no distinguishing facial features such as the dimpled chin. That meant one of two things obviously. They were not the same person or the guy wore a disguise. The Volvo had yet to be found even though an APB was put out in all of Metro Atlanta. They would search for the car high and low.

Her phone was vibrating on the desk. Looking at the display, she had a text from Mark. He wanted to know her plans for tonight. Watch Channel 5 News, you'll see my plans, she thought. Instead, she texted him back saying she had a lot on her plate, but would call him later. She'd like to see him, but her thoughts were consumed with this new assignment. She hoped he was patient. Just then, her phone vibrated again. The text was again from Mark and it read "DON'T FRET. I'M PATIENT. GIVE ME A CALL." Where had he been all her life?

The press conference was being held at the old North Fulton County Annex which sat on Roswell Road about a mile south of Northridge Drive, a highly used exit off Georgia 400. The building was old and used to house the small regiment of North Fulton police officers before Sandy Springs was incorporated. The building now held the tag registration office, claims courts, and several other government entities such as the city planner and so forth.

She pulled into a semi-full lot and stopped her Crown Vic between a news van and an identical twin of her own car. Coming up the back walkway, she could see that the media was here in full force. Every local station she could think of, a couple nationals, and even a couple radio. A female anchor stood by the back entrance in front of a camera, speaking into a microphone. She was supposed to go to room H-105 on the front entrance level but upon walking toward the elevator, a uniformed police officer approached her.

"Agent Hunt?"

"That would be me."

"I'm officer Starks. I was sent down by Chief Skinner and asked to bring you to conference room three."

"I thought I was supposed to meet him in room H-105?"

"There was a change of plans Ma'am. Everyone is meeting in the conference room now before heading to one of the courtrooms where the press are waiting."

"Well, let's do it then."

Linda disliked things being changed at the last moment. The conference room was located down the hall from the elevators upon entering, she saw that the room was pretty packed. Noticing his rank by his uniform and insignia on his lapels, she walked directly over to Sandy Springs Police Chief Wade Skinner and stuck out her hand.

"I'm Agent Hunt."

"And I'm Wade Skinner," he said shaking her hand. "I didn't know they made FBI agents as beautiful as you. You're as cute as a newborn kitten."

"And I thought everyone who made it to Chief of Police had experience in law enforcement. Now we both know we were misinformed."

He glared at her, his face turning red. Linda had done her homework. Chief Wade Skinner was the new elect that was appointed only the year before by a record slight majority. Before becoming Chief, he was a business owner whose enterprises stretched from liquor stores to shady strip clubs. He had no experience and, in her opinion, no business in law enforcement. She wasn't going to say anything, but, well, he started it. Yep, making friends already.

"Listen here, Ms. Hunt. I don't…"

"It's Agent Hunt," she said interrupting him, "and while I'm okay with this being a joint effort, I'm not here to listen to you tell me anything. I'm here to help in the apprehension of a murderer and possible serial killer. Everything else is beside the point and in my way. Now, are you gonna help or are you going to be in the way?"

The Chief turned and stormed off toward a group of men who hurriedly looked down at the papers in front of them, acting as if they didn't hear the exchange. A man walked toward her. He was around 6 feet tall, solidly built, and walked with a swagger as if he'd seen a thing or two. He stopped in front of her trying to hide a smile. He was handsome in a rugged type of way; sandy blonde hair with stubble on his face. He had great, light-brown eyes that were mesmerizing.

"I envy you," the man said.

"Oh, yeah? And why is that Mr.…."

"It's Brennan -- Detective Brennan. That was my boss you just tore a new one and, well, I guess I wish I could do the same thing."

"I'm Agent…"

"Hunt. Yeah, I heard."

"I didn't mean to cause friction. It's just that…"

"Oh, no. I totally get it. He's an ass and you had to make sure he knew upfront that you weren't here to take orders from him. It's cool. You were right on point by the way." With that, he strode away toward somebody calling his name.

"All right people, it's showtime," someone shouted. "We'll go in through the judge's chambers and come out where the microphones are set up on the bench."

Linda was expecting some kind of briefing on how the release was going to run, but she guessed that her laying of the law left her to fend for herself. That was cool with her.

The majority of the people in the room hurried out the door she just came through. That left Detective Brennan, some type of public relations guy, the Chief, and herself. The PR guy took the lead and they followed through several doors coming out onto the platform of the judge's bench. The big chair was removed and there were about 10 different microphones with various call letters on their stems, sticking up through a makeshift podium. The lights were blindingly bright. Even with the huge chair gone, there was barely standing room. Feeling highly uncomfortable, Linda put on her best, professional face while at least six cameras were pointed at her, the PR guy motioned to the Chief.

"Chief, they're ready." Wade Skinner stepped to the microphone.

"Terror has struck our community. Senseless killings and cold-blooded murder. The people of Sandy Springs will not stand for it. We will find those persons responsible and let them feel the full weight of justice. The Sandy Springs Police Department is now correlating with the FBI and, from here on out, there will be a joint effort in this investigation. I have no doubt that those responsible will be apprehended expeditiously. Thank you." He turned to Linda. "Agent Hunt," he said motioning her to the microphone.

"Thank you and good evening. I'm going to take this time to ask that anyone who may have information regarding the shootings please call the hotline we've set up. We will flash some illustrations here in a second and anyone who thinks they know or may have seen this man, again, please call the hotline. He is wanted for questioning. We are investigating this with the utmost diligence and we will find those responsible. Thank you." With that Linda stepped away and the PR guy explained that there was an emergency and there would be no questioning at this time. Again he took the lead, leading back through the maze of doorways and out into the corridor.

Mr. Fletcher had gone over with her what needed to be said and what not. While they were not hiding the fact that the huge accident was directly caused by a sniper and connected to the other shootings, they were not trying to broadcast it yet either. It was crowd control. They didn't want folks panicking, hiding in their homes, and not going to work. Everyone seemed to have somewhere to go because she was left standing there by herself. She walked out to her car to find the handsome detective leaning on the Crown Vic parked beside hers.

"Nice car," she said, unlocking the door.

"Yeah, they keep us civil servants comfortable, don't they?"

"That they do," Linda replied.

"I'm looking forward to working with you, Agent Hunt. I know there is some past stigma on the relationship between locals and the Feds but I just want you to know that it's beneath me. You and I want the same thing and I have no problem whatsoever getting some help doing it."

"I'm glad to hear that. The feeling is mutual."

"I thought it might be. I'm also to relay to you that a work area has been cleared for you and your agents at headquarters." Brennan took a card out and handed it to her. "Let me know when you're organized so we can put together what we have and brainstorm."

"Sounds good. We'll get together tomorrow a.m. and see where we stand. And thanks for the hospitality, Detective Brennan."

"You got it." With that, they both got into their vehicles.

CHAPTER 28

Initially, after seeing the press release with the sketches of his face, he was panic stricken. He recorded the newscast. He called in to work that next day and claimed to be sick. He didn't want to see anyone. He sat in his home office all day and went over elaborate escape plans. He was prepared for this. He had over $40,000 in cash in his safe and a little over $200-grand in an offshore account. He had also bought a fake driver's license and Social Security card a few months back that would stand up to general scrutiny. Those had set him back $10-grand by themselves. He also had started renting a decent house in Mexico using the same identity. It was outside the city of Reynosa and sat half a mile away from the nearest neighbor. It had running water and electricity, which suited him fine until he put together a more permanent plan. He had never been there himself, but he had pictures of the property along with the keys that were sent to a P.O. Box also bought with his new identification. He was ready. Catch me if you can.

The next day Jared went back to work expecting odd stares and peculiar looks, ready to take off if need be. But there was none of that. Just business as usual. Having pumped his confidence back up, he prepared for his next move. His wife had been nonstop bitching because his constant absence. "Jared, we need to talk." Jared this and Jared that. He swore to himself that if he, in fact, did have to hightail it, he would have the satisfaction of killing her. Choke her and watch the life drain out of her like a caught fish. Leave those stupid kids to fend for themselves. Hell, maybe he would choke them too. They were just miniature versions of his nagging wife. God, how he despised them.

The 'Walk for Autism' was not a huge event, but it would still attract several thousand people. Following the event via Internet, he saw that there were over 800 registered participants. Of course, all of those weren't autistic, but they were just as pathetic. They were the parents and friends of the retarded kids. All of them with their "woe is me, my poor child" shit. Weak, just plain weak. You had to be tough in this life to make it, Jared's father always said. These people were not tough. They were a drain on society and always looking for a handout or special treatment. Well, Jared was going to give them what they needed. The path of the walk was only a kilometer long. It started at the intersection of Northridge Drive and Dunwoody Place. It traveled north up Dunwoody Place and ended on the same road at the mouth of a Publix grocery store plaza. There would be all types of booths set up in the parking lot selling hats and T-shirts, milking honest working people out of their hard-earned money for their 'cause'.

There were some highly wooded neighborhoods that sat on the east side of Dunwoody Place that Jared saw would be the best place to take a shot on the starting line of the walk. There were highly manicured lawns to some pretty big houses that sat on the few side streets that bordered Dunwoody Place. Yesterday, he had parked at the Quiktrip down the street and went walking through the wooded area that separated those houses from Dunwoody Place. It was only barely elevated and the best place to shoot from was around 400 yards away. It wasn't ideal, but he thought he could do it. To make things even more problematic was the escape route. Not far from the very spot he would shoot from was a barely distinguishable path. If you followed the path a couple hundred yards, it led to a chain-link fence. Someone had already taken the liberty of pulling the chain link away from the support posts. Once past the fence, there was a steep hill of briars that led down to the service area behind a plaza that sat on Roswell Road. He would leave the car parked right there. No one would even see him leave. Once around the corner of the building, he would be just another car in a parking lot of a plaza. Camouflaged. He would use the Volvo, but the cops had linked him to the car and he knew every "pig" within a hundred mile radius would be looking for it. The Volvo was simply too hot. Now that the police had linked him to the Camry and Volvo thefts, they would be on high alert to any automobile thefts and immediately turn the heat up on the description. Stealing a car this time was not an option. He would have to buy one. He had plenty of money. That wasn't the problem. The problem wasn't even with supplying his identity. He had a fake one. The problem was with the guy selling him the car. Signing all the necessary paperwork, he would get a good look at Jared and remember the all-cash sale. He would have to go disguised again. More than likely, the car lot would have cameras anyway. The disguise would have to be good.

Walking up the steep, inclined driveway of Atlanta Costume, he saw that Friday afternoons were one of their busier times. He went in and immediately saw 'Cipher' who had helped him last time. You couldn't miss him. If it was somehow possible, it looked like he had added even more piercings to his face since last week. Jared wanted to cover more of his face this time and went directly to the facial hair, looking at beards. Thirty minutes later, Cipher, who showed zero recognition upon seeing Jared, was ringing him up. He bought a shaggy, dark wig with matching full beard and mustache. He was getting his Paul

Bunion on.

Jared went out of Fulton County to buy his car. He picked a place at random and chose Etowah Motors. The sign said 'Buy Here – Pay Here' and that was exactly what he wanted. With added sunglasses, you almost couldn't see his face. The full beard and wig were perfect. He didn't notice any cameras as he walked up and started surveying the cars. He needed something dependable. It didn't have to be fast, but being quick wouldn't hurt. He was looking at a dark-blue, 10 year old Nissan Sentra when a short, Hispanic man with several gold chains walked over and with surprisingly good English said, "That's the fast one, too."

"I didn't know they made a fast Sentra," Jared replied. "How dependable is it?"

"A Nissan? Hell, it'll probably be around longer than me. You wanna give her a spin?"

"I guess I should," Jared said. He didn't want to cause undue suspicion and buying a car without a test drive probably would.

The car was very peppy. It was like driving a big go-kart. It would do nicely. When they got back, Jared told the guy he would pay cash for the $3500 Sentra. Somehow after hearing that, his English got even better. They went inside to fill out the paperwork when something the man said froze Jared in his tracks. Something Jared had not thought of. The man wanted a photo copy of Jared's license. The man in the picture of the license would not match the guy sitting in front of him. He handed over his fake ID and waited for some kind of comment about the discrepancy. The salesman didn't even glance at it. He took it over to a copying machine, came back, and put the piece of paper in a manila folder with the other sales forms and handed the license back.

"Okay Mr. Norton, we're all set. Here are your keys and…" This Hispanic looked at him oddly for a second. Oh, Shit, he thought. Did he recognize him from the newscast? Was his beard coming unglued? Then the guy smiled and showed off three gold teeth. "Almost forgot. Let me go to the back and get your drive out tag."

Jared breathed a sigh of relief and smiled. "That would be great." When the salesman went through a doorway, Jared hurriedly found the photo copy in the open folder on the desk. He was stuffing it in his pocket as the guy came back out. He stood and took the tag from the man and headed for the door.

"Come back anytime Mr. Norton. We'll always have a deal for you at Etowah Motors."

"I sure will."

Taking the hot beard and wig off, Jared winded through the gears of his new Nissan Sentra. Sport Edition, no less.

CHAPTER 29

Mark had compiled quite the collection of exercise equipment over the years. Most weeks, he worked out for an hour at least 3 days. Here lately though, he'd been sweating it out 5 or 6 days. As he finished his last set of bench presses, his mind wandered back to Linda as it had been most of the day. It seemed as if she was reluctant to see him again. She told him she was super busy at work with something important and time consuming, but not even enough time to spare for a drink or a meal? He found himself feeling like he was back in high school. The more you cared and showed attention, the less it seemed they liked you. But if you paid them no attention and treated them like shit, they were all over you.

Throughout the years since Jenny, he had put up a wall to most women; so not to fall in love with them and have them taken away again. Now, it seemed he had let that wall down and he felt almost insecure. He found himself wondering if he did something wrong. Was he horrible in bed? She said it was wonderful, but it had been a long time since he'd last had sex. Maybe she had just been humoring him in her confirmation of a good night.

He did see her momentarily in a newscast about the

search for this so called 'supermarket slayer'. He also heard on a news radio station that the huge accident that took place on I-285 somehow was connected. Something about a motorist being shot through their windshield and therefore losing control of the vehicle and creating a pile-up. Authorities didn't confirm this, but they didn't comment on it either, so who knew.

He hadn't called Linda since yesterday, at which point she told him she would have to call him back. That didn't happen. Should he take that as a sign to leave her alone? Maybe he should go buy one of those men's magazines where they answer and philosophize about such questions. It was just after noon. Figuring he might catch her on her lunch break, he decided to try one more call. If she didn't answer or return the call, then he would leave well enough along. She answered on the fourth ring.

"Hi, Mark."

"Hey there."

"I'm sorry I haven't been able to return your call. This assignment is running me ragged and we aren't making much headway. My boss is breathing down my neck 24/7 like I have a crystal ball with all the answers. I'm barely getting 4 hours of sleep at night."

"This is the thing with the sniper?"

"Yeah, and it's exhausting."

"Well, I'm no psychologist but it sounds like you need some R and R."

"You're right. I do. I've been going full speed for almost a week now. I think I'll take off early today."

"That's exactly what you should do. And…"

"And?"

"And, you should go home, take a hot bath, and put something comfortable on – while I go pick up some things from the grocery store for dinner. I'll come back to your place, make us dinner, and we can lounge lazily over drink and conversation."

"That sounds wonderful. What are you, a romance

novelist?"

"No, but I quickly recognize a woman's worth."

"You always know the right thing to say, don't you?

"Mama didn't raise no fool." He said in an exaggerated Southern drawl.

"Okay, then. Here's the plan," said Linda. "I'll go home in another hour. I'll get comfy and we can have an early dinner. I still need to get to bed early so I can… Oh, shit!"

"What?"

"I totally forgot."

"I'm lost, Linda."

"I'm sorry, it's just that I forgot my best friend is flying into town tonight and I have to pick her up from the airport."

"Oh," Mark said, sounding defeated.

"No, no. Listen. It may still work out. If you don't mind my friend, Beth, tagging along."

"Not at all."

"Great. She wanted to meet you anyway."

"How did she…"

"Not that I said anything to her about you," she said giggling.

"I'm flattered."

"Don't be. You're a cool guy and I like you."

"Now, who always has the right thing to say?"

"I try," she said in good humor. "I'll just check when her flight comes in and call you when I get home."

"Sounds great. Talk to you later." Mark hung up the phone.

Mark was elated. Here he was feeling sorry for himself when she really liked him. He got ready to go to the grocery store. He would fix a great meal and he would aim to impress her friend, Beth. He skipped out the front door and into his Chevelle, mumbling words to a song he was making up as he went along.

* * *

Linda's kitchen didn't have some of the extravagance

of his own but she had the essentials. The meal he was preparing was one of his favorites and pretty easily prepared. Basically, it was bone-in, stuffed chicken breast. It was served over a bed of rice sautéed with spinach and feta. Mark preheated the oven, and then on the stove he heated two tablespoons of olive oil in a cast-iron skillet. The stuffing was a blend of ricotta cheese, chopped chives, and minced rosemary and thyme. Already stuffed, he placed the chicken breast, skin side down, into the hot oil until it browned. After repeating the opposite side, he transferred the skillet to the oven to roast for 20 minutes.

Shortly after he put the chicken in the oven, he opened a bottle of Sharaz red wine. As he poured himself a glass, the girls came through the door.

"We're home," bellowed Linda.

Mark made his way into the living room to meet them. Beth was a very attractive, light-skinned black woman. She wore extremely short, denim shorts and a tight t-shirt that pressed against a voluptuous chest. She had long, blonde braids that obviously were not her own. She smiled. He followed suit and shook her hand.

"I'm Mark."

"You sure are and I'm Beth."

"Nice to meet you. How was your flight?"

"Good, thanks. You're right, Linda. He is hot."

"Beth!"

"What? He already knows. How could you look like that and not know?" Beth said, smiling mischievously.

"Okay. Introductions are over," said Linda, pushing Beth toward the couch and giving Mark an 'I'm sorry, but that's how she is' face.

"I envy you, Beth. I could never get into an airplane and leave the ground," Mark said following.

"You're scared to fly?"

"Ever since I was a kid. I get horribly airsick. Something about not being in control. No matter what I see happening, it scares me."

"I never thought about it like that," Beth said looking thoughtful.

"I just opened a bottle of wine. Dinner won't be ready for another fifteen minutes, but would anyone care for a glass?" Two yeses shot from the living room, as he went to the kitchen. He brought their glasses to them and sat opposite them on the loveseat with his own.

"So Mark, I know how my girl, Linda, here feels about you, but how do you feel about her?"

"You don't have to answer that," Linda blurted. "You'll have to excuse Beth, she can be very direct at times."

"No, it's fine. I like her bluntness. Actually, I'm becoming very fond of Linda," he said, looking into Linda's eyes. "She's a very unique and passionate woman. Not to mention a great kisser."

"Okay then, you go girl," Beth said.

"Don't get her started, Mark."

"What? I'm just being honest. You are truly a breath of fresh air," Mark replied.

The timer on the oven went off and Mark went to tend to dinner. "You ladies want to dine in the living room or at the er... table?" Linda still had not gone shopping for furniture and only had a four seat fold up dining table from her apartment.

"In here is fine. You want some help?"

"I'm fine. Stay seated. I got this," Mark said bringing in three plates piled with the chicken and rice.

After taking a bite, Beth loudly expressed her approval with a "Mmmm, yummy," then said, "Hold it. Before we go any further, I have to ask." She paused looking at Mark intently. "Do you like black women?"

CHAPTER 30

Nobody used the phone for its original purpose any more. They were uploading photos or video to Facebook, texting, or listening to music, using it as an MP3 player. Brennan's sixty-two year old father was no different. The picture was of his father squatting down on a golf course pointing inside the pin. The caption above his father's head was, "A hole in one, Buddy."

His father, Gary Wayne Brennan had remarried after divorcing his mother Sarah almost twenty years previous. His old man retired from the bar/restaurant business and married a former girlfriend who, ironically, had been the woman he dumped thirty-five-years ago to start a relationship with Brennan's mother-to-be. His father now spent his days landscaping his lawn and playing golf. His step-mother Katrina, or Kat as she liked to be called, had convinced his father shortly after tying the knot, to leave the Metro Atlanta area and move to Rome Georgia where her family owned some land. Gary was skeptical at first having lived in the city his whole life. Then he found out that the subdivision they would be moving into sat in a surrounding golf course. They moved to Rome two weeks later. He dialed his father.

"Hey there, Buddy!" Everything was Buddy with his dad.

"Hey, Dad. Looks like a nice shot you hit there. Congratulations."

"Yeah, my first hole-in-one and it was a beauty. A 136-yard par three on the back nine. I hit an eight iron off the tee and it one-bounced right in the cup. Damn, I wish I'd had someone videoing it with my phone." Told ya. The phone becomes a video camera.

"That's great, Dad. So, how's Kat doing?"

"She's with her mother in Tunica playing the slots and whatever other game they can waste away money on. They're up there for the weekend, be back Sunday. What's up with you, Buddy? Still working that case with the Feds?"

"Yep. It's slow going, too. Not a lot of evidence to work off of. We were hoping to get some help from the press release, but so far just a bunch of misleading info. We'll get our man, though."

"That's the spirit, Buddy Boy. Well, I've got a foursome behind me giving me the evil eye so I better get going. When you get time, you should come up. Kat and I would love to have ya."

"I'll see what's up after I nail this case down, Dad. Good luck out there on the course."

"Thanks, Buddy. Talk to ya later."

"Bye, Dad."

Today was Saturday and Brennan's day off. Like he had told his Dad, the case was pretty much at a stand-still. Agent Hunt's team of agents and three detectives of Sandy Springs PD, including himself, had been turning over every rock in sight to no avail. They had yet to find the black Volvo from the carwash, nor had any real leads been created by the press release. There were no useful prints from the Camry other than a couple Toyota salesmen's and they had received no mail or messages from the perpetrators claiming their work. Not only was the guy smart and careful, but catching a killer who murders people from random spots, shooting from a couple football fields away, was incredibly difficult in itself. He would slip up or get over confident, Brennan was sure. They always did. It was just a matter of time.

He and Agent Hunt were both in agreement that they needed some help from the public. Somebody had seen this guy. He was not invisible. Even if he was disguising himself, somebody, somewhere had seen him. Brennan liked working with Linda Hunt. He didn't think he'd ever say that about a Fed, but she was good. She was an extremely competent investigator with exceptional organization skills. Her order of priorities inside the investigation was spot on. And man was she passionate. He could see how she made it to where she was being so young. A lot of guys had problems taking orders from an attractive woman, not Brennan. He would go into battle with this lady. In fact, he already was. Thinking of another attractive woman, he called Maria Flemez.

"You're up early," Maria answered.

"I was awakened by a maniac with a golf club."

"What?!"

Laughing, Brennan explained about his father sending the photo.

"At least somebody is doing what they love," she said.

"Oh come off it, Ms. Flemez. I've seen you in action at the lab. You love what you're doing, too."

"Don't get me wrong. I enjoy my work. It's definitely a challenge at times, but I'd rather be doing something else."

"And what would that be?"

"You."

"Well, I can't deny that you are very good at that."

"I knew you would agree, but seriously, I get tired of working around such tragic events. Don't get me wrong. I like helping to put the puzzle together that captures those responsible. I just hate having to think about and deal with sad case after sad case."

"It does get to you," Brennan offered.

"I mean, every week it's a rape or a robbery. I know this is reality, Brennan, but sometimes ignorance is bliss. Ya know?"

"I do. I think about it all the time. I also know that I'm good at what I do. Through all the evil out there, I like to think I slow it's decent. I've been doing it so long, it doesn't even feel like a job, but an obligation."

"And I know that, Brennan. I love your passion and commitment. You are definitely in your element."

"It's not always invigorating, but it all makes sense when I'm able to prevent someone from getting hurt or stop someone from taking another's life. I'm saving people. At least that's how I trick myself into putting the badge on every day."

"You are and you do. You're so cute! Let's stop talking about work and start talking about what you're gonna do with your day off."

"Well, I was thinking of asking a beautiful woman to have a picnic with me at Piedmont Park. I thought maybe we could rent a couple bikes from a place called Skate Escape and I would take her on a tour of the nearby neighborhood that I grew up in."

"Wow. Did you just come up with that?"

"Actually, I've been planning it for a couple days."

"And who is this beautiful woman, if I may ask?" she said giggling.

"I'll pick you up in an hour. How does that sound?"

"I can't wait."

"See ya."

"Bye."

Piedmont Park was huge. It was Atlanta's Central Park. It had a botanical garden, a lake, a humongous swimming pool with diving boards, miles of skating and running paths, and acres of grassy fields. Brennan grew up in the neighborhood across the street. Midtown Atlanta was a great place to live. Not only was it an epicenter of business and social activity but it was beautiful. It was a mixture of magnificent architecture and vibrant vegetation. Between Ponce De Leon Avenue and Tenth Street, where the park started, the streets were lined with dogwoods and the short driveways led to elegant Victorian or Georgian homes. Some had tall columns holding up wrap around verandas while others had six or eight pairs of French doors in their façade. The trees were lush and green in the spring and summer, while autumn brought with it a cacophony of colors.

They sat on a flannel blanket in one of the fields. It was May First and beautiful, so there were a lot of people in the park. They skyline of Atlanta sat to their left. It looked close enough to touch, skyscrapers rising up out of the ground like majestic entities. Brennan brought with them a basket filled with cheeses, crackers, and pre-made sandwiches. They also stopped on the way and picked up a bottle of white wine.

"This is perfect," Maria said, leaning back on her hands and letting her head hang backwards. "It's like a scene out of a movie."

"I'm glad you approve, but don't get too relaxed yet. We still have a bike ride to take."

After they talked over snacks and a glass of wine they dropped the basket and things off at the car that was parked street-side on Piedmont Avenue. A short walk took them to a place Brennan had frequented as a teen.

Skate Escape had been around since the seventies. They sold all types of roller skates, skateboards, and bicycles. On the side of the store, there was a counter set up under an awning. This is where the place did its rental part of the business. As they walked past a selection of used bicycles toward the counter, a young, highly tattooed man in his twenties came out.

"Can I help you folks with something?"

"Yeah. We wanted to rent a couple bikes for maybe an hour or two," Brennan said.

"That's no problem."

He then showed them the hourly rates for skates and bicycles. Five minutes later, they were rolling down a path in the park on a couple Beach Cruiser bicycles. They took the path out of the park and onto Charles Allen Avenue which ran between a row of Victorian homes sitting up on a bank to their right and Grady High School to their left.

"That's my old high school," Brennan said, pointing to the old structure.

"It's beautiful," she said admiring the three-story main building. "It looks well maintained, but old."

"It is. It was the first high school in Atlanta to be built with a stadium and sports field. Let's go around the other side. I'll show you."

They rode on, making a left on Eighth Street. They stopped on the left side of the street right before crossing over Monroe Drive. Looking through the chain-link fence, they admired the green field striped for football. On either side of the field were concrete-tiered seating stands. They looked like two stairways leading upward for giants.

"That's cool. Did you ever play there?"

"No. I was a shrimp in high school. I played basketball. I was a decent point guard all four years of high school, but not good enough to get a scholarship for college."

"So, what'd you do after high school?"

"I went to a community college called Georgia Perimeter. I worked nights at my Dad's bar in Buckhead, either bar-backing or cooking and earned my associates in criminal justice."

"Had you always wanted to be a cop?"

"Actually, no. I wanted to be a psychologist if you can believe it, but that didn't pan out."

"Lost the passion?" she asked

"No, I just couldn't handle all the school. I wanted to get out there, ya know. I wanted my own place and wanted to be on my way to the white picket fence and 2.4 kids." Laughing, he shook his head. "After I got my degree, I saw an ad in the paper with A.P.D. and thought my knowledge in criminal justice might help joust me up the ladder. Been slaying the bad guys ever since. The rest is history."

"Well, you turned out alright."

"You're pretty alright yourself," he said pulling her to him. They started to kiss when Brennan's phone began to ring and vibrate. He mumbled, "They'll call back," through a tangle of tongue and lips. Then, Maria's phone rang also.

"We're popular," Maria said, breaking their embrace and looking at her phone. "Oh, shit!"

"What?"

"There's some kind of emergency. Something about the Walk for Autism."

Brennan looked at his own phone.

"I got the same thing asking me to come in, ASAP

"What's the Walk for Autism?" she asked.

"I saw it on the bulletin board yesterday. They are closing off Dunwoody Place for some autism charity event."

"Oh, no! You don't think…"

"I hope not. Let's go."

CHAPTER 31

He would have liked to have left the Nissan running behind the shopping plaza, but the last thing he wanted to happen was to come running down the hill to find that some homeless guy took off in his getaway car. He settled for leaving it unlocked.

There was still a little over an hour before the walk started. Jared laid in wait. The gun wasn't as powerful as the Great Alaskan 338, but it would get the job done. He had been practicing and he consistently hit his target up to 500 yards away. The starting-line of the walk was 420 yards. He couldn't miss. Of course, he knew each shot would become more difficult. Maybe not the first two or three but after that, everyone would start running. Seeing people's heads explode in front of you will do that. They could run but there was nowhere to hide. Besides a couple vehicles, there was nothing to provide them shelter. The rifle he was using had a ten-round magazine. He planned to burn through two clips plus the one round he had chambered in under 45 seconds. The distance between him and the car, through the path, was 130 yards. To pack-up and cover that distance would take another 45 seconds. He would be driving through the plaza parking lot in under two minutes. The cops might not even comprehend what was going on in that amount of time. It was foolproof. People were gonna die… lots of them.

There was only 10 minutes until show time. Jared was doing breathing exercises as he was taught. Five seconds breathing in, five seconds breathing out. He was nervous. Not so much nervous, as he was anxious.

He lay looking through his scope with his left hand under the stock and his right on the grip. His finger was on the outside of the trigger guard and the butt of the big rifle pressed against his shoulder. There were around a thousand people at the starting line – some walking, yet others were there just for support. There were people all up and down Dunwoody Place and at least another thousand or two at the finish line.

Looking through the $400 scope, he saw that they were about to start. He looked for his first victim. He would try to shoot as many children as possible because he knew that the parents would then try to protect them or at least try to drag them out of harm's way. That's what he wanted. That way he would still have slow or unmoving targets to shoot once all hell was breaking loose. He found his first target. She had blonde hair and big blue eyes. Her mouth was twisted in a grimace even though she looked to be laughing. She was probably around eight or nine and the blonde woman pushing her wheelchair was most likely her mother. The little girl couldn't even walk. Pathetic. Pathetic and weak. Hell, he was doing her and her family a favor. He drew a bead on the middle of the little girl's forehead and slipped his finger around the trigger. He took a deep breath.

CHAPTER 32

He couldn't go to the nearby Quick Trip to get a slushy, which sucked. It was like 80 degrees outside and a cold, blue-raspberry slushy would hit the spot. His mom said the reason he couldn't walk to the gas station was because they were having a big race-marathon-thingy on the main road. He knew she wasn't lying because he could see a bunch of people through the woods using his binoculars. Sometimes parents did lie, though. A couple weeks ago, he wanted to see a new movie at the theater but his mom said it was for adults only, that they wouldn't even let him in because he was only eleven. Then a couple days later his friend, Brian, told him how cool the movie was. Brian's dad took him to see it and he had seen boobies like three times.

His own dad was in the army and hardly ever home. He was a really important person. Even people older than his dad called him 'Sir'. His rank was colonel, something to do with a full bird. Whatever that meant. He was a Junior and that meant that he and his dad had the same name. Robert Curtis Fuller Jr. was his whole name, but his mom called him Robbie. His dad never called him Robbie, only Robert. His dad was overseas right now protecting the USA from terrorists. Around the time Robbie was born, the terrorists blew up two ginormous buildings in New York and they killed a lot of Americans. His dad said he was making sure those ragheads stayed where they belonged. Whatever that meant.

"Ghost, come in. Ghost, come in. Over." That was Brian calling him on their super cool, walkie-talkies. They weren't the toy ones either. They were real ones.

"Ghost Face here. Over."

"Are you locked and loaded, soldier? Over."

"Ghost Face is locked and loaded. That's an affirmative, Hawkeye," Robbie replied.

Today was another rematch. Robbie had lost the last three, but today was going to be different because he had a new rapid loader for his paintball gun. There had been something wrong with his other loader and it had cost him several matches. Brian lived seven houses down from Robbie. There was nothing but woods behind the houses all the way to the shopping center, so they made that their battleground. Brian tied a green flag around a tree deep in the woods behind his house and Robbie tied a brown one around a tree behind his. Robbie's flag was brown because that was the color of his paintballs and Brian's was green because that was the color of his ammo. Green and brown were the only colors their parents would let them use. Something about blending in with the surroundings.

Robbie was in his full jungle fatigues complete with his equipment belt and camouflage face paint. They each had to start from their flag and work their way to the other's and capture the flag without getting shot.

"Ghost Face is engaging. Prepare to die, Hawkeye!"

"You don't stand a chance, Ghost. Hope you brought your body bag."

Last time Robbie had stuck to the tree line bordering the yards. It had proved fatal. This time he was going to go really deep into the woods. He ran quietly through the heavily wooded area, trying to gain ground at the beginning. He wanted to find a good place to lay and wait for Hawkeye to go for the flag. He found a spot between two big tree trunks that were growing closely together. He pulled out his binoculars and settled in. He was surveying the surrounding woods while pulling jelly beans from his cargo pocket. That's when he saw it. Something white. Surely Hawkeye wouldn't bring something white with him to a match. Using his binoculars, he looked for the flash of white he had just seen. There it was. It was a sneaker. Wait, two sneakers. He could barely see them because there was a tree in his way. Hoping it wasn't some kind of trap laid by Hawkeye, he slowly crawled to a better position to see what it was. He pulled up his binoculars and looked again. Holy cow! There was a man lying there. What was he doing? Was he dead? That would be so cool to find a dead body. Like that old movie with the kids walking on the train tracks that his mom liked.

"Hawkeye, come in." Brian didn't answer. He most likely thought that Robbie was trying to get him to give away his position.

"Brian, I'm calling a time out. Come in, this is important."

"What is it?" replied Brian.

"There's a man lying in the woods."

"What? Where are you?"

"I'm directly behind the Donaldson's house about halfway deep. I'm right by two big trees that look like they're growing out of each other."

"I'm coming to you. Over."

"Be really quiet, Brian."

"Roger that. Stealth mode engaged. Hawkeye out."

Robbie tried to sit up a little to get a better view of the guy. As he gazed through the binoculars he saw the man's leg move. He was alive. Then he saw a gun. It sure looked like one and he had seen plenty. He'd even been to a gun show with his dad. The man lying in the woods was holding a rifle. He heard a sound and looked behind him. Brian was crab walking toward him.

"Where is he?"

"He's lying down," Robbie said pointing. "You'll see his white Reeboks," he said handing over the binoculars.

"Oh, yeah. I see him. Holy cow, he's got a gun."

"I know. I just saw it , too."

"Do you think it's real?"

"I don't know. It looks real."

"Come on. Let's get closer so we can get a better view." Robbie didn't like it, but he crawled along side of Brian.

The heavily wooded area was dense with over-growth. Pines, oaks, and sporadically placed magnolias. The smell of earth and plant life invigorated Robbie. It excited his sense of adventure, but at the same time the surrounding vegetation made him feel safe. Except he didn't feel safe right now. He wouldn't tell Brian this because he didn't want him thinking he was a wimp. It was hard to move quietly because of all the sticks and old leaves, but after a while they came as close as they dared. The man lay unmoving about 40 feet to their left. The guy was almost lying on the path that the older kids used to go to the shopping plaza. He and Brian had used it once to go buy candy at CVS but his mom had found out the next time he went with her. The old lady behind the counter told her about seeing him the previous day and that was all she wrote. He was grounded for a week.

"Are you sure you saw him move?" Brian asked.

"Not 100 percent, but I think so."

"Well, he sure looks dead to me," he said looking through the binoculars. "How about this, Ghost. I'll stay here with my trusty R390 pointed at his head while you go poke him with a stick to see if he's alive."

"No way."

"Come on. If he moves, I'll hit 'em fully auto right in the face and we'll run to your house 'cuz it's closer."

"Why do I have to poke him?"

"Because you're quieter than me. You're a better point

man."

"I am?"

"Sure you are, Robbie."

"Ok. But if he moves, you have to blow him to smithereens."

"Scouts Honor," Brian said, doing a two finger salute.

"Screw the scouts," Robbie whispered. "Pinkie swear."

They did. Robbie was very slowly crawling toward the trail on his belly. He got to about 20 feet away and stopped. He was so scared. What if the gun was real and the man shot him? What if the guy was crazy and tried to eat him and his friend. Surely paintballs weren't going to stop him. He took a deep breath. Okay, I can do it. I'm a good point man. Even Brian said so. He crawled one more step.

* * *

This was the moment he loved about shooting long distances. If he even trembled a minute amount, the shot would be off. Breathing calmly, totally relaxed, he began to apply pressure to the trigger. He heard dry leaves crackling behind him and to the left. It was close to him. He registered, but in such deep concentration as he was, it seemed far away. There it was again, even closer. He looked over his shoulder to identify the sound and what he saw almost made him shit his pants. A soldier with face paint and a machine gun was crouching not 10 feet from him. He scrambled to get up and run when something hit his neck. Oh my God. I've been shot, thought Jared. He reached up with the hand that wasn't carrying the rifle and felt wetness when he was hit in the chest. Once, twice, and again in the arm. Jared ran for his life crying out as he went, sounding like a wounded animal.

He was dying. His neck stung like crazy and his chest was throbbing. He had to make it to the car. The army guys had to be right behind him, but he didn't dare look back. Coming to the steep hill declining to where his car was parked, he stumbled and fell through the dense briars, ripping his skin and clothes. He made it! He didn't see any army or police. He hurriedly put the key into the ignition, slinging the rifle into the back seat and stomped the accelerator.

CHAPTER 33

Brennan called his captain on the way in. Some kids had spotted their shooter. He dropped Maria at the station on the way to the scene. It seemed that their perp, in a rush to get away, had left a rifle case behind and Ms. Flemez was needed for her lab expertise.

He could barely control his excitement as he raced to a well-to-do neighborhood that sat between Roberts Drive and Dunwoody Place. Some fellow officers were already at the scene. Brennan was called as soon as the kid's mother called the police, but he had to drive from Midtown and drop Maria off.

He pulled onto Meadow Grove Drive and he saw the usual upper-middle class fare. Nice yards, nicer houses, and a German car or SUV in every other driveway. He saw a collection of squad cars and Crown Vics about half-way down and to his surprise he didn't see a media van yet. The front door was open to the Fuller residence with two uniforms just outside.

"Did one of the Fullers want this door open?" he asked pointing to the front door and looking quizzical.

"Uh, I don't think so," replied one of the uniforms.

"Hmmm." Brennan looked at the door as it might hold

some key to the case. The uniforms moved to either side to let the detective see the doorway more clearly.

"Ah ha!" Brennan said. The officers looked up waiting for some revealing info. Raising his index finger Brennan continued.

"Take notes, boys." He stepped outside the doorway. "You'll notice that just outside the door it's hot." The officers were hanging on every word. Brennan stepped inside the doorway. "Now, you'll notice that it's cooler on the inside." They looked at him quizzically. They didn't get it. He slammed the door in the uniforms face.   Idiots. 'Keep-the-door-closed-when-the-A/C-is-on 101'.

In the kitchen two of the other three detectives in the department were speaking to two boys of about twelve with their mother, Brennan assumed, standing by looking panic stricken. Detective Jenkins, usually working car theft and burglaries, saw Brennan and excused himself.

"What have we got?" asked Brennan.

"What we have is our sniper. The kids found the guy lying in the woods with his rifle, if you can believe it. They thought the guy was dead, approached him, and get this, shot him with a paintball gun."

"You've got to be kidding me."

"I shit you not, Brennan."

He filled him in on what he had already gotten out of the kids and mother.

"CSI is still all over the woods photographing and processing," said Jenkins.

"Okay, why don't you guys go talk to the techs and I'm gonna run through it again with the kids."

"You got it, chief," Jenkins said playfully, slapping him on the shoulder.

As the two detectives took their leave he introduced himself to the mother and explained that he just wanted to ask the boys a few more questions.

"By all means. I can't believe that a murderer was behind our house. I mean, this is a great neighborhood," said the mother.

He turned to the boys. "So, I hear you boys had an exciting morning."

One boy nodded, the smaller one. The bigger kid said, "Yep. We were on a real mission, like Robbie's dad."

"Are you Robbie?" he said nodding toward the smaller one.

"Yes, sir."

"And what does your dad do?"

"He's in the army, sir." Jenkins had told him that the Fuller Kid's father was a colonel.

"That's very honorable. You must be proud of him."

"Yes, sir."

"And what's your name, son?"

"Brian."

"Okay, I know you already told the other detectives, but I want you to tell me everything that happened this morning starting when you woke up."

"Are you a detective, too?" asked Brian.

"Yes, I am." Brennan pulled out his badge and showed it to them. Simultaneous 'Cools' were expressed.

"Why don't you have a suit on like the other detectives?" Brian again. He still had on his shorts and polo from his and Maria's day at the park.

"I was undercover." More enthusiastic 'cools' this time.

Brennan took notes as the boys replayed each other's version of their adventure. He thanked them and told them he might have more questions later and would be showing them some pictures to see if this guy was a 'bad guy'. He gave each of them a card, along with the mother, and asked them to call if they thought of anything else. If this guy was their sniper, these kids were very lucky.

As he walked out the back door to make his trek through the woods, he spotted a huddled group of Feds with Agent Linda Hunt speaking authoritatively, gesturing with her hands. He walked over as they were breaking up.

Shaking Brennan's hand Linda said, "Saw you

interviewing the kids, and thought it better not to interrupt."

"Thanks."

"I got the story from your colleagues. Brave kids."

"Lucky kids, if this is our guy."

"I concur, well, let's go see what we have."

They made their way through the woods and found the spot where the man with the gun had laid. There were evidence markers everywhere. They both donned gloves and booties for their shoes.

"So the two boys thought he was laying here dead?" Linda asked.

"Yeah, they saw the rifle of course, but they say he didn't move a muscle for a good ten minutes while they observed him."

"He was concentrating on his shot," she said shaking her head.

"That was my thought too," he said as he crouched next to the spot where the killer had laid. Linda was beside him. They both looked through the last 20 yards of wooded area and could see the festivities still going on at the starting line, though the Walk was officially over.

"Sick fuck was gonna shoot into the Charity Walk."

"This is one demented guy," Linda replied looking at Brennan's features. His jaw muscles stood out and he was breathing audibly through his nose.

"Hey," she said, putting a hand on his shoulder. "We'll get him. Let's stay objective here. I have a psychological profile being drawn up as we speak. We have two new witnesses and we have the rifle case. We'll get him."

"I just hope we get him before he shoots somebody else." He took a deep breath and stood up. Detective Jenkins approached.

"Agent Hunt," he said nodding his head in greeting. "Come check this out." He pointed with his thumb over his shoulder.

The three walked down the path, stepping agilely

around the yellow evidence markers. The sun was out in full force now trying to penetrate the canopy of leaves overhead, only barely succeeding. Regardless, it was stifling hot and humid. They walked a hundred yards or so and came to a steep decline, choked with briars that led to the service way of a shopping plaza. There were crime scene techs everywhere. They were meticulously combing the briars for fibers and trace evidence. There was no way someone got through those briars without leaving something behind. The three of them skirted farther down the crest of the hill and picked their way through to the bottom. There was another tech photographing a set of long burn out marks, obviously left by someone in a big hurry.

"I'm sure the rubber left behind by the tires will be too common a size to really trace their origin, but of course we'll send it to the lab," Jenkins said as he grabbed a plastic evidence bag from the photographing tech. "This however should prove to have a closet full of leads." Jenkins handed the bag to Linda. Inside was a mildly worn, white Reebok sneaker.

"The kids said he had white Reeboks on." Brennan said.

"Exactly," replied Jenkins.

CHAPTER 34

"That's right, Candice. Chief Wade Skinner of the Sandy Springs Police Department has confirmed that his department is working closely with the FBI in the investigation of the double homicide that took place not two weeks ago on Roswell Road. Channel 5 Investigates is now on the scene where a suspect in this investigation was not only spotted but derailed in another attempt to take people's lives."

The camera moved to the left and two young boys of about twelve filled the screen. You could see that it was dark outside behind the kids, but even so you could see they were in a wooded area. Now the screen held the news anchor and the boys.

"This is Robbie Fuller Jr. and Brian O'Reilly. These two brave, young men found the suspect lying in the woods with a large rifle. It's not confirmed yet, but sources say he was aiming and about to shoot into a crowd of people who were through the woods here partaking in a charity event for autism. The boys, who were playing paintball in the woods, scared the man off before he could do any harm." The camera zoomed in a little and the anchor spoke to one of the boys.

"Tell us Brian, were you scared?"

"No, Ma'am."

"How about you, Robbie?"

"No. We were just trying to catch the bad guys like my dad. He's in the army."

"There you have it from two local heroes that…"

He turned the TV off and threw the remote control across the room. "Idiot!" he said through clenched teeth. "God damn idiot!" louder this time. He paced around his living room fuming. He went to a drawer in his kitchen and retrieved an untraceable, pay-as-you-go cell phone he had purchased at Wal-Mart. He turned it on and punched in a number.

"Hello?"

"What the fuck are you doing? Are you trying to put us in jail, you idiot?!"

"Of course not. I'm sorry. It's just…"

"Sorry? Sorry doesn't cut it, Jared. We had a plan. We stick to the plan. The next target has meaning. Just like the first two. You can't just go killing people for no reason, just because you think you can. Which, by the way, doesn't look to be the case. You listen to me and you listen good. You be where you're supposed to be, when you're supposed to be, so we can follow through with our objective. Do you understand or do I need to draw it in crayon for you?"

"I understand," Jared said with a tremor in his voice.

"I'll keep my ear to the ground to make sure they aren't getting close to us."

Jared didn't want to tell him but he had to. They would probably broadcast the fact, but the guy had the connections to find out anyway.

"I dropped my rifle case at the scene." He wouldn't say anything about the shoe. That could have been anybody's, thought Jared.

"You what?"

"I freaked out when those kids saw me."

137

"Was there anything in it? Anything at all?"

"No, nothing."

"We're okay, then."

"But it'll have my prints or dead skin or something that could lead to me. How are we okay?"

"Who cares about them having your prints or DNA? What would they compare them to? You're not on file. You're not a government or federal employee. You're not a convicted felon. They can't do squat. We'll talk about this in further detail when we meet. Just lay low and I'll see you then."

"Okay," Jared said hanging up the phone.

He was shaking. The guy scared him. He never knew why, but he had never been more frightened by any other person in his life. It was as if the guy had two personalities. One minute he seemed like a genius and was often awe-inspiring in his eloquence. The next, he would stare at you with such hatred, such intensity, that it seemed to define evil. He hoped the man would accept his apology.

CHAPTER 35

"This case is exhausting," Linda was saying. "I mean we now have the guy's DNA, we have carpet fibers most likely from his house. Hell, we have a slew of trace evidence. If we ever capture the guy, we will be well on our way to a conviction, but none of our evidence points to his whereabouts. I'm sorry I'm dumping all this on you. It's not your problem."

"No, it's fine. Really," said Mark through the phone. "It's therapeutic for you to vent. I'd like to give you some feedback that would help, but I'm afraid I'm out of my element with this."

"Thank you, Mark. You're so sweet. It's okay, though. Something will break. At the same time, I have Beth to entertain. She's flying back to Baltimore in the morning. I swear, I love her to death, but a little bit goes a long way with her."

"I like Beth. She is full of personality and quick to speak her mind. I wish I was more like her sometimes when it came to dealing with my customers. Just able to be blunt with no worries of repercussions."

"Yeah and you'd be broke, too."

"Well, there is that." Linda was laughing. Mark always

put her in a good mood. "How about I make you two dinner again. This time at my place?"

"No, I don't want to put you to the trouble. It's my turn to treat anyway."

"I'll act like I didn't hear that and expect y'all at 8:00?" he said letting the question hang.

"Well, since you insist, kind sir," she said, still giggling like a school girl.

"I do."

"Okay then, we'll see you at 8:00."

"Just call when you are ready and I'll give you directions. It's only about a mile or two from your place."

"Sounds great. Talk to you later."

"Bye," Mark said, setting his cordless down.

He was starting to really like Linda. He wished she could come over by herself. He wanted to make love to her again. Her friend, Beth, probably wouldn't mind watching. Though nowhere near his type, Beth looked at you like she wanted to tear your clothes off and eat you. Which he was sure she could do. She was a very sexy woman with curves in all the right places. She could fit into quite a lot of his fantasies but not his realities.

Mark chose to make a three-cheese lasagna with Caesar salads and he also made a pitcher of vodka gimlets. The women showed up right on time and Mark showed them to the living room.

"Dinner is just about done, Ladies. Let me get you a drink while you wait."

"Is he for real, girl? You sure he's not some robot programmed to be the perfect guy?" Beth asked Linda.

"I can assure you, he is real."

"Yes, let's talk about that. Give me the juicy details."

"Details about what?" Mark said, coming into the room and setting their drinks on marble coasters.

"Nothing!" Linda said a little too quickly. "Your house is beautiful," she said, diverting the conversation. "Did you decorate it yourself?"

"Thank you. I did, with a little help choosing the furniture. Okay. Ladies. Dinner is served. You can bring your drinks with you."

Mark had a huge dining room with an antique teak table in its center. There was a matching china cabinet that sat to one side and a large display case on the other holding several vintage rifles.

"Wow," exclaimed Beth. "You're rich."

"Beth!"

"What? I feel like I'm on an episode of MTV Cribs or something."

"I don't know about rich," said Mark, "but I do well thanks to a lot of hard work and frugal living in my past."

"I'm sorry, Beth…"

Interrupting, Mark said "No, it's fine really. Sometimes I have to sit back and appreciate it all myself."

"Whatever," Beth said. "These vodka thingies are really good, too."

"Wait 'til you taste my lasagna."

They ate their salads and the main course while talking mostly of the women's days of high school and their inevitable friendship. When they finished, they each got a refill on their drinks and retired to Mark's back deck.

It was dark out and instead of turning on the lights, Mark lit several Tiki torches. He and Linda sat in a wicker loveseat and Beth sat opposite them in a matching chaise lounge.

"Look at you two. If I didn't know better, I'd think you two had been together for years."

Everyone sat in a comfortable silence enjoying their after-meal contentment. The air was a little humid, but it was pleasantly warm and smelled of magnolia and honeysuckle. The shadows were doing their dance as the Tiki torches' flames jumped this way and that, fighting a slight breeze. Beth sat up and set her glass on the table then picked up both Linda and Mark's phones.

"What are you doing?" asked Linda.

"Nothing, just admiring you rich people's iPhones. I have a Blackberry but these iPhones are something else. They're just like little computers." She was really looking for this free app that another friend had shown her. She found it and downloaded it first to Mark's, then to Linda's phone. They would see it later on their menu screen and thank her.

Snapping out of her state of relaxation, Linda sat up and stretched. "Well, we better get going. I have to have Beth at the airport at 7:00 a.m. and then take my butt to work."

Mark walked the women to their car where Beth gave Mark a hug, squeezing his butt in the process.

"I just had to see what you were working with. Not bad. Nice meeting you, Mark. I'm sure I'll see you at the wedding."

"Wedding?" he asked.

"Yours and Linda's," she replied, giggling and ducking inside Linda's Honda.

"Thanks for a great evening," Linda said, shaking her head. "The lasagna was great." Mark leaned in and they kissed deeply with cheers from inside the car.

"Later, Agent Hunt. I'll call you."

"Bye, Mr. Glover."

Mark watched them pull out until he couldn't see the car's taillights anymore. He exhaled loudly. "Linda, Linda, Linda." He said thinking to himself.

CHAPTER 36

The thirty-two year old woman screamed through her gag as he brutally sodomized her. It wasn't very loud. The TV that was turned up inside the motel room and drowned her out. The motel was of the seedier places only costing him $30 for the night. There was only one pillow that came with the queen-size bed and the ceiling tiles were falling into the tub, but it suited his purposes.

The woman, Stacy Kemp, and he were on top of that stained, urine-smelling, queen bed, but with a plastic sheet covering it. Plastic covered almost the whole room actually. The floor, chair, and nightstands all taped and covered in painter's plastic. The woman was already bleeding onto the plastic sheet. After donning two pair of latex gloves he had beaten her badly, breaking her nose and knocking out a couple of her straight, white teeth. Her hands were tied behind her back using plastic zip-ties. Her wrists were slippery with blood from her struggling and earnest attempts to flee. But that's not where the majority of the blood had come from. Most of the blood had come from the wounds on her chest, though he had put duct tape over the gushing wounds so she wouldn't bleed out. He had slowly cut her nipples off her chest with a serrated bread knife he picked up at Wal-Mart. The bleeding from her breasts had slowed to a trickle. Now, blood was making its way around the sides of the Louisville slugger as he rammed it in and out of her anus. He didn't derive any pleasure from this, for it was a means to an end. He just wanted those that loved her to know that her death was painful and brutal.

It took him a little over four hours to clean the motel room properly. Every surface was wiped down and sanitized. The carpet, drapes, chairs, and bed were all meticulously vacuumed. He wasn't trying to hide traces of the girl, for they were sure to find her. He didn't want them to find any fibers, hair, or trace evidence that could link him to the room. He couldn't be caught yet, for it was just the beginning.

CHAPTER 37

Detective Mike Dugan of the Atlanta Police Department had never seen anything like this in his career. As a 22 year veteran, that was saying a lot. He thought he had seen it all. Thought that a murder scene couldn't affect him after all he'd seen and been through.

The odor was what got most people. Decaying flesh was hard to get used to. He need not worry about that with this scene though. The victim hadn't been dead that long. There was a strong odor, though. So strong, in fact, they eventually had to set up an exhaust fan with a filter. The odor was chlorine bleach. A lot of it. The female victim lay in a bathtub full of it. Though that was the least of the young woman's problems. Most of her teeth had been knocked out and someone had made a mess of her breasts. It was hard to make an inventory of all her injuries because of the detached limbs floating in disarray. Both arms and legs had been severed in a not-so-neat fashion. You could see hack marks on some of the protruding bone. Jesus Christ. Who could be capable of something like this? This was rage on a level he had never seen.

"Detective Dugan?" Someone calling his name shook him from his reverie. "Detective Dugan," a scene tech

145

continued. "We're ready to drain the tub. Are you finished in here?

"Yeah. Go ahead, Cooper. I have to question some witnesses. I'm done with the body until she goes to post."

He would come back to the room once all the techs were gone and process the scene again. So far they had only found evidence of the removal of evidence. There wasn't a speck of dust in the entire room. Not one print or smudge on any surface in there. Whoever did this went to great difficulty to leave nothing behind. Leaving the body wasn't any kind of symbolism; it was just more method to his madness in covering his tracks. The bleach would eliminate any trace evidence whatsoever. Not only was the guy obviously crazy and meticulous, but he was extremely smart and hip to what crime scene techs would look for. He made a note to himself that it was a good possibility their perp was ex- or currently working in law enforcement. Who knew? It seems everybody knows how to get away with murder these days. All you had to do was turn on your TV.

There were only a couple people to interview. Several of the motel's occupants had long since checked out and the only record the owner kept of these customers was a first name he wrote beside the room number in a log book. He spoke with three occupants that remained. Not only did they not seem to know anything about the person in 107, but they seemed to be the type that wouldn't talk to police about it even if they had. The owner was a small Indian man in his late forties. He had mostly gray hair that was receding and wore wire-rim glasses pushed tight against his face. He had owned the run-down motel for eight years and this wasn't the first time someone had been murdered at his place of business.

"I tink I told you already, Detective. Dee man was white. Ee's name from dee log ees Bob. He had a walking steek."

"A walking stick, you mean a cane?" asked Dugan.

"Yes, a cane."

"If you had to guess his age, what would it be?"

"Maybe upper forties or low fifties eef I had to guess. But like I say, I no see him very good."

The Indian told him the man came in during early afternoon yesterday, which was Monday, May 3rd. The owner's description of the perp was not only the best thing he had to go off of, it was the only thing. No one else saw this older white guy at any time between the time he checked out of the room and the discovery of the girl's body. The guy was a ghost.

CHAPTER 38

Linda sat in her makeshift office at the Sandy Springs police department. She was waiting on Detective Brennan to come in so they could go over the evidence left behind by their sniper. Two of her agents were in the field checking into some of those leads and another sat at a cubicle partitioned off from where she sat. The room was most likely used for conferences at more normal times. It was large, maybe 20' x 30' and the walls were bare except for a couple award plaques bestowed on the department for this and that. It was sectioned off into 4 parts by carpeted partitions. Three smaller and a larger section for herself.

She was staring dreamily out of one of the 4 windows watching heavy traffic at the intersection of Barfield and Hammond Drive which, ironically, was part of her new jogging route. Brennan walked in.

"Federal Agent Hunt, come in. Earth to Agent Hunt," Brennan said playfully as he sat in one of the chairs on the other side of her desk.

"Sorry, I was daydreaming about what I was going to do to this guy once we find him."

"Well, I'm with you on that one, but the odds right

now are probably more like 'if' we find him."

"Don't come in here with that negativity, Brennan," she said in a more pleading voice than authoritative. "We are going to get him. What do you have besides what I already know from CSI?"

"Let's see here," he said looking at his notes. "I don't know what all you have, so I'll run through what I know. The rifle case is negative for anything foreign besides a couple partials and some gun oil. As you know already, we have enough of the guy's skin off the briars to help a burn clinic. And let's see... the tire marks were left by a Michelin Model F2 size 17 R35 205, which I might add are available on 8, count 'em—8, various models of cars from Fords to Hondas."

"You're just full of positivity," she said sarcastically.

"I'm not finished. That brings us to the shoe. We have carpet fibers, a slew of human hair, about ten types of dirt, and then we have a couple slivers of paper that have laser printed ink on them."

"Is the printing unique?"

"It is and it isn't, according to Flemez. The pattern is consistent with certificate printing and coupon design printing."

"That's a pretty wide scope," she said. "It could mean anything from cut up mailbox stuffers to a printing company."

"I know."

One of Linda's subordinate agents walked in just then. The agent's name was Michael 'Big Mike' Ogles. And big he was. He stood 6'7", 270 pounds. He had put on 20 pounds since his days of playing tight-end for UCLA, yet he wore the extra weight well, but he still struggled with some doorways. He stood before Linda and Brennan with obvious good news.

"I think I got something," he said.

"Well, don't keep us in suspense," said Linda.

"I was combing the tow truck yards while awaiting a

call back from the sample we sent to Quantico, you know looking for intakes that came in after the Walk for Autism episode. Maybe an unreported hot car with our guys M.O. Well, there was a car that caught my attention. It used to be a '91 Nissan Sentra, now it's just a burned-out shell. I asked the Super when the car came in, and get this—6 hours after the walk episode. The Forsyth County Fire Department was called out by some nearby neighbors of an abandon property because of a car that was aflame. No one knows whose car it is or where it came from. The car has no tag and I've already ran the VIN. It's not registered." Agent Ogles' phone rang. "One minute," he said.

"Yeah, what ya got. Uh huh, uh huh, spell that. Okay. Thanks a lot. Bye. That was my VIN inquiry. The title is in the name of an Etowah Motors bought over 3 months ago."

"Okay," said Linda, "so what are we thinking here? That our guy stole this car off the lot somehow and used it as his getaway?"

"Maybe," Brennan said rubbing his chin in thought. "But would this guy want to steal another car knowing the heat was on? Remember, he's smart and very organized."

"Maybe he thought…" Linda started.

"I'll bet he bought it!" interrupted Brennan.

"I just told you the title is in Etowah Motors name," Ogles said patronizingly. "No, listen. If he just bought it and didn't register or transfer the title then it still would be in their name."

"You're right!" snapped Linda, "And if this place is even remotely upstanding, they would need papers signed, social, Driver's License, etc. Ogles, get me Etowah's location. Get the guy out of bed or whatever you have to do. We're going to go see a man about a dog."

CHAPTER 39

Jared sat at the abandoned construction site that he used for his target practice. The guy was supposed to meet Jared here 10 minutes ago, but he was always late. Jared was a little scared. Jared had really fucked up and betrayed a trust between them. He thought if he could have made that last shot on his own, that maybe the guy would respect him more. Look at him more as an equal. But it had not been in the plans. The plan was to do the supermarket victims to get local attention, then do the highway shots to obtain national attention – then they could get to the good stuff. The highway shots had been a thing of beauty. The guy really could shoot. He had been teaching Jared and he was getting better, but this guy was a fucking machine. Jared had witnessed him shoot a truck that said Big Brother Movers on the side from over a mile away and put 9 out of 10 shots inside the 'O' in Movers. A fucking machine. Not only could the guy shoot but he was a genius. He planned everything down to the last detail and that was why he was mad at Jared. Rightfully so, thought Jared. He hated to disappoint him. Especially now that the plan was about to get good. Now people would not only remember him but they would lock their doors because of him. They would keep their kids inside and they would leave lots of lights on. Jared hoped he still would be part of it all. There was so much fun to come. He hadn't got to kill anybody, yet. The machine had done all the trigger pulling. But Jared had helped. Yeah, he set everything up and he knew he had done it well.

"Why did you deviate from the plan?" a voice said, coming from behind him. He spun and saw the guy sitting on a tree stump 20 feet from him. There was no telling how long he had been there.

"I made a mistake. It won't happen again. I just wanted to cause more attention. I wanted to prove myself," replied Jared.

The man walked closer to Jared, stood in front of him and smiled. He looked at Jared with repulsiveness on the inside but showed a genuine grin. He knew he would now have to kill Jared sooner than he had originally planned. He had always planned on killing him once he served all his use, but now the idiot's own actions would cause him to expire sooner.

"It's okay, Jared. I understand your motives. They were just, but we are so far into our mission, now, that we must be very careful and stick completely to the plan."

"Can I still kill one of the important ones?"

"Of course, Jared."

"I already saw what happened to the Kemp girl in the paper," said Jared. "I wanted to do her. You said I could have fun with her before we killed her."

He wanted to kill Jared right there, right now. Slit his belly open and strangle him with his own intestines. Cut his testicles off and choke him with his own genitalia. He was but a selfish child in a man's body. He despised him.

"The schedule had to be moved up due to unforeseen obstacles. You can have your fun with the next one. I've already obtained transportation. We have three days until the next scene unfolds. You will meet me here at the planned time."

This meeting place which he had shown to Jared was full of purpose. There was not a house or business for several miles and there was only one road in and out. He could watch from afar and see if Jared was being followed. He had to put a certain amount of trust in Jared. He needed Jared to be his puppet to get the heat away from him. It was working. The cops were looking for Jared under every rock. You couldn't turn the TV on any channel without hearing about the search for him, but he himself was a ghost. He knew that the authorities would soon find Jared and he would be watching.

"So everything's cool?" Jared had thought the guy would be a little angrier, maybe even threaten Jared.

"Yes, we're still on track, but try to lay low. Take a couple days off work if you can."

"Okay. I'll do that and see you back here in 3 days."

With that, the man walked into the woods and out of sight. Jared got into his car and turned on the air conditioning. He wouldn't mess up again, thought Jared. If he just stuck to the plan and lay low, he was going to be remembered as a devastatingly smart killer who not only out-smarted the cops and FBI, but got away not leaving a trace. After these next killings would come the grand finale and it would turn the country on its ear. It would change the justice system as they knew it. People are gonna die… lots of them.

CHAPTER 40

The rain was coming down in sheets. The sky was the color of ash as far as the eye could see, the highway only a few shades darker. The big storm drains on the road's shoulders were raging war with the downpour. The car's tires cut through an inch of water as they made their way north on I-575. They were going to meet with Hector Sanchez, the sales manager at Etowah Motors. Brennan rode in the passenger's seat of Linda's P.O.S. Crown Vic. It was technically his day off, but he felt they were finally getting close to having a bead on their man.

He was supposed to be meeting with an old friend in support of his friend's sobriety at a place called Ridgeview in Smyrna. His friend, Todd Smalls, had been battling a heroin addiction for the past 12 years. He and Todd had played basketball together at Grady High and had stayed close throughout the years. Todd was a smart and funny kid, quick to tell a joke and quicker to help out a friend. Todd's father was a prominent pediatrician who was strict, but very supportive when Todd had voiced his ambition to follow his father's footsteps into the medical field. Todd had a promising career ahead of him. Then, half-way through medical school, his 15 year old, baby sister was killed. A log came off the back of an 18 wheeler striking and causing her and her friend's car to overturn, killing his sister and severely injuring her friend. Todd took the loss extremely hard. He and his sister had been very close. Not long after the accident, Todd was in a crash himself while drunk and, though the wreck didn't involve anyone else, Todd broke his arm after striking a parked car. He did a short stint in the hospital and was sent home with a cast and some pain killers. The cast came off but the pain killers not only stayed— got stronger. He was hooked. Todd would tell you it was his escape, his escape from the pain of losing his baby sister. Lortabs turned into Roxycontin and Roxys to Oxys. Swallowing pills turned into snorting them and snorting turned into shooting. Todd's habit, after exhausting all avenues of funding, soon became impossible to maintain. Prescription pills were expensive, so he turned to heroin. A $10 bag of heroin's high was equivalent to almost $50 of prescription pills. He was hooked again. That habit got out of control as well and he soon needed $200 a day to keep an even keel and not get sick with withdrawals. Of course, as a heroin addict, he was irresponsible and unable to stay employed. He had long since leeched all he could from family and friends and, at that point, turned to a life of petty thefts and burglaries to support his habit. He was in and out of the Fulton County Jail, unable to complete many attempts at rehab programs. His last attempt at procuring funds to support his habit was more serious and involved a gun. The judge was done with the slaps on the wrists and wanted to send Todd to prison. But with pleading from Todd's family and Brennan himself, he was sentenced to a 9-month, in-patient rehabilitation program at the Ridgeview Institute.

Todd was taking his recovery seriously this time around and Brennan, as his only friend still standing, signed on as his sponsor. He loved Todd like a brother. Brennan frequently was at his friend's side through counseling sessions and Narcotics Anonymous meetings. Today, he was scheduled to attend one of Todd's last therapy sessions, but this current case was becoming almost like an obsession. He had to find this guy and would not stop until he did. So, after giving his apologies for flaking on his prior engagement, he sat entangled in this killer's web, trying to place the next piece of the puzzle.

"Agent Ogles is having the burnt car towed to your precinct," Linda was saying as she concentrated on the nasty weather and the road ahead. "Damn it Brennan, I hope this is our guy."

"I have a feeling it is. I've been running it through my head all day and I can't come up with any other feasible alternative."

"Well, we'll know something shortly. We're 10 minutes from the prestigious Etowah Motors."

"Etowah. Isn't that a tribe of Indians," Brennan asked.

"Yeah, I Googled it and read briefly through some stuff. The Etowah originated from right around here. They have some type of burial mounds around Cartersville and Red Top Mountain that still bring tourists."

"Man, am I sheltered. I've lived 40 minutes from Cartersville my whole life and have never even heard of the Etowah Indians, or Red Top Mountain for that matter. Had you heard of them, Linda?"

"No, but I'm from Maryland, so I get a pass. You, sir, are guilty of some serious home-turf negligence." They were both laughing as they pulled up a long driveway off of Hwy 92. "This is it," announced Linda.

"About what I expected," Brennan said looking out the window at the small collection of cars. "And the rain has stopped."

Etowah Motors sat off Hwy 92 on a slight incline on the north side of the street. The lot of maybe 30 cars was surrounded by waist-high steel posts preventing theft and on each post was a colorful balloon. There was one of those big air-inflated, dancing, attention-grabbers shifting wildly street front. Brennan couldn't figure out what it was though. A big worm maybe? Etowah's only building had a rough-looking deck out in front that was in serious need of paint. Upon walking to the front door, he noticed the deck was the least of their worries. Mismatched shingles littered the roof and one of the front windows was of the plastic, garbage bag variety.

They entered and a cheap bell tied to a string announced their arrival. The interior was little better than the exterior, Brennan noticed as a short, pudgy, Hispanic man approached.

"My name is Hector Sanchez," the man said smiling, exposing gold teeth to match his many chains and shaking their hands. "What can I do for you folks?" Linda took the lead.

"My name is Agent Hunt, Mr. Sanchez. I'm with the FBI," she said, showing her badge. "This is Detective Brennan." He showed his creds. The man was suddenly pale, even though he had been expecting them.

"Oh, right. You're here about the Nissan Sentra."

"Actually, we're here about the man who bought the Sentra."

"Okay, I remember him. Mr. Norton. Really nice guy with the big beard." Linda and Brennan exchanged glances.

"Mr. Sanchez, can we see any paperwork you may have concerning this Mr. Norton and the sale of the car?"

"Sure, sure. Have a seat right here and I'll go get the file." They sat in uncomfortable chairs across from a cheap desk with an old computer monitor on top.

"Big beard?" she said.

"Probably a disguise like with the chin at the Volvo theft."

Hector came back carrying a thin manila folder and sat at the desk opposite them. "This is everything," he said, sliding the folder to Linda. It included the sales history of the car, a couple pictures of the Sentra, a bill of sale, and a couple other company record-type documents. The bill of sale had the buyer's information as a Mr. Jerry Norton. It listed a driver's license number, a date of birth, a social, and an address listed as a P.O. Box in Dunwoody, GA.

"You never copied his driver's license?" This was state law. She checked.

"Of course. It's in there."

"But it's really not, Mr. Sanchez," she said, motioning him to look for himself. He flipped through the thin folder.

"I swear I put it in here. Someone must of taken it out."

"Who would to that, Hector?" said Brennan.

"I don't know," said a confused Hector. "I don't know why anyone would want to take it out." Brennan did, but didn't say anything.

"Do you have any cameras on the premises, Mr. Sanchez?" Linda asked already knowing the answer.

"No. Nada."

"Okay. Listen, Hector. I want you to think back to the day you sold Mr. Norton the car."

"Okay"

"Now, I want you to describe him in as much detail as possible, including what he was wearing."

"Okay. I remember. He had on tan pants and a button-up, long-sleeve shirt, but it wasn't tucked in."

"Go on. What about his hair and face?"

"He had kinda long, dark hair but he wore a hat and a thick beard and mustache."

"What about his eyes?" Brennan asked scribbling notes furiously.

"He had on sunglasses."

"Even inside?" Linda asked incredulously.

"Yep. In here, too."

"That didn't seem strange to you?"

"Look, I'm just trying to sell cars here. I don't ask for reasons. He had money, paid in cash. He can wear a racecar helmet in here if he wants to." They wouldn't learn anything else here. They got up to leave.

"Thanks for your time, Mr. Sanchez."

"No problem, no problem. Say, have you looked outside? I got some great deals. A discount for the police."

CHAPTER 41

He got her machine again. He understood Linda was a busy woman but he could also see how her work might run off potential men in her life. Was that what he was? Mark never really understood the whole thing growing up. What distinguished a commitment between two people? The consensus was that the term 'dating' was free of commitment, but if you said 'we're going out', those words somehow made the relationship of a deeper status. But didn't 'going out' literally mean dating? It confused Mark. He wondered what status he and Linda were in. Were they just 'dating' or were they 'going out'? Mark guessed he was more old school. He felt that if you were having sex, that it was a mutual understanding that your sexual partner be monogamous. Did Linda feel the same way?

Mark had to go to New York for a day to attend his little brother's wedding. He wanted to tell Linda personally, but he went ahead and left it on her machine the second time around. He had not been up to visit his family in almost two years. The last time was for a family reunion which, for whatever reason, Mark always felt uncomfortable attending. There was a fake feeling to it. Like a movie set or something. Everybody was overly nice to everybody. Hugs flowed like water and older women felt obligated to pinch cheeks. Everyone ran around acting like they remembered you from some other long ago family function. "You remember little Mark don't ya? He's Patty's oldest. Of course, blah, blah, blah." Whatever. He loved his family, but he felt it hard to love family members he didn't even know existed.

His younger brother Brett was 27; seven years younger than Mark. Even with the age difference, they were close before he left New York. They spent endless days riding three-wheelers, snowmobiles, and sleds. As boys, they had stayed outside a lot. His parents' house sat on 20 acres of grassy hills and was bordered by heavy woods. There were countless things to do and get into.

They talked from time to time, mostly exchanging messages via Facebook. A picture here, a picture there. Brett favored Mark a lot, though he was shorter and more stocky, following their father's genes. Mark took more after his mother who, at 5'11", was tall and athletic. Both of his parents were in their mid-sixties and in good health. His mother had retired years ago due to his father's success at receiving a settlement. His dad spent his time trying to make more money flipping small real estate deals, but most of the time broke even.

Mark's father had worked at a machine shop for a little over 20 years when an electrical surge caused a pressing machine to malfunction and activate on its own, crushing his father's hand. His father would have been fine with the company just paying his medical bills and maybe a small compensation package, but the company denied any wrongdoing or fault, even suggested that his father crushed his own hand on purpose. Workman's Comp would pay the medical bills no matter what, but after such behavior by the company, his father sued. The jury had seen it his father's way and awarded damages for another million. That was 12 years ago and his father still told somebody the story every day.

Hartsfield-Jackson International Airport in Atlanta was the busiest airport in the world. Airports were already chaotic, even worse after 9/11, but Atlanta's airport was special. Where with most airports you needed to be there an hour or even an hour and a half before take-off, you needed a good three at Hartsfield. He had just got off the speeding concourse train and stepped onto this concourse when his phone rang. Setting his small carry-on down, he saw that it was Linda. Excited, He answered.

"You're alive!"

"Mark, I'm so sorry. The truth is we've had some new developments and I've had to do a lot of organizing. I've been really busy. It's still not an excuse, but I apologize."

"You had me at 'Mark'," he said laughing. She laughed, too, nervously.

"I thought you might be mad at me. Thanks for being understanding," Linda said, yawning through the phone.

"Say no more about it. You sound like you need some rest."

"You have no idea. I wish I could go to New York with you. When's your flight?"

"I'm at the airport now."

"You're only going to be gone for one day right?"

"Yes, Ma'am."

"Good. When you come back, how about you come to my place and we just skip dinner and go right to dessert."

"Didn't your parents teach you to eat your vegetables?"

"I don't want any vegetables. Show me the beef!" Oh, my God. Did she really just say that? What the hell was wrong with her? She waited for a response, wincing.

"It's a date, Agent Hunt. Tomorrow night, then?"

"Yeah, but let me call you tomorrow with the time. It might be a little late. Maybe 9 or 10."

"Sounds good. Well, let me get on this plane. They're boarding, Sweetie."

"I'm looking forward to tomorrow Mark and again, I'm sorry."

"Stop apologizing or I'll punish you tomorrow."

"Promise?" she asked.

"You're so bad. I gotta go. See ya tomorrow."

"Bye, Mark."

Hanging up, Linda couldn't believe her behavior. She was becoming too comfortable with Mark. The truth was she missed him. Was she falling for him already? For the first time in her career as an agent, she couldn't wait until she found this murderous creep so she could spend some time with the man. She'd never felt as if she could find a balance between work and home life, but it was seeming easier to imagine now. She really was falling, wasn't she?

Mark boarded the Delta 727 airliner and got comfortable in his first class seat. He sat in the window seat and shared the row with an elegantly-clad, elderly woman. Normally he wouldn't fly but due to taking time away from the store for this trip he had a doctor prescribe a pill to help him sleep for the duration of the flight. Mark popped the pill in his mouth, swallowed, and waited for it to take effect. He and the elderly lady exchanged smiles and nods, and then Mark closed his eyes, deep in thought and drifted off to sleep.

* * *

He awoke as the tires made their protest with the pavement. With no baggage but his carry-on, he made his way to the Enterprise counter and rented a mid-size sedan. Walking outside to find his car, he took a deep breath, taking in his home-state air. The weather was cool and clear, somewhere in the low sixties. He found his Chrysler 300 at the end of the huge lot. It was not the hemi-edition, but the car was still attractive. It was silver and had nice, shiny wheels on it. He got in and tried to remember how to get into Manhattan from LaGuardia. Though he had been into the city plenty of times, it had been awhile. He was from upstate New York, outside of Albany which was over two hours' drive away. Mark planned on buying a suit for the wedding in the city. He had several suits of course, but it had been years since he'd bought a new one... plus he loved the hustle and bustle of Manhattan. He drove over the Hudson River and onto the island entering into the 100's. Soon he was in Harlem passing the famous Apollo Theater. He made his way over to Broadway so he could drive through Times Square.

As a child, Times Square was the center of the world. All the lights, screens, and people. He felt like everyone was trying to get there and he wanted to be there too. It was magical to a young Mark. It had changed a lot since back then. There were even more lights and more screens, but it lost its magical appeal. Maybe the experience of life had made him a pessimist. All he saw now, as he took 42nd Street toward 5th Avenue, was the homeless and an abundance of police. It was no longer exciting or joyous but, instead, depressing. As he stopped for a light, a street hustler ran to his car squirting something on the windshield and started wiping furiously with a handful of newspaper. Mark took out his wallet, grabbed a bill, and lowering his window handed the man a hundred bucks. Just the look on the man's face was worth it. The hustler was still thanking him as he drove off.

Mark ended up buying everything he needed at Saks Fifth Avenue. He bought an olive, single-breasted suite by Prada, a striped shirt by Armani, a couple pairs of socks, and a pair of crocodile loafers by Bally. $2,500 later, he was on his way to the small town of Altamont. The wedding was tomorrow at 10 a.m. in the morning and he had an early flight back at 5 p.m.; meaning he would need to head back to the airport no later than 2 p.m. He would stay the night at his parents' house and pray they would keep their constant life inquiries to a minimum.

After Jenny died, his parents, full of good intentions, just wouldn't stop with the pity. Mark grew sick of it quickly, which was part of the reason he hadn't been up in so long. But as Mark thought about it, he kind of wanted them to ask questions now. He wanted to share about his new… whatever Linda was to him. Who wouldn't? She was beautiful, successful, and classy; not to mention, intelligent. Mark's mood improved as he figured out this wouldn't be the same ol' pity party – originally dreading spending time with his family and having to deal with all the looks and how-are-you-doing-really questions.

He made good time from the city and made it to the house he grew up in a little before suppertime. As he made his way up the gravel driveway, seeing the house and its surroundings, he was forced back in time and was flooded with memories. It was a simple, two-story home painted a pale yellow with dark green shutters. The house was old but his Pops kept it in good repair. The gravel driveway led to the left side of the house where a two-car garage took up almost half of the bottom floor. There to meet him as he stepped from his rental car were his mother and father. While his father had not changed in the last 2 years, his mother looked to have aged 10.

"Hi, Mom."

"Oh Mark, it's so good to see you," she said, hugging him and pecking him on the cheek.

He hugged his father also and they went upstairs carrying Mark's bags. They ate a nice dinner and talked mostly of Mark's little brother and what a nice girl he was marrying. Surprisingly, they asked little of what Mark had been doing and his reasons for not visiting as often. After his mother had retired for the night, he and his father sat in comfortable chairs in the den and shared a drink.

"So, who is she?" his father asked, after several minutes of silence.

"What?"

"Who is she? I haven't seen you this content in a while and I'd bet dollars to doughnuts it's because of a woman." The man was good.

"Well, if you must know, her name is Linda. I started seeing her a couple weeks ago," Mark said, failing to hide his smile.

"Well, when are you getting married? Because you're getting old and I want grandkids," he said playfully.

"Hell, Dad. I don't even know if we're a couple yet. All I know is she makes me happy and I enjoy spending time with her."

"Say no more." With that his father gulped the last of his scotch and stood up. He put his hand on Mark's shoulder and said sincerely, "That's all that matters to me, my boy." His father then walked to his room and shut the door.

The wedding was a big success. His brother looked the happiest he had ever seen him. Drinks were in heavy rotation and flashes from cameras were plenty. Mark genuinely had a good time and he vowed not to take so long making his way back up here next time.

His flight back to Atlanta was right on time and he couldn't help himself from urging the plane faster. He was going to see Linda in a few hours and he couldn't wait.

CHAPTER 42

Linda was up early. She put on her gym shorts along with a baggy t-shirt. After having a wonderful cup of Kona coffee, she started her stretching and began her run. She had not run in two days, not feeling motivated. After last night with Mark though, she was refreshed, determined, and ready to go. They made love like two eager, hyperactive teenagers. Clawing and tearing one another's clothes off. She even went down on him, which she had only done one other time in her life. She felt alive when they were together. Spunky even. She found herself wanting to try new things and test boundaries.

Arriving back at her house she was surprised to find a text awaiting her. Leaving a sleeping Mark in her bedroom, she went out to the kitchen and re-read the text. It was from Agent Ogles. SAMPLES TAKEN FROM BURNT NISSAN STEERING WHEEL CONFIRMED AS A MATCH TO THE PAINT USED IN THE KIDS PAINTBALL GUNS. IT'S OUR MAN. ALSO FOUND THE P.O. BOX. IT'S OUT OF A MAIL BOXES ETC. ON CHAMBLEE DUNWOODY NOT FAR FROM PERIMETER MALL. WAITING ON INSTRUCTIONS.

Could this be it? Could it be that easy? A very smart

guy goes to all this trouble to hide his identity after murdering five people and injuring two dozen more, just to be caught checking his mail? It seemed a little too good to be true, but who knew. Sometimes you caught a break.

She took a hot shower and dressed quickly. She talked to Ogles and told him to get everyone together at Sandy Springs PD. She was careful not to wake Mark as she left. He definitely deserved his sleep after his performance last night. She left him a note thanking him for a great night and encouraging him to hang out at the house as long as he wished, but to lock up with the spare key she kept on top of the porch light if he left. If this kept up, she might just have to get him a copy for himself, she thought, giddily.

It was only a little over a mile from her house to the police station. When she walked in her make-shift office, she was happy to see everyone present, including Brennan and Detective Jenkins.

"Good morning everyone," she said and was met with a room full of smiles. "Okay, Agent Ogles the floor is yours." Big Mike stood up with his notes.

"With the help from everyone on this joint task force, we've nailed this guy down to a P.O. Box in Dunwoody. I've already spoken with the manager of the Mail Boxes Etc. where a Mr. Jerry Norton keeps his box and he actually knows Mr. Norton by sight. Says he comes in regularly, at least two times a week, always late afternoon."

"Did you get a description?" Brennan asked, scribbling in his own notes.

"Yes and they, of course, have security cameras everywhere in a business like that. The guy – I'm sorry…" Ogles referred to his notes and continued "The manager, Mr. Ricky Howell, knows what he's looking for and is finding the footage for us as we speak. The man he knows as Mr. Norton is on the short side of 6 feet, white, about 160 pounds with shortish, dark brown hair. Said Mr. Norton was a pleasant enough guy."

"Alright," said Linda. "We will obviously be staking out his P.O. Box. Assuming he checks his mail while we're watching, how should we proceed?"

"Well, your guys will of course do the stake out on the P.O. Box," Brennan started, "being as Dunwoody's out of our jurisdiction, but do we take him down? I don't think so. I mean all we have is him lying in some woods with a rifle and some similar descriptions for some stolen cars. I know we will probably learn his true identity after we book him and maybe we will have the murder weapon just sitting at home, but again maybe not. Where would that leave us?"

"I agree." It was Ogles again. "Our case at this point is entirely circumstantial."

"We have him cold on false identity and forgery," this from Agent Lucas out of Linda's office.

"Well that's not good enough," said Linda. "He's going down for murder." She said this with such force that it changed the mood of the meeting. "Now, what plan are we putting forth to ensure Mr. Norton's capture and inevitable path to lethal injection?"

"We have no choice but to follow," said Brennan. "Tail him to his house, find out who he really is. We have to be patient. Maybe we see him loading guns into a car or we tail him to another target site and witness him set it up. Either way, we have to follow and lay low to have a better chance at prosecuting this guy."

"Okay, do we all agree this is our best course of action?" A murmur of yeahs. "Ogles, I want you and Lucas to start surveillance now and text me hourly with updates." Ogles and Lucas took their leave. "Brennan," she continued, "I don't know what's left for you to do until we see where this guy lives. Could be he lives right here in Sandy Springs, but all we can do is wait and see."

"Yeah, it sucks. This is where I wish I was a Fed and I could follow the case wherever it went."

"I'll keep you updated, Brennan, and thank you for all

your insight and hard work."

"Anytime, Agent Hunt."

"Call me, Linda."

"See ya later, Linda." With that Brennan walked out of her office, taking Jenkins with him.

CHAPTER 43

Big Mike had the more average-sized Agent Lucas go pick up the recorded security DVDs from Mr. Howell at Mail Boxes Etc. Sending him in would definitely cause less attention than his own 6'7" frame. They now sat in the back lot of a Burger King, which was in front of a huge plaza on Chamblee Dunwoody Road. The anchor stores were a Publix and a Home Depot. There were probably 20 other smaller business filling the shopping center out. Mike saw a Sally's Beauty Supply, a Dollar General and of course the store they were watching, Mail Boxes Etc.

They both had binoculars, though you couldn't see them using them thanks to the tinted windows in his government-issued Chevy Impala. He and one other Agent were the only ones with Impalas instead of Crown Vics. He never had a Crown Vic, so he didn't know if he were lucky or cursed.

Mail Boxes Etc. sat at the left end of one of the plaza buildings. They had a great view of Box number 4105, which was owned by their suspect, through huge plate-glass windows. They had been there all day and had already eaten twice of the ultra-healthy menu of the gourmet Burger King. It was closing in on 7 pm and they had yet to see their man. The place closed at 11 pm and while Mike would put in the extra hours to catch this guy, staking out a store, he thought, was a waste of his talents. So, in 4 hours, his ass was going home.

"So, what do you think of our boss's ass?" asked Lucas. Here we go again with this conversation.

"I think if we talk about it anymore it, might just appear. I know she's a chick, Lucas, but the more I work with her, the more I'm growing to respect her. Let's look at her as our boss and it will be easier to do our jobs in the future. She does have a nice ass, though." They both laughed good on that one and as Ogles was wiping tears from his eyes, he saw a man enter their store. He looked through his binoculars and saw an average white guy heading toward the front counter.

"Look alive. This could be our guy."

They both studied the man. He was talking with a female employee with an animated face. The guy was the right build to be their guy. He had the short, dark hair, also. Big Mike didn't have to wonder long. After wrapping up his conversation with the female, he went straight to box 4105. While keeping his eyes on their suspect, he called Agent Hunt on speed dial.

"Agent Hunt."

"We've got him. He's at his box now."

"Good. Follow him. Make sure you keep your distance. I'm sending additional agents now. Don't let this guy see your tail."

"Yes, Ma'am."

"I'll call you back after I report to Fletcher." She hung up.

The guy was now leaving the store. He got into a late-model Acura and was backing out.

"You get his tag, Lucas?"

"Got it."

There were only two exits out of the plaza and the Burger King sat at the nearest one. Their man was pulling toward it. They got into position and pulled behind him 3 cars back. They took a right on Roberts Drive toward Sandy Springs. Up ahead, the road turned into a 'Y'. If you went left, you would stay on Chamblee Dunwoody. If you went right, it turned into Roberts Drive. Roberts Drive went through the corner of Dunwoody and ended in Sandy Springs at Georgia 400 and Northridge. Staying several cars behind him, they followed the Acura over Spalding Drive and into Sandy Springs. Shortly after, the Acura turned left into an upper-middle class subdivision called 'Club Springs'. They also made the turn, staying back. They lost sight of him for a minute before passing a side street and seeing the Acura pulling into a driveway about five houses down. They kept straight while Agent Ogles called Hunt.

"What do you have, Ogles?"

"Mr. Norton lives at 627 Carriage Park Lane, Ma'am."

"Good work, Mike. Real good work."

"No sweat, Boss."

"Okay, I'm sending another car to you. Set up the best way you can for now. I'll work on getting us a house to watch from. If he leaves, tail him."

"Roger that."

She hung up and immediately called Brennan. She owed it to him. He wanted this guy as bad as anyone and had definitely put in the work.

"How's the hunt, Agent Hunt?" he answered.

"Well, I could really use a good detective to work his own part of town."

"No way. He lives in Sandy Springs?"

"Well, somebody does." She brought him up to date on what they knew.

"I know the neighborhood. The guy's rich."

"We profiled him to be and it's not too surprising that he lives in the same area. Maybe it's a comfort thing or convenience."

"It's strange to me, because he's so organized and

intelligent in some aspects, then in others he's amateurish. I mean lying in the open woods in an urban area? It's almost as if there are two of them, ya know?"

Yeah, I see what you mean, but I think he is definitely our guy. Maybe just makes mistakes like everyone else."

"You're probably right or maybe this Mr. Norton has an identity crisis."

"That would be the least of his problems. I've got to report to my boss here. Get everybody on board on your end and find out what you can about getting us inside a house with a view of our guy. From what I hear, it's not the kind of neighborhood where cars park on the street."

"That it's not. I've got it. Do what you gotta do, and thanks."

"No, thank you. Your investigation got us here."

She hung up with Brennan and called Fletcher, the SAC (Special Agent in Charge.). He wanted a face-to-face at the soonest and had a negotiator en route from Quantico in case it heads in that direction. It was all coming to a head. She hoped she could end it all without any more bloodshed. Even though, she wouldn't mind at all if they had to take this sick bastard out.

CHAPTER 44

He knew they would find him. It was all in his plans. The police didn't have enough evidence on Jared to charge him yet, that's what it was. They would follow him everywhere, bug his home and phones, never letting him out of their sight. They wanted Jared to set up for another kill. Of course, they had no idea about him. He was always one step ahead. That's how you never got caught. Knowing what your opponents are going to do before they do. That's what the police were at this point. Just unworthy opponents. They hadn't a clue what was really going on. They, like Jared, failed to see the big picture. It was coming though. Live in 3D.

He rented a house about 6 months ago on Carriage Park Lane. It was 3 houses down and across the street from the Millers, but he still had a good view. Right this second, he was looking through an UltraVid scope out of one of the upstairs bedroom windows. A Chevy Impala sat four houses further down Carriage Park from Jared's. In the driver's seat was a giant of a man. He would bet money the guy played college ball. Another guy sat in the passenger's seat, small in comparison. These were not locals. These guys were Feds. He knew, by sight, every detective on Sandy Spring PD payroll and, of course, everyone knew after watching the press release with the saucy FBI chick, that the Feds had taken over. Sure, they may let the locals hold the ball, but the Feds would do the scoring.

This new development was a slight dilemma. The next step in the plan started tomorrow. Jared was supposed to meet him at the old construction site. Now the cops would be following his every move. It was almost enough to drive him into a rage and just kill both Feds in their car where they sat. That was the problem though. Every time you altered something in a controlled experiment there were counteractions; like ripples in water from a disturbance. He didn't like the unknown and killing these two cops would most definitely have unknown and unplanned for repercussions.

A plan started to form in his head. If he got Jared out of the house now, before more cops came, it could work. He pulled out an untraceable cell phone and punched in a number.

"Hello?"

"The plan has changed. You need to tell your wife to drive you to a hotel. Get…"

"A hotel, what are you talking about? I thought…"

"Listen to me like you've never listened to anyone before in your life. It's time for us to move. I told you this may happen. I've planned for it. We're okay. Get everything you can in the next 5 minutes and have your wife take you to the Comfort Inn on Shallowford Road. They won't ask any questions. Give them a fake name. Don't use any ID that you've been using. When you get in the car, lay down in the back seat. Stay down the entire way. I'll explain everything later. Keep your cell phone on. Is there anything you don't understand?"

"What… I mean, what do I tell my wife? My kids are just going to bed."

"Jared, you better not be going soft on me."

"No, no. I just don't know what to say."

"Figure it out. You have exactly 5minutes to be in the car and moving."

He hung up the phone. He didn't know if Jared could do it, but for his sake, he better. His other alternative was to die tonight in front of his wife. He watched and waited. He was extremely patient when it came to achieving his objective and his objective right now was securing a possible leak. He couldn't let the police get to Jared. Jared would fold up like a cardboard box. Yes, Jared had served his purpose. Time to die.

Exactly 5 minutes and 40 seconds later, he watched Jared's wife, Debbie, pull out of her garage. No one else was in the van. He moved the scope to the Impala to see what they would do. The big guy was already on the phone. Probably asking what to do. Follow or stay. Debbie's Dodge Grand Caravan took a left then a right onto Roberts Drive. The Impala stayed. They thought Jared was still in the house. Just as planned. He was so much smarter than them.

Ten minutes later, he left the rented house on Carriage Park. He pulled out in a black, super-charged Jaguar XK8 and made his way to Chamblee before he left. He saw the Feds' backup arrive and get situated down at the other end of the road, away from the Impala. Too Late. Amateurs.

He didn't think they would, but in case the Feds went forward and questioned Mrs. Miller when she arrived home, she too would fold and tell them where she took Jared. He called Jared.

"Hello?" said a muffled voice.

"When your wife drops you off at the hotel, wait until she leaves, then walk across the street to the BP Gas Station."

"Are you…" He hung up.

Twenty minutes later, after he had made sure there was no kind of police waiting and that Jared's wife was in fact gone, he pulled around the back-side of the gas station where Jared sat with a duffle bag.

"Get in."

They rode in silence for the next couple minutes. Jared was the first to speak.

"Where are we going?"

"Right down the road here to another hotel. A lodge actually."

"Why, though? What's going on?"

"What's going on, Jared, is that you have led them to you. I don't know which idiotic action actually did it, though I can think of a few. But either way, they were watching your house." That quieted Jared for a minute.

"So, do we continue with the whole plan?" Jared asked.

"Yes."

"Where will I stay?"

"With me. They'll be watching the hotels and such after tonight."

"But you said I would get to kill my family," Jared said louder than he meant, sounding like a whining child. He shrank back as if expecting to be hit. It never came. Instead, he spoke calmly to Jared.

"Of course, you can. I'll even help you plan. Right now, we need to concentrate on our next objective, which is Mrs. Stanley. Tomorrow, she will die a horrible death. But her pain will be nothing compared to the pain her husband will feel when he sees what we've done to her."

CHAPTER 45

"The wife is leaving?" asked Linda.

"Yeah, you want us to follow?"

"Is the husband with her?"

"No."

"Stay with him and the house. God damn it! Your backup should be there any minute. Let her go, Ogles. There's nothing we can do."

Four agents were watching the house early Monday morning. Ogles and Lucas had pulled an all-nighter. Ogles was on his third thermos of coffee and his eyes were still starting to droop.

"I wonder what time this guy goes to work."

"I hope it's soon," answered Ogles. "Because I'm about to fall asleep or freak out from boredom. The info we got on this Jared Miller, a.k.a. Jerry Norton, is that he runs a marketing firm off Roswell Road. Those guys are pretty nine-to-five, so I'd think he'd be leaving the house pretty soon."

An hour later, at ten till eight, they watched as Mrs. Miller and two kids backed out of the driveway in her van. Ogles called Linda.

"Wife's leaving again. This time she has the kids with

her."

"Okay, you follow, but leave the other car on the house."

"Roger."

They followed the van first to an elementary school not a mile from the house, where a little girl of 9 or 10 got out and went inside. Mrs. Miller then drove to a pre-school called Little Buddies, where a younger girl was left. Mrs. Miller then went directly home.

"We're back at the house."

"And?"

"Mrs. Miller dropped her little girls off at school and came right back. Parks and Womack said there was not so much as a light turned on or off at the house."

"That's strange. It's 8:30, he should have left for work by now."

"I agree."

"Okay, I give it until 10. At 10, call his office and ask for him. If he's not there, call the house under some false pretense. If the wife says he's not home, we will go in. I'll get Sandy Springs PD ready. Let's just sit tight and see what they say at 10."

"You got it, boss."

After 30 minutes of her boss saying that it was the right move, she called Brennan to see if everyone was in place.

"How are we looking?"

"Locked, cocked, and ready to rock, ma'am."

"I'll be there in five. Did the negotiator get there?"

"Yeah, I met the guy. He's over talking to Big Mike. Scared to death, if you ask me. Says he's a profiler, never been in the field."

"Well, hopefully we won't need him. I'm going to call Mrs. Miller myself and see if maybe she wants to go ahead and let us come in without Jared's knowledge. It's worth a try."

"Let's be happy the kids are out of the house if things go nuts," Brennan said.

"Nobody's going nuts, we will promise him the world and everything in it. Have some faith."

"I'm riding with ya, Hunt."

"Okay, I'm pulling in now," Linda said, hanging up.

There was a big church around the corner from Jared's house where a SWAT team, 8 police officers, and 6 federal officers sat waiting on the signal to go in on the Miller house. Two snipers were already in position in the front and back of the house.

Ogles had called Point Marketing to find out that Jared wasn't in today and no one knew when he might be. He also called to talk to Jared at his house and learned from Mrs. Miller that Jared was not at home either. This was strange because he was never seen leaving.

Linda now sat in the back of the Sandy Springs SWAT mobile command center. It was basically a Greyhound bus where the back half was surveillance equipment and electronics and the front weapons, armor, and seating. She was in the back half taking a minute to herself before she put the call into Mrs. Miller. Was Mrs. Miller part of it? Was this a Bonnie and Clyde thing or was she just ignorantly sitting by while her husband was savagely killing people? She took a deep breath and dialed. The profiler was listening in.

"Hello?"

"Mrs. Miller?"

"Speaking"

"Mrs. Miller, my name is Linda Hunt. I'm an agent with the Federal Bureau of Investigation. I'm call…"

"It's about Jared, isn't it? What's happened? Is he okay?"

"Mr. Miller is not in the house with you?"

"No, I took him to a hotel last night. He wouldn't tell me why. I've never seen him so panicked. What's happening?"

"I'm going to send some officers over to talk to you in just a minute ma'am." Linda gave Brennan and company the thumbs up and 15 law officers took off around the corner.

"Ma'am, for your safety, I need you to hang up the phone with me, go to your front door, and put your hands straight up in the air."

"What?"

"Ma'am, please. I'll explain everything in due time. Now go out front with your hands up."

Linda heard the woman hang up and Linda dashed to her car and floored it, lights blazing. When she pulled in front of the Miller's house they were already taking Jared's poor wife into custody. The SWAT team was combing the house ready for anything. Mrs. Miller could be full of shit. They went from room to room until the whole house was cleared. Linda walked out and opened the rear door of one of the patrol cars.

"Mrs. Miller, I'm Agent Hunt who you spoke to on the phone. This…"

"What's going on?" Debbie Miller said through racking sobs. "I don't understand." Tears ran down her face and she used her cuffed hands to wipe them away. Linda undid the woman's cuffs and showed her a piece of paper explaining the search warrant.

"Does Jared own any firearms, Mrs. Miller?"

CHAPTER 46

Jennifer Stanley had been married for 32 years. She was an at-home-mom for eighteen of those years and in the ten years since their son, Brian, had left home, she had made it her goal to try to keep her size-six figure. Okay, size-seven. At 56 years old, it was beginning to seem like an exercise in futility. Her husband, Steven even bought her all the latest exercise equipment. They had an entire room dedicated for Jennifer's workouts.

She stood naked, looking at her body in the mirror. What did it really matter? Steven and she rarely had sex anymore, not that she didn't want to. Steven was always busy working and when he was at home, he was too tired to do anything. Don't get her wrong. She loved living comfortably, which Steven's hard work provided, but she wanted a little booty, too.

Her platinum-dyed, blonde hair was cut a little shorter than she normally wore it, coming down around her jawline. She could probably use a face lift, she thought, but her gold-flecked, hazel eyes still sparkled brightly. Her tits were in good shape too and, for twenty-five grand, they should be. Steven had bought them for her. Why, she didn't know. He didn't even look at them anymore. Oh well, the massage she had scheduled would take all these thoughts away, she thought, stepping into the shower.

Steven Stanley was a partner at a semi-prestigious law firm named Covan, Allen, and Stanley. He had only been with the firm a little over four years and had been a partner all four of them. He came into the firm a partner partly because of his trial experience and courtroom tenacity, but a lot of it had to do with his previously being the Senior Assistant District Attorney of Fulton County. Not the big man himself, but only one rung below.

Though he liked being on the other side of the fence, being a defense attorney sure paid better. As an Assistant District Attorney, he was lucky to clear a hundred grand a year. Since joining the firm, he hadn't taken home less than a million five. He felt he deserved it. He graduated from the University of Chicago's law program in the top ten percent of his class and then slaved for the Fulton County Superior Court for 27 years. Yeah, he deserved it. He was about two years shy of retirement. He would be sixty. Where did the time go? It seemed only yesterday he was graduating law school.

Retirement was going to be nice. He had bought a nice 55-foot yacht last year and was having it refitted to his liking. He and his poor, neglected wife, Jen, would cruise the islands without a care in the world. Ah, what a life. Cold margaritas, the sun shining, beautiful blue waters as far as the eye could see. Only two more years. He got excited just thinking about it. He felt like celebrating the simple fact that retirement was close. In fact, he would. He'd take his beautiful wife out to her favorite steakhouse, Champs. They'd have dinner and relish the thought that the time was near.

CHAPTER 47

The shower felt good after almost an hour on the treadmill. Jennifer could feel the tension seeping out of her. The massage she had coming in a couple hours would feel even better. As she turned the water off, she thought she heard their squeaky, storm door slam shut as it was prone to do.

"Steven?" She yelled as she pulled a towel around her. "Steven, is that you?" She padded across her carpeted bedroom floor and looked into the hallway. "Steven!" she tried again. Huh, she thought she had heard the door.

She took her towel off and wrapped it around her wet hair. She liked looking at herself in the mirror. Some people thought that was conceited, but she thought it was a good thing that she liked the way she looked. She was squeezing her tits looking at their shifting shapes when she felt something stir inside her. She reached down between her legs and felt that she was wet. She scooted her butt up onto the counter and spread her legs. She toyed with herself, slipping a finger in and out, rubbing the wetness all over her folds. Using her other hand, she forced three fingers inside her with a moan as the one hand rubbed her clit furiously. She was on the verge of orgasm, moaning loudly, when she heard the unmistakable sound of a man laughing. Her eyes shot open. There in front of her were two men wearing some kind of plastic suits. For a moment she froze, unable to do anything. Then she frantically got up and tried to close the door separating her vanity area from the bedroom, screaming at the top of her lungs. She almost got a grip on the door knob when she was struck on the top of her head. Then, there was darkness.

Mrs. Stanley was starting to come around as he and Jared finished tying and taping her to her four-post bed. Her eyes bulged wide as she saw her captors and her predicament. She thrashed wildly against her restraints accomplishing nothing, but causing herself pain. She tried to scream through the many layers of duct tape that was wrapped around her head to no avail. She calmed substantially when she realized she was at the absolute mercy of these two men.

Jared was looking at the naked woman while rubbing himself through his suite.

"Let me fuck her before we kill her."

"No."

"Come on, what does it matter. I'll wear a condom."

His plan changed in his mind. Let the idiot play.

"Okay."

"Really?"

"Sure, you deserve it. But leave your suit on."

"Alright." Jared then reached inside his suit and retrieved his wallet from his pants and took out a Trojan condom.

"You brought your wallet to the murder scene?" he asked Jared. He couldn't believe he had allowed himself to be in cahoots with this moron up to this point. It made him want to throw up.

"Yeah, well, it was inside the suit y'know." He acted as if the answer would suffice.

Jared then got on the bed and atop a spread eagle Jennifer Stanley. Jared roughly fingered her vagina with one hand while stroking his cock with the other. He stood there watching them, parts of his plan changing with every second. Jared put the condom on and began thrusting inside her. Tears ran down her face.

"You like that. Don't you, bitch," Jared said over and over again as he took her throat in his hands and began choking her, thrusting faster and faster.

The killer took from behind his back an unpainted Louisville Slugger and walked behind Jared. He raised the bat and even through her watering eyes as she was being choked he saw the surprise in them. He reached back and swung the professional baseball bat as hard as he could and struck the back of Jared's head. You would expect a fantastic noise but it really wasn't impressive. Sounded more like hitting a watermelon. Jared slumped over onto Jennifer, quite dead. There was only a small amount of blood that ran out of the dent in the back of Jared's head. His heart had stopped pumping it.

After a moment, Mrs. Stanley started bucking again. He calmly walked over to her and cut her throat deeply with a serrated knife, scraping vertebrae in the process. He watched as the blood ran out of her and she pointlessly gasped for breath.

He was glad to be rid of Jared Miller. Jared was a sick man. Sure, he knew he was homicidal himself, but he had a cause, a purpose. He was doing what he was doing for a reason. Jared, on the other hand, just raped the poor woman because he derived pleasure from it. It excited Jared to rape and murder. It did not excite him. He had an objective and he would achieve it. Period. He would take as many lives as it took until people got his message. The more the merrier, as far as he was concerned. The more people that died, the more the people would pay attention to what he had to say. The supermarket shootings along with the highway shootings were merely a prelude to assure his audience's attention. Mrs. Stanley and Stacy Kemp were pieces to a puzzle. A puzzle with many pieces.

People are gonna die… lots of them.

CHAPTER 48

He and Maria sat on her back deck, which literally came 20 feet from the water's edge of the Chattahoochee River. They had a late lunch and now sat in what was sure to be another blistering day. They were under the cover of the many trees straddling the river bank, enjoying their cappuccinos.

The subject of discussion was the possibility of Brennan moving into Maria's apartment. While he liked to think he was falling in love with her, it was just too soon. They had only been dating a couple weeks and Brennan again liked to think he had a little experience with moving too fast. That in itself is what he contributed to the ridiculous fallout between him and Sam.

"It makes sense Brennan. I want to be with you, you want to be with me. We work for the same agency and both understand what comes with the job. We're compatible in bed and want the same big house with the white picket fence. Give me a reason why not."

"That's a trick, Maria. I'm not gonna play pessimist, while you play optimist, making me look negative and doubtful."

"Uh, huh. How about because you know it makes

sense, too."

It did make sense. He wanted to move in and for Maria to be right, but he needed protection. He didn't want to end up heartbroken and an empty shell again. Caution was that protection.

"It does make sense. I'm not disagreeing with you. I just think we should give it more time."

"Okay," she said enigmatically, stretching the word out.

People were complex creatures. Ask anybody who has started a relationship with the person of their dreams only to later separate from them feeling as they didn't even know them. Insecurities turn to hatred. Secrets and embarrassments turn to fuel that enrage the next argument. Suddenly, after however much time, the person you once saw yourself spending your life with is but a curious stranger. And you'd only be fooling yourself to say, "Yeah, but she, or he, is not like that." Right.

"How about we revisit this conversation after we get this maniac Miller off the street?" Brennan said lightly.

"Deal. Now come over here and give me a big, wet kiss."

"You're closer. You come over here."

"What? We're the same distance from each other," she said, looking confused.

"If everything is gonna be an argument with you, I can go ahead and..."

"Oh, fuck off," she said as Brennan hurried over to her chair and covered her in kisses.

Laughing, he said, "I think I love you."

"I think I love you, too."

Brennan settled back in his chair. "I hope we get this creep soon. I really thought we had him yesterday at his house. The poor wife. It was so sad. She had no idea."

"I can't imagine," she said mimicking a shiver. "You think your husband is off working hard at the office and he's really out killing people for sport. It's spooky."

"Which is why I need time thinking about shacking up

with you," he said laughing. "You could be a stone-cold killer." He dodged a balled up napkin that was aimed for his face. "Seriously though, the guy was definitely leading a second life. You'll see tomorrow when you go into work. The guy had eleven rifles, two fully-automatic assault rifles, five handguns, and an assortment of scopes and shit. He even had a class-2 body armor vest. This guy is a serious nut job."

"At least we took all that from him."

"Yeah, and Linda Hunt is closing all his bank accounts, but leaving his credit cards open to see if he'll alert us to his whereabouts. When we opened his safe, we found some shit about a property in Mexico. He might be running there now, for all we know."

"Nah, I think the guy's pride is hurt. I bet he'll stick around. Remember, all those crazy serial killers really want to be caught anyway."

"I hope so." Brennan's phone rang. He looked at the display. It was Captain Kirby. "What's up, Cap?"

"We found Jared Miller."

CHAPTER 49

He didn't like leaving things to chance or in the hands of someone whose competence had yet to be proven. If he could do it himself, he would. Even if it meant going above and beyond. It was second nature to him by now. All those years in the ranks of the district attorney's office had trained him well.

It wasn't a myth that being physically attractive got you places. Steven Stanley had seen it time and time again. Not just females either, the attractive men moved up the ladder faster as well. And while Steven knew there were small grounds for this, in that the juries were more compelled to agree with an attractive person, he didn't like it. He supposed he was biased because he wasn't what you would call an attractive guy. He was short and a little pudgy with a plain face that perpetually held an expression of disbelief.

Regardless, he was now in a position where it didn't matter. His wife had told him on several occasions that he was hard on certain individuals for no apparent reason. After analyzing his actions toward those people, he noticed that they were attractive, mediocrely competent individuals. After further analysis, he discovered he wasn't hard on them for no apparent reason or because of them being overly attractive, but because he comprehended the tool they had at their disposal and, as his subordinate and foot soldier, he wanted to see better use of their available arsenal. Wow, he took his job too seriously. He needed some time off or, better yet, to retire. It wouldn't be long now, he thought, immediately putting him in a better mood and reminding him why he was coming home early.

Steven drove his Mercedes S600 down Brandon Mill Road admiring the huge homes and gargantuan lawns. He and his wife had moved to the Brandon Mill section of Sandy Springs shortly after his partnership to Covan, Allen, and Stanley. Their previous home in Roswell had slowly turned into an area of constant, Hispanic fiesta music and hordes of immigrants gathered at gas stations and plazas looking for labor. They were happy to now live in the more secluded Brandon Mill.

Their house was a five-bedroom, two-story structure sitting 50-yards or so from the street taking up three acres of land. He smiled every time he pulled through his remote-operated, wrought-iron gate. His wife was probably working out. As Jennifer got older, she tried harder and harder to keep her nice figure. While he appreciated this, he would love her the same no matter what her appearance turned out to be.

He walked into the house through their three-car garage and sat his briefcase and keys on an island in the kitchen. "Honey?" She didn't answer. She probably had her iPod pumping full blast through her ear buds. He took the carpeted stairs up to the second floor and looked into the exercise room only to find it empty. Huh.

"Babe? You here?" he asked as he went to their bedroom. In the shower, he thought. He pushed open the bedroom door and was about to call for her again when his words got stuck in his throat. Seeing what was in the bedroom, his first instinct was to run. There was a man in the room. It took a second to figure out he wasn't a threat. On the bed was a mess of blood and a person he knew to be his wife, though he couldn't bring himself to fully realize it. He instead concentrated on the man as he took careful steps into the room. The man was seated upright in one of two sitting chairs to the left of the bed. His chin was on his chest and his head listed to one side. The man wore some kind of biological, plastic suit and as Steven got closer, he saw that the man's crotch area was a bloody mess. He slowly turned to the bed and fell to his knees crying. Who could do such a thing? Jennifer had been the sweetest person he had ever known. Who could hurt such a gentle soul?

He got up from the floor wiping tears from his face and, with all his strength, held back the others that were sure to come later. He took out his cell phone and called the police. After numbly telling the police what he'd found, he sat on his front stoop with his head in his hands and asked to nobody in particular, "Why? Why?"

CHAPTER 50

Brennan pulled his unmarked car up to an open gate at the entrance of what he assumed was the Stanley residence. There was a uniform posted there who lifted a line of yellow crime scene tape to allow him to enter and waved him through. Several neighbors had walked down their long driveways to see if they could sneak a peek at whatever was going on.

Parking off to the side behind four other vehicles as to allow passage out, he noted a crime scene van, a detective's car, two patrols, and backed into the garage was a coroner's van. He couldn't help but think about the mileage that van was getting here lately.

He walked past a tech working by the door-way and entered the house. Nice place. The activity must have been upstairs because the huge, first floor was deserted. At the top of the stairs, he was spotted by Captain Kirby.

"Brennan, over here."

"The victim is definitely our guy, huh?" Brennan asked.

"Victims with an 's' and, yes, one of them is definitely Jared Miller, a.k.a. Jerry Norton. It's not pretty, so be prepared."

Brennan walked toward the open doorway where all

the activity was and peripherally saw Detective Jenkins talking to a puffy-faced, middle-aged man. He continued on into the room where several techs were at work photographing and collecting evidence. Matthew, a guy who worked closely with Maria Flemez back at their lab walked over to him.

"Boy, you got yourself into one here."

While the guy was a nice kid, he was 100% nerd and often uncouth, missing a lot of social cues and the like.

"It sure seems that way, Matt. You wanna give me some preliminary info and your take?" The kid was smart as a whip and Brennan, through experience, had grown to value his opinions.

"Okay. First, I thought it was the husband for sure. The guy over there was hit in the back of the head with something the size of a baseball bat and he wasn't in that chair when it happened."

"The body was moved?"

"Definitely. Come look at this." They walked over to the bed where Mrs. Stanley was bound by wrists and ankles to the bed posts. The restraints were plastic zip ties and several had to be used at each post to stretch from post to wrist or foot.

"If you look closely at the vagina, you'll see that all the blood isn't from her – it's from him. His penis is still inside her." Brennan swallowed some bile and looked closer. Sure enough, there was a piece of flesh that wasn't supposed to be there. Matt continued, "Now, I can tell you that it was cut off with a fairly sharp instrument, but what we don't know for sure, at least not yet, is…"

"Whether he was inside her when it was cut or if it was put there after the fact," finished Brennan.

"I think it was inside when it was cut off," Matt said.

"So what? The guy is fucking her with this space suit on and the husband catches them and hits buddy with the bat? I'm not buying it."

"That's why I said I thought it may be the husband at

first. The suit kinda fucks that up."

"Yeah, what's up with the suit anyway?"

"This is where my next theory comes in," Matt said, looking conspiratorial. "The suit is simple plastic with shoe cover booties. There is tape connecting the suit to the booties. It looks to me like he was really trying to make sure he didn't drop trace."

"Wait a minute. How did we get I.D. on the guy?"

"Oh, you'll love this. His wallet, complete with cash, credit cards, and driver's license was laying right here on the floor. Open, if you can believe that."

He couldn't believe that. There was something they were missing. Why would a guy who's wanted for several murders and had went to the trouble of wearing a protective suit even bring his wallet along with him? It didn't add up. None of this crazy shit was adding up. What the hell was a serial sniper doing raping some rich lady in her house? This is way off his M.O.

"And the husband just happened to come home to this?" asked Brennan.

"Yeah, he left the office about 45 minutes before the 911 call from his cell phone. His office confirms it. He says he was coming home to surprise his wife with dinner arrangements."

"Jesus."

"Yep. And another crazy thing is the guy's testicles."

"What about them?"

"They're gone," Matt said. "I mean, we found his penis, but where are his balls? Everything was cut off but we've yet to find the jewels."

"Brennan!" Detective Jenkins almost yelled coming into the room. "Downstairs. You got to see this."

"I think we found his balls," mumbled Brennan.

Brennan went downstairs and was led into a huge kitchen with two floating islands. The floors were marble and the counter tops granite. The tech he passed walking into the house when he arrived was dusting for prints on the refrigerator. Jenkins motioned toward the fridge.

"Go ahead, take a peek."

Brennan opened it and saw most of the stuff you usually would: milk, juice, cheese, eggs. But, in between the juice and milk on the top shelf was a white, paper, doggy bag with blood all over the outside. The bottom of the bag was saturated through and dripping onto the yogurt on the shelf below. Attached to the bag by duct tape was a note. The note was handwritten and read: "Here you go, Mr. Stanley. Now, you won't have to grow a pair." Brennan looked over at Jenkins incredulously.

"Well, let's call Agent Hunt."

CHAPTER 51

They just got back to her place. They had taken Mark's old pickup in anticipation of using it to take her newly bought furniture home, but after making her choices and feeling the solid quality of the furniture, Mark made a deal to have it delivered that day. Linda had never heard of the place, but fell in love with the store quickly upon entering. Jordyn's Boutique was a specialty furniture store that specialized in modern-designed furniture that used a lot of steel and glass.

Mark called her around noon almost insisting on going shopping for her furniture. Reluctant at the time, being her only day off to rest, she was glad now that she accepted. Linda really enjoyed spending time with Mark. He was witty and charming and had the best manners she had ever observed. While being a little old fashioned in his ways, he was still down to earth and able to laugh at some of the raunchier subjects. She decided she was definitely falling for him.

Between this case – and this case, she'd had little time to think about anything else. After the raid on the Miller residence, she had talked with Debbie Miller at length. She didn't have any information that would help them understand why Jared was killing these random people. She had said he was a good father, but more of a provider than a nurturer and that went for being a husband as well. She said that she was unaware of any psychological problems, but did say he had seen a therapist a number of years ago about having reoccurring nightmares. She said they had gotten worse recently, but that Jared refused to ever talk about it.

The night before the raid, she said Jared had gotten a phone call, and then became frantic to leave. When asking what was going on, Jared told Debbie that it was very important that he leave unnoticed and that he would explain everything later. Debbie didn't want to leave her girls alone, but he had been so adamant that she was genuinely frightened.

Linda had gone to the hotel off Shallowford Road, but no one even remotely fitting Jared's description had got a room close to the time in question. She had felt good about wrapping this case up soon. Thought they had him. Now the trail was once again cold. Linda fell into her old loveseat, which was soon to be replaced, and drank from a bottled water.

"You look exhausted," Mark said smiling.

"I am, but it was worth it. I really like the stuff we picked out."

She and Mark had taken over two hours choosing things for her new house. They ended up choosing a couch and loveseat that was brushed stainless steel and black, hand-stitched leather. They chose a matching coffee table of glass and the same brushed steel. The dining table was a bigger version of the coffee table and the chairs' black leather matched the sofas. She completed her shopping by choosing a black mahogany headboard for her bed and matching, black night stands with white and grey marble tops.

When Mark asked what she planned to spend, she said her max was $6,000. When the bill came she signed a receipt for $5,999. She knew it was Mark's doing. But she didn't know the real total was around $15,000.

"I'm glad you like it. You'll be happy. It holds up really well. I've had my living room set for almost 10 years and it's still like new."

As Linda put her arms around Mark, her phone rang. It was Detective Brennan. She told Mark to give her a minute and she walked into the bedroom.

"Agent Hunt."

"Hey, Linda. We've had some new developments."

"Tell me."

"Jared Miller is dead."

"What? How?"

"Well, he was castrated…"

"Castrated?" Linda said interrupting, sounding bewildered.

"Yes, castrated. But what killed him was a bat to the back of the head."

"Where was this?"

"Inside a home in a wealthy neighborhood right here in the Springs. Linda, there's more."

"More?"

"Just come on down to the station. We're all down in the lab."

"Be there in five."

Linda went back into the living room where Mark was looking out the window.

"The furniture people are here, Linda."

"Great," she sighed.

"What's wrong?"

"Something at work has come up. Is there any way you can stay here for a while and supervise?"

"Of course. Go do what you have to."

She walked over and pecked him on the lips. "You're the best. I'll call you."

Linda made it to the Sandy Springs PD in record time. As Brennan recommended, she went straight down to the lab. It was probably the nicest, most modern lab she had seen outside of Quantico. There were all types of machines and gadgets on the plain, white counters that Linda couldn't even begin to guess what their functions were. There were two tech people she had never met along with Jenkins, Brennan, and the Hispanic hot tamale that she knew Brennan to be sweet on.

"Welcome to our nightmare," Brennan said, handing Linda a hairnet, facemask, and booties for her shoes. She looked at him skeptically, taking the items.

"It's policy."

"So, what do we have?" Linda asked donning the safety gear.

"Okay. First, let me bring you up to date." Brennan told her about the woman and the scene. "And now, let's look at our most interesting piece of evidence." They walked over to a section of counter where Maria Flemez was looking at something through a microscope. Off to the side of the microscope was a bloody, white paper bag. Beside that was another tech who was looking at a handwritten note through a magnifying glass. "Maria, why don't you tell Agent Hunt what we know."

"Hello, again, Agent Hunt," Maria said shaking hands.

"What we know is that the person who did this is good. They are very smart and very careful. The note," they all moved over to where the tech with the magnifying glass was taking notes, "in my opinion, was written by a right-handed person using their left hand, making it nearly impossible to match to anything. There are no prints or fibers anywhere in the bedroom…"

"You've already cancelled out the wife and husband's prints?" Linda said interrupting. "Did they have a maid?" Thinking it was too fast to have already done this on a crime scene that was less than six hours old.

"Agent Hunt, what I'm saying is there are no prints whatsoever. Whoever did this not only wiped every surface, but vacuumed the bed, the floor, even the victim's hair. Like I said, the guy is very smart. He even wiped the wife's skin off. He knows his stuff." A lot of people didn't know that prints could be left on skin with the right amount of oil and pressure present. Apparently, this guy did.

"Who the hell is this guy?" Linda asked to know one in particular.

"I don't know," said Brennan, "but we know he is somehow connected to Steven Stanley. The note is most definitely personal and about Stanley performing some action cowardly."

"How does Miller tie in to all this?" asked Linda.

"I've been thinking about it and the only thing that makes sense is that he had an accomplice."

"Wait. Are you talking about just at this scene or the shootings as well?" asked Maria.

"I'm thinking the whole time," said Brennan. "And I'm thinking this other guy is the alpha male. I mean he used Jared Miller like a prop in this, like he was nothing. And it's obviously he's the one who has the beef with Stanley."

Everybody let that sink in. Was it this other guy orchestrating this series of killings? Was this Stanley ordeal linked to the shootings?

"You know, I was having problems seeing Miller as the shooter that took the first shots after investigating the scene we found off Dunwoody place," Linda said.

"Me too," said Brennan, "but all the evidence was there. And we took it."

"Don't be hard on yourself," Detective Jenkins said speaking for the first time. "We're not psychic. We go where the evidence leads us."

"I know, but it felt disconnected from the first two. I mean, besides having a car doing nothing on video tape, we have nothing on the first two shootings." Brennan shook his head. "Then we have the charity walk scene. It's as sloppy as it gets. He left every type of evidence possible. We should have seen it."

"But Miller was the guy in the video driving the car and he was the thief. We know that for sure," added Maria.

"The guy was using Jared as a puppet," said Brennan. "He probably planned to get rid of him the whole time."

"It makes sense," said Linda. "That would explain the phone call that Jared got right before he left his house the night we were watching. This guy was watching us, watching Jared, and gave him the heads up. No wonder he saw us coming."

They again all sat in silence and marinated in the new hypothesis.

"Okay," Linda said clearing her throat. "So where does that leave us? Where do we go from here?"

"We have to dig into this Stanley guy. He knows our man. He may not know he knows him, but he does." Brennan paused. "The guy was an Assistant District Attorney for a lot of years. He's gonna have a lot of enemies. That should be our angle, I think."

"I concur," Linda said. Everyone else nodded their head in the affirmative. "Okay, let's tear Stanley apart and see what we find. I'll get my guys up here ASAP. Now, if you'll excuse me, I have to go report to a man who is not gonna be happy."

CHAPTER 52

He had a whole list of people to kill. He knew he would probably be caught sooner or later. In fact, he planned on it. How else would they figure out the puzzle and therefore his message if they were missing the main piece? His plan was more to get found rather than get caught. He had a nice exit strategy all planned out for when the time was right. Nah, they wouldn't catch him. He was too smart, too careful.

Carmine Gallasi was a Canadian citizen and had been for three years. Formerly from South Africa he decided to retire early to the Ontario region and spend his days sailing the Great Lakes and enjoying his favorite sport, ice hockey. His father had owned a big game ranch and gave safaris to rich Americans and the like. He did very well for over 30 years. Then, when Carmine was 30 years old, his father had a heart attack while hunting and couldn't make it to the hospital in time. He passed and Carmine was motivated to keep the ranch going only to figure out, several years later, that he was tiring of the company – tiring of Africa. He sold the game ranch unexpectedly and, well-off now, moved to Ontario, Canada. This was all true, researchable information. Except for the fact that Carmine was actually at the bottom of Lake Michigan with no hands and no teeth. He would never surface but if he did, they wouldn't be able to find out who he was.

He had taken over Carmine's life. Even had access to his money. Making people wire entire fortunes was easy when you had a gun to their head. This was his well thought-out escape. Once in Canada, he would be untraceable with a documented history as Carmine. The police didn't stand a chance. The next victim's death would cause even more heat to befall him, but he wasn't concerned.

His killing spree was about to get major attention once they put a couple more pieces of the puzzle together, the media frenzy would be an unstoppable force. The next victim would be an undeniable shot at the justice system. They must not only be alerted of their wrong-doings, but a hypocritical justice system, that cared more for the criminal than their victims, needed to be held accountable and put on display. He would do just that. Fate had chosen him and he would not ignore fate.

CHAPTER 53

"Let me get this straight. What you're sitting here telling me is that the perp you've been chasing, while burning up uncountable man hours and spending money as if we print it ourselves, is not even the killer?"

"He may not be…" Linda tried to get in.

"Agent Hunt, do you have any idea how badly this looks on me? On our office? And you in particular?"

"With all due respect, Mr. Fletcher. No one could have foreseen that there were two perpetrators. And while he is now dead, Jared Miller was involved in these crimes and that was where the evidence led us. No one can fault you, this office, or me for that."

Linda and Special Agent in Charge Jeff Fletcher sat in his office after he asked her to come in for a face-to-face. The recent turn of events obviously was not what he wanted to hear. Linda felt that Fletcher most likely gave confirmations to some higher-ups that the situation was under control and, now, would have to go back with only excuses.

"I wish it were that easy, Agent Hunt. I wish it was as black and white as logical findings. But it's not. I have the Deputy Director breathing down my neck on this and all he cares about are results. I'm almost certain that regardless of my painting you and your team as competent investigators, he will be sending in a specialist."

"Sir, I…"

"Depending on his orders," Fletcher continued, raising his hand to quiet her, "you may, or may not, continue to supervise this case."

"Sir, that's bullshit."

"I didn't say I agree with it. But when it comes to the politics of the Bureau, I'm a pawn just like you."

Linda sat and fumed. She couldn't believe this shit. She and her team had done damn good work, did it while operating with local law enforcement, and did it by the book. She didn't care what kind of specialist they were, no one could have done it better.

"Linda," Fletcher started. She looked up. He had never in seven months called her by her first name. "I want you to plan on the worst case scenario that he employs a specialist here. That won't happen for two or three days and I'll try to stretch it for what I can. I'm giving you free reign in the meantime. Go get this son of a bitch. That's an order."

Linda beamed, "Yes, sir."

CHAPTER 54

Mike Dugan was an attractive, middle-aged African-American, or black, depending on your political correctness. He would be 50 years old next month and yet his hair had just started to gray around the temples. Trying to save money for retirement one day, he had been bringing his lunch to work with him for the past 10 years. Usually lunch was leftovers from the previous night's dinner, but sometimes his loving wife would make it special. He didn't know if it was his wife's cooking or the fact that he ended up throwing a lot of it away, but he kept his weight in-check and was decently fit for an "old geezer.

Detective Dugan had been with the Atlanta PD for over 20 years and, despite his nonchalant demeanor, he was passionate about his job. He had just cleared a drug buy – turned robbery/murder case thanks to a girlfriend of the perpetrator calling in and giving a play-by-play account of what happened. He wished they were all that easy. He had several open cases he could work on, but the brutal and sadistic murder of Stacy Kemp stayed on his mind. It wasn't that she had been the fiancée of a Superior Court Judge; not even about the additional pressures that came along with a high profile murder. It was the fact that he had absolutely nothing. He had logged nothing into evidence except meaningless witness statements, photos of the scene, and of the body. Motive? What's that? Suspect? Not a one.

He sat at a computer terminal that was inside the homicide squad room. There was a national database setup for all law enforcement officials where one could enter in information on active, closed, and cold cases. There was a similar database called ViCAP standing for Violent Criminal Apprehension Program that the Feds used. But being a lowly city detective, he didn't have access to that. The program he used was called CODIS which stood for Combined DNA Index System and, though it started as just a national databank for DNA, it now was set up more like ViCAP allowing investigators to enter and search all types of criteria. He had entered the Kemp case into the active cases and would sporadically come back to it with thoughts or to further his notes. This time he was looking for cases with similar circumstances. The program gave you a great deal of options to filter your searches. He typed in a series of keywords: 'female', 'sexual', and 'no physical evidence'. He got cases nationwide. He further filtered the cases by adding 'Georgia' to his keywords. 57 hits. He thought how to filter it even more. He didn't want to guess or add really particular details that may rule out a match, such as adding 'white female' where Dugan didn't even know the killers M.O. yet. Maybe Kemp just happened to be white, but the same killer brutally raped and killed two other black females the same way. He added 'Atlanta area' and came up with 34 cases. Eight were active, 12 were closed, and the rest were cold cases. He wasn't concerned with the 12 closed cases, of course, so that left him with 22 cases to work with.

He started with the active cases because there were fewer. He read through five cases which took him over an hour before coming to a newly entered case out of Sandy Springs. It was an older, white woman and her throat had been cut almost to the point of decapitation. Reading on into the notes, he saw that there was a second victim. Seeing that it was a male, his hopes plummeted. Then, as he read on in the case notes, he saw that the scene had been meticulously cleaned by the perp. He read on until he saw that not only had their perp wiped for prints, but also went as far as vacuuming the bed and victims. This had to be his guy. He looked for the date of the crime and saw it was only the day before yesterday. The Kemp woman had been murdered three days previously. He looked for the lead detective's name and badge number, then called Sandy Springs PD. Detective Brennan wasn't in, but after telling his fellow detective, Jenkins, what it was about, he gave Dugan his cell.

"Brennan," he answered.

"Hi, my name is Mike Dugan. I'm a detective down here in Atlanta."

"Yeah, what can I do for you?"

"I think we need to talk."

CHAPTER 55

The Country Club of the South was an elite, gated housing community that sat tucked off in a seclusion of trees in Alpharetta, Georgia. The Atlanta Braves baseball hall of famer, Chipper Jones, lived there along with recording artist Axon and several other stars and well-knowns. The community held close to 200 homes and was guarded like Fort Knox. There was only one way in and one way out, which was manned with guards and secured by remote control gates. There would be no following behind someone and slipping through the gate. No, tailgating would get you pulled over and surrounded shortly thereafter by their private security company. This security company was not your average flashlight cops. Each of them carried side arms and most were ex-military. They also had an arsenal of AR-15s and shotguns. If you were even moderately good at reading people, you could tell they were itching to use them.

The residents of Country Club of the South enjoyed their privacy and had no problem paying for it. Not one of the almost 200 homes was under a million bucks, while some were closer to five. The club dues alone were $30,000 a year.

He didn't have a problem with people living in this manner, he wouldn't mind it himself. Nope, most of the people here were just living the American dream, causing no harm to the rest of the world. Except one guy. This one guy was a part of the problem. He was at the head of a facet of justice that was the main contributor. He was in a position to control and see justice done, but like most in his position, he allowed politics to control his decisions. He held a lot of power, more power than a lot of people thought. He was basically in control of the entire Fulton County's law enforcement. More powerful than a police chief, the commissioner, or sheriff. He was the District Attorney for the richest and most crime-filled county in Georgia.

He had been Steven Stanley's boss. The big cheese. While Stanley was a veteran prosecutor himself and made a lot of decisions in his day to day cases, every plea negotiation had to be approved by his boss, Jeremy Elcombe.

Jeremy Elcombe graduated from Harvard Law and, soon after, went to work for a hot-shot firm down in Miami, Florida. He made his millions in a short time as a criminal defense attorney and as a litigator in a few mass tort cases. Between his firm suing pharmaceutical companies for administering bad drugs, he defended mid-level, organized crime figures. He quickly made a name for himself as a cutthroat litigator and a bulldoggish trial attorney. He loved the limelight, loved putting on the show for the press. It made him feel powerful and he wanted more. The next tier of power after being rich was politics and he saw his opening when the position of District Attorney was offered to him.

He moved into the Fulton County Superior Courthouse like he owned the place, which in some regards he did. From DA, he would catapult to mayor or maybe even governor. After that, who knew – the possibilities were endless. Elcombe ran the District

Attorney's office like a lot of politically ambitious DAs. All he cared about was the conviction rate. This was what was wrong with our criminal justice system. The focus was off. It was no longer about bringing criminals to justice. It was what kind of deal can we make with them to get a conviction. Fuck the fact that they destroyed a family or took away someone's wife, kid, sister, or father. The only thing that mattered was the conviction.

The guilty pleas that most criminals take instead of going to trial are called negotiated pleas. They usually involve the charges being reduced and the defendant serving a lesser sentence in exchange for a guilty plea and conviction. While there was sure to be cases where this practice was feasible, it was now the preferred way to handle almost every case. This was unacceptable. This was how the guy that raped your 14-year old daughter would get out in five to six years. This was the reason the guy that robbed your mother, who now is too scared to leave her house, only spends three to four years behind bars. This was why people had to die. Letters to your congressman and support groups didn't do shit. Something drastic had to be done and he was doing it.

He knew that he could have concocted a plan that would have gained him entrance to and exit from the country club, but there were too many uncontrollable variables to go that route. He was trying to be smart, not brazen.

He sat uncomfortably in the forest that surrounded the Country Club of the South. There was a 12 foot, electronically-monitored, chain link fence that also encompassed the grounds, but it wouldn't hinder him in the least. He was a good hundred yards behind it and would be shooting over it. He would be using his trusty Alaskan again. After the performance it gave him shooting into the cars on I-285, he owed it to the big rifle to be brought on another outing. The rifle broke down and the bi-pod was collapsible, but it was still 14 pounds. At 42-

inches long fully assembled, it was awkward to tote around in the dense woods.

He was shooting from an elevated position and at only 300 yards, he could do it in his sleep. The back of the Elcombe residence faced the woods and sat at the end of a large expanse of green grass, past a small creek. On the back of the two-story mansion was a three-level deck that overlooked a swimming pool the size of a small country. Jeremy Elcombe wasn't home, but his beautiful, Brazilian wife, Sueni, was. In fact, she could have been looking right at him. Her glistening, caramel-colored body sat facing him as she lounged at the pool. She had enormous, modified breasts under a string bikini that was at least two sizes too small. Her black sunglasses were almost as big as her breasts and sat snuggly on her adorable face. She was 25 years old and had been married to Elcombe for three of those years. She was his third wife and 23 years his junior. Sueni was a trophy of his position and bank account and she was about to die.

He would be using Lapua Magnum rounds that at any closer of a distance might cut her in half. He didn't know if Jeremy truly appreciated his beautiful wife, but he was sure about to miss her. The tiny red dot at the middle of the crosshairs slowly made its way down from that pretty face to the center of her impressive bosom. Sometimes before he pulled the trigger or took a life, in another way his conscience got him. He wondered as he gazed through the quality scope if this woman had sinned. Was she an exceptional wife or was she a hussy? Did she enjoy life? Could she sing? Did she like to cook? These thoughts ran through his mind even though he knew them to be harmful to his focus.

She had just set down a cold, tropical-looking drink on a small patio table to her left when the powerful round entered the center of her chest. Before her face could register surprise the force of the round hitting her body kept her sitting upright, but slid the lounge chair back two feet. Seconds after her hand went to her chest, she was dead.

He collapsed the bipod, threw the rifle over his shoulder, and calmly walked through the woods toward a side street. There sat an abandoned house and a white GMC van with a counterfeit steam cleaning decal on its sides. As he got into the driver's seat of the van, he marveled at how easy it was to get away with murder.

CHAPTER 56

Brennan sat with Maria alone at a table in "Linda and Company's" temporary office at Sandy Springs PD. Both were using laptops and Brennan was just hanging up with a clerk of court.

"Okay. I have a list of cases that both Judge Kemp and Stanley, acting as prosecutor, were both involved with being emailed to us as we speak."

"Why didn't they just give it to you over the phone?" asked Maria.

Because it's over a hundred," he said nonplussed. "Jeremy Elcombe was the DA over Steven Stanley starting in 2002 and ending when Stanley retired into private practice in '08 so, that will eliminate a lot of the cases. But, otherwise, Elcombe will be involved in any case Stanley and the judge were in some regard."

"So, we're looking at the criminals they all had a part in convicting?" she asked.

"I don't think so. The note on the bag was implying that Stanley needed to grow a pair of balls. In other words, he was calling him a coward. As a defendant, I can't see a reason that would be plausible. It makes more sense if we were looking for a victim in the case. Maybe the District

Attorney's office failed to prosecute because of one thing or another and the victim wanted blood."

"Could be, Brennan. That it's a very disgruntled family member of a victim. Maybe the DA's office was scared to take a murderer or child molester to trial and that's what they meant by growing a pair."

"Exactly," Brennan said, starting to get animated. "And now they are taking out the loved ones of those responsible. It fits."

"Not just loved ones, Brennan, but wives. The first murder was the fiancée of Judge Kemp, right?

"Yes, and then Stanley's wife and now Elcombe's wife. Holy shit! Let's go through this list."

As they sifted through the cases on the e-mail, only 42 of them involved all three husbands and they began March 2003 and ran to July 2008. They needed to go to the courthouse and look at the files themselves. As Brennan made that possible talking to Judge Kemp and his clerk, Linda beeped in on the other line. He thanked the clerk and took the call.

"Brennan."

"We've got nothing here. Another long-distance shot without a trace of evidence," Linda said numbly.

"Well, we have a great lead." He filled her in on their research and logic and Linda was 'gung ho' about dissecting the county case files.

"Me and my guys will meet you there, Brennan. Give us about an hour."

CHAPTER 57

Paul Grier grew up in Atlanta Georgia. Not in the suburbs, but in the city itself. He didn't live directly in the ghetto. In fact, thanks to his father, they were relatively well-off. Living in the city, you were never more than a hop, skip, and a jump from the bad parts no matter what section you lived in yourself. He and his father rented a house on Charles Allen Avenue and the house was only a block from the intersection with Ponce De Leon Avenue. Across Ponce, Charles Allen turned into a road called Parkway. Parkway was the beginning of the ghetto. Another road ran parallel to Parkway called Boulevard and these roads and others were the stomping grounds of street hustlers and 'Dope Boys' of the notorious Forth Ward section of Atlanta.

Paul lived on the nicer side of Ponce De Leon but the close proximity allowed young Paul a glimpse of the street life – and he liked it.

His father, Gary, was a good man that worked hard and loved his son. Gary owned a small construction company where he was the foreman of every job. While he made decent money, Gary was hardly ever home. He often had jobs out of town in nearby cities such as Savannah or

Columbus and being a two or three hour drive from Atlanta, he often chose to stay in local motels to save on time and money. Being an absent father a lot of the time, he compensated by trying to buy his son's affection with new shoes and toys. At the time, Paul didn't mind. In fact, he thought his dad was the best for buying him all this stuff. But, as he started to get into junior high and high school, he used his father's absence as a license to do whatever he wanted. Paul started out hanging with the wrong crowd. His daily activities were getting high, stealing cars and merchandise, and selling drugs. He was in and out of juvenile, often manipulating his dad and the court judges that he had a drug problem. The problem was his criminal mentality. He didn't see any problem stealing cars from people, because the insurance would pay for it. Stealing from a company's store that made billions in profit, even forging other people's checks because the bank would credit it back.

Paul believed this to be sound logic and fair-play morally. Well, the DAs and judges didn't, and sent him to prison. The first time he only did a year for six counts of first degree forgery and theft by taking a stolen auto. His second prison term was much more substantial at seven years. He had been shocked at so much time for only being a participant in a snatch robbery, but he had taken it to trial and lost.

He came home from that prison bid and put forth serious effort to change his life. Paul wasn't stupid, in fact, he was extremely quick, but after six different places in a row fired him for being a convicted felon and lying about it on his application, he went back to the street life.

He did really well for a while this time. He had made some money selling dope, but he was staying away from the street life. He would sell the drugs through his cell phone, driving to meet most of his clientele. He started out selling weed and Ecstasy and moved up to Meth. Yep, he was doing real well until one of his customers got pulled over with a gram of Meth and told the police everything about Paul Grier. Shortly after that, his customer worked with police and set him up. He was charged with possession with intent to sell Methamphetamines and possession of a firearm by a convicted felon. He, again, was going to prison; this time for only five years. While he was in prison this time, he realized what had to change to keep him out of trouble. It was him. He had to change who he was. He concentrated on this moral change and practiced self-discipline. He took staying out of prison seriously.

He met a girl via Facebook on a smuggled cellphone while there. Here name was Ashley Henley and she adored Paul. He only had a year to go when they met and he talked to her almost every day of that year. She came to visit and even sent him money. She loved him and he loved her. She picked him up the day he was released and he directly moved into her home where she had two children by a previous, dead-beat, baby-daddy. She was even able to help Paul find a job. Everything was looking up. God had sent him an angel. They were married three months later at a small church with only immediate family and a few friends. They were compatible in every way. Perfect for each other.

Upon receiving a promotion from work, Ashley wanted to surprise Paul with the news and have a small celebration. She stopped at Green's Liquor Store on Ponce De Leon which sat street-front behind a Kroger. She was standing in line with champagne when a masked man came in with a gun and robbed the cashier. Ashley put down her alcohol and put her hands in the air. As the man ran out the door he fired two blind shots behind him and one of those unlucky shots hit Ashley in the middle of her forehead. She died there.

The Atlanta Police Department caught up with the 'crack head' robber down the road not five minutes after the robbery. He was apprehended on foot after running from a stolen Jeep that was reported to be the getaway car. They locked the man up for murder, armed robbery, and car theft.

Paul had been absolutely crushed by the loss. He studied the case against the 'crack head' and as a veteran of the workings of the system, he felt sure it was a slam dunk case for the prosecutor.

The prosecutor's name was Stanley. He had assured Paul that the perpetrator would feel the full weight of the law. He would do everything in his power to see that the guy got a life sentence. That's what Paul thought he deserved for taking his wife. It may not have been murder, but it was definitely voluntary manslaughter, as well as armed robbery.

Paul showed up for the guy's trial in Judge Kemp's courtroom on the fourth floor of the Fulton County Superior Courthouse. It was set for trial, but that's not what took place. In fact, all Paul saw for most of the day was everybody else's cases. Midafternoon, Mr. Stanley walked over and said that a resolution had been reached in their case. A resolution? What the fuck did that mean? He said that the defense, the judge, and the prosecution had made a deal where they could spare having a trial and the defendant would plead guilty. How much time will the guy get? thought Paul. Exasperated, not knowing what else to do, Paul sat and watched as they made a plea deal, dropping his armed robbery to simple robbery and the murder to manslaughter. Then, Judge James Kemp sentenced him to eight years. Paul had screamed out in open court. How could they do this? How could they just let him get away with eight years? Paul kept screaming his obscenities and ended up in jail for contempt of court.

Paul had never been a big fan of the justice system growing up. Some of that came from ignorance, but mostly he hated cops because he had been a criminal. Now, as a tax paying, productive member of society, he loathed the system. It was supposed to be there to protect you. Its obligation was to be fair and make sure that wrongs didn't go unpunished. It was really just more bureaucracy. Another way to create jobs and enable them to say "Hey look. We're doing something." In other words, it was bullshit.

CHAPTER 58

Linda was just leaving the Country Club of the South with Ogles and Lucas following. Alpharetta Police, along with the club's private security firm were still knocking on doors and combing the surrounding woods. She knew they would come up empty-handed. She knew that Mrs. Elcombe's killer and the man they had spent 3 weeks looking for were one and the same. Linda didn't know it was the same guy because of the target or because of the method of murder, but more than anything, she knew it to be him because of the lack of evidence. No one had seen anything. There was no trace of him being anywhere. Sueni Elcombe was just here one minute and gone the next.

Linda was exhausted and she was sure her whole team was also. Not only physically, but mentally. They were chasing a phantom. The killer was playing with them. This was some kind of sick game, she thought.

She dreaded calling Fletcher and informing him of the latest murder. The DA's wife for God's sake. The media was still having a field day over the shootings earlier in the month. They were always quick to remind the public that no suspect had been apprehended. The press knew about the motel slaying of a judge's fiancée. They also knew about the double homicide in Brandon Mill involving another county employee and they were about to find out about the DA's wife. It wouldn't be too much longer before they put it together and all hell would break loose. As of this morning, the director of the FBI had yet to make a decision on sending in more troops on this. Once it hit the newswire about these new murders, whether they were in connection with the sniper killings or not, she would lose control of this investigation and her fast track career would come to a halt.

She needed to talk to somebody. She tried to call Beth, but she only got the machine. She dialed another number.

"Hello? Linda?"

"Hi Mark," she said miserably.

"Hey, what's wrong? You sound down."

"I shouldn't have called. I just needed someone to talk to." She was just short of sobbing.

"Of course, you should have called. I'm here for you, Babe. Day or night. What's wrong?"

The floodgates opened and she cried like a baby right there on the phone. She explained all that had been going on and how important it was to her.

"I'm sorry for acting like this. I swear, I hardly ever cry."

"It's okay to cry, Linda. You can't always be tough and hold it in. We all need release."

"You're so sweet. I'm so glad that we met."

"I am, too. Let me know the minute you have some time off so I can come kiss your face."

"Aww, I will. It should be later tonight. Maybe you could swing by."

"I'm game. Call me."

"Okay. Bye."

Linda sat there and listened to the phone click as Mark hung up. She had almost said it. Almost told him she loved him. Was it too soon? Did he feel the same? Either way, he brought a smile to her face. She pulled into some open spaces reserved for police on Pryor Street in front of the courthouse.

Atlanta was a crazy city, thought Linda. Here she was an FBI agent standing in front of the highest courts in the county, not to mention the ten or so Fulton County deputy sheriffs that strode the sidewalk. Then, right across the street, she witnessed a young, black male, maybe 15 years old, sell some type of drugs to a street person. One hundred feet from him was a guy selling bootleg DVDs out of a large suitcase. She guessed it was hard to worry about things like this when you had guys out there like she was after.

In the lobby, there was a short line of people waiting to step through a metal detector and have their bags go through an X-ray machine. Fulton County's courthouse had a major security mishap in 2005 which resulted in the deaths of a Superior Court Judge, a Court Recorder, a Deputy Sheriff, and a Federal agent.

In the spring of 2005, a Fulton County inmate named Brian Nichols was on trial for the rape of his ex-girlfriend. It was the second time the court was taking this case to trial. The first trial had a hung jury that voted in favor of the defendant 8 to 4. Needing the jury to be unanimous in convicting Nichols, they tried again. One morning, while being escorted up the elevator by a Fulton County Deputy Sheriff, the 6'4" and 260 pounds Nichols over-powered the female officer escort. He hit her several times with his fist that was loaded with a heavy piece of metal. Almost killing her, he then disarmed her of her firearm and keys. Making his way from behind the courtrooms out to the lobby, he shot a court recorder and the judge in his case. Nichols somehow managed to make it outside where another Deputy Sheriff tried to stop him and was shot to death. Nichols left the area using the public transit and happened upon an off-duty Federal agent in an unfinished home that was being built. Nichols shot him as well. While the biggest manhunt in Atlanta history was underway,

Nichols forced his way into a woman's apartment where she fed him and talked him into giving up and turning himself in. Twelve hours after the first shot was fired, Brian Nichols was right back at Fulton County jail.

Because of that incident, Fulton now kept a small army of deputies standing by in the lobby, of roaming the corridors. The three agents badged their way through and Linda immediately spotted Brennan and Jenkins standing by the elevators.

"Glad you could make it," Brennan said shaking hands around.

"Sorry we're late. Alpharetta was a real circus," she said, pulling her red hair back into a ponytail.

"It's cool. Look, I've spoken to the powers that be and we have free access to the files as long as we need them. We'll be using Judge Kemp's chambers as he is just as determined to find this killer as we are."

"Does everyone know about Elcombe's wife?" This from Ogles.

"Yes. A select few are aware and some have even left home early to check on loved ones."

"I can understand that," Linda said.

Brennan pressed the elevator call button and the five of them boarded. They had a short ride to the 4th floor and made their way through Kemp's courtroom, passing several courtroom employees. The judge's chambers were empty and files sat stacked on a fold-out table. Several chairs had been brought in to accommodate them.

The room was full of dark woods with muted drapes and carpets. An entire wall of bookcases sat to one side of the room, holding volume after volume of law books. The desk was mahogany, but a modest size for a man of Kemp's position. On the very organized desk sat a brass lamp, a planning calendar, and a framed picture of the judge and a beautiful woman.

"Look at that. It's so sad," Brennan said, pointing to the photo.

"What? The picture? Why is it sad?" asked Ogles.

"That was the judge's fiancée who was just murdered." Everyone had a moment of silence on that one. Linda grabbed a file.

"Okay, let's go over what we know and what we are looking for. Brennan, fill us in on the Atlanta case."

"The woman's name was Stacy Thurston but she had already assumed the Judge's name. She was found tortured, killed, and cut up in an Atlanta motel. She was the first to be killed since the initial shootings and I believe this to be the killer's first meaningful kill."

"Meaningful?" asked Agent Lucas.

"At this point," Brennan continued, "I think the killer used Jared Miller to set up the sniper shots while he himself took the shots. This is just a theory. But I think the shootings were just a show. An attention grabber. I don't think he had even enlightened Miller to his real intentions. The next victim, as you know, was the wife of Steven Stanley who was a prosecutor and we now have the killing of Mr. Elcombe's wife; Elcombe being the DA himself. All three were involved in just over 40 cases in a span of roughly five years. There is no way this is a coincidence. Our killer is somewhere in these files. I'd bet my life on it."

"Okay," said Linda. "What are we looking for here? I think everyone agrees that this is a man rather than a woman, right? And as our collective thinking goes, I think we can also eliminate the defendants and their families. At least for the time being, I want our main focus to be on victims and their loved ones. That means brothers, fathers, boyfriends, husbands, uncles. Any male that is mentioned as being in support of the victim. The guy is killing people's wives, so I think we are looking for a husband or fiancé. Pay close attention to every case. Pull anything that even leans toward our guy. What I believe will be the most promising will be cases where there was a female victim injured or killed. Everybody with me?" A bunch of affirmative nods. "Alright, then. There are 42 cases. There's five of us, so everyone grab eight files. I'll take the odd two."

Everyone grabbed their respective folders and began sifting through pages and pages of data. Some folders were only a half inch thick while others were four with corresponding attached folders. Linda noticed with her first two that the large ones were the ones where there was a trial and the thinner ones were the plea outs.

No one spoke for almost an hour and after 3:00 p.m., Linda called a break. Everyone used the bathroom, some throwing water on their faces, Brennan massaging his eyes. They got snacks and drinks and then made their way back to their seats. Linda had claimed the judge's desk and from there she asked for a status update.

"I've got one that looks good," Ogles started.

"Nothing yet," Lucas added.

"I have one of interest," Jenkins said, in turn.

"I've got a pretty good one," Brennan remarked.

"And I haven't seen one yet. Let's finish it up. At the rate we're going we'll be finished in an hour or two."

They all went back to their reading. Linda had two more than the rest and had been scanning pretty quickly. She had been through seven of the files and the only one that came close was a woman that was beat half to death with a hubcap puller. The case never went to trial because of identification problems. The perp took a ten-year plea to serve five. There was no mention of a spouse.

She started her last one and noticed the others were all through. She held up one finger at them and trudged ahead. She scanned the information faster now, having become good at it as of recently. She saw something that made her stop completely. She looked up and saw that no one was watching her. She read on capturing every detail. Fifteen minutes later she was done and put the rest of her files with the others on the table.

"Sorry that took me so long. Some of these cases make

interesting reading and they reach out and grab you," she told them.

"You can say that again," Brennan said. "I think we should go over our findings and look closer at the best ones. What do y'all think?"

"Sounds good to me," Ogles said, "How 'bout you, Linda?"

"I like it. Who's first?"

"I got this," said the giant of a man. Big Mike Ogles stood up and cracked his knuckles and handed his most promising file to Linda. "Alright. Last year around Christmas, April Ford, out of Roswell, GA, called the police and reported a suspicious person walking around outside her apartment. She told the officers, once they arrived, that she was pretty sure the guy had been trying to look through her partially-closed blinds. The officers looked around and didn't see anyone, but told her to close her blinds, lock her windows and doors, and that they would be patrolling the area. Call if she had any other concerns – yada, yada, yada. So, this April Ford woman lives with her husband but he's overseas in Afghanistan; army specialist. The husband is due home in two weeks, by the way. Anyhow, two hours after the police leave her apartment, she thinks it is a good idea to take her recycling to the complex's designated area which is only 50 yards from her front door. As she goes back into the apartment she is grabbed from behind and led into her bedroom where the crazed man punched her several times and proceeded to rape her. When the guy was done, he hit her in the head with a single brick that she had in the house for some arts and crafts project. She was able to call the police, though badly hurt. The perp was found hours later in his own apartment, which was in view of Mrs. Ford's. A witness saw him run into his apartment shortly before the police arrived again. They charged him with aggravated battery, rape, sodomy, and kidnapping. The husband, army specialist Brian Ford, comes home and gets very involved with the prosecution. They've got a slam dunk case until Mrs. Ford suddenly dies of an aneurism. The doctors say it was definitely caused by her injuries, but it was very untimely and tragic. Without a victim, the prosecutors had to cut a deal and the perp, Tally Ringold, got off with a fifteen to serve seven years sentence." Ogles drank some of his water. "Now, Stanley prosecuted the case with Judge Kemp presiding over the case and this is during Elcombe's reign as DA. This Ford guy is full of hatred, he's a trained soldier, and no stranger to violence. I like it."

"Very good," said Linda. "Let's look at his whereabouts at the times of the last three murders. Ogles, I want this information ASAP"

"Done," Ogles replied.

"Okay. Who's next?" she asked.

"I had one, but I just went back to look at something and saw that the husband is partially paralyzed and 63 years old," said Jenkins.

"Well, still check his whereabouts if everything else fits. You never know. Anybody else?"

"Nothing from these cases," Lucas said.

"I have a great one. It's so good, I really want to go find the guy right now and lock him up." Brennan said with a big smile on his face. He had everyone's attention. "The guy's name is Paul Grier. His wife was shot and killed in an armed robbery of a liquor store. The shot wasn't intentional, so the guy was charged with manslaughter along with simple robbery. There was some identification issues in the case because of a mask the perp wore, so the DA's office cut a deal and the guy pleaded out and took eight years. Mr. Grier was livid and actually went to jail for contempt of court because of his behavior inside the courtroom. It shows in the prosecution's notes that this wasn't Mr. Grier's first time in jail. He has served 3 different prison terms; everything, from forgery to robbery to aggravated assault. This guy is a career criminal. I like him as a number one suspect. We have documented threats toward the court for not doing their 'so-called job', we have a convicted violent offender, and, I bet if we check, he won't have an alibi anywhere in sight."

"It seems too good to be true," Linda said. "Though the killer is a really smart guy. This guy is a street thug; a repeat, convicted felon. Do you think he's capable of pulling this off?"

"I haven't a clue. I don't know the guy, but from what I have read here, he looks to be our best candidate."

"Alright. Let's get a bead on him as well. I didn't see anything worthwhile in the files I read, so let's get on this Grier and Brian Ford. If they don't have concrete alibis for these murders, let's tear their last couple weeks apart."

CHAPTER 59

"We have one more stop to make."

"Let's make it quick, homie, I don't like riding around with all this heat in the car."

"It's cool. The car's legit. I just need to ride up to Sandy Springs to see if we can get off these pistols to a couple Mexicans I work with."

Paul Grier and his friend, Tony, left the Cotton Mill Lofts taking a left on Boulevard toward I-20. Paul and Tony were like night and day. Paul was a skinny, white guy of average height while Tony was a six-foot, black guy who tipped the scales at right around 400 pounds. Paul was a quick-witted, street hustler while Tony's biggest achievement on any given day would be rolling a blunt of weed. Somehow, despite their differences, they had been best friends since meeting each other in prison some years earlier.

"I think that blue car back there is following us," Tony said.

Paul looked in his rearview. "Come on. Don't start getting paranoid on me."

As they merged onto I-75 North, Tony looked back and couldn't see the blue car any more. Maybe he was being paranoid.   He wasn't.

Big Mike Ogles and Agent Lucas were following the silver Dodge Charger up I-75, but they were a good 10 cars back. They had just come from the west side of Atlanta in an area known as "The Bluff". It was a high traffic drug area known to everyone including the authorities. They witnessed Grier dropping off packages to two separate locations. After the drug deals, they followed the charger to the east side where several gentlemen with dreads came out to look at something in the trunk. On I-75 now, Ogles pulled out his phone and hit a speed dial.

"What do you have, Ogles?" Linda answered.

"Well, there's no doubt the guys should be behind bars, but I don't think this is our guy."

"Shit! That's both of our suspects down the drain."

They had inquired as to Brian Ford's whereabouts soon after leaving the courthouse only to have it confirmed that Brian had gone back overseas on a tour nine months previous and was still there.

"We have to go back to the files. The connection has to be there," she said.

"I'm with you, Agent Hunt. We must have overlooked something."

"Go on home. We'll attack the files again tomorrow."

"Good night, then."

CHAPTER 60

Linda felt sick to her stomach. She couldn't believe it. With her head in her hands she wondered what to do next. She was at the Sandy Springs PD writing a report when Ogles had called-in the dead-end with the Grier character. Now, she sat at her desk dazed and confused. It just didn't make sense. Then a thought struck her and she started pushing things around on the desk's surface until she found what she was looking for. She opened the file up and scanned for a phone number. Finding it, she grabbed her phone and dialed.

"Hello," said a sleepy voice after ten rings.

"Debbie, this is Agent Hunt with the FBI. I'm sorry if I've woke you, but I need to ask you some more questions."

"It's okay. I was really just laying here thinking."

"Alright. Now, I've already asked you about Jared's recent behavior changes and anything new that he'd been doing, but now I want you to think further back in time. How about a year or two ago? Maybe even before that. Did he meet any new people? Join any clubs? Anything like that?"

"No. I don't think so. It seems that Jared pretty much

had the same routine shortly after our honeymoon."

Damn. There had to be a link between them. Somewhere, somehow they met, thought Linda.

"How about friends from his days at Georgia?"

"No, he was pretty self-contained. I mean, he had gone out for drinks after work with his employee's but... wait! He did do something different for a while. I don't think he did it for long though. Because he never talked about it afterward."

"What was it?"

"He started going to a target range after work to relieve stress."

"A target range? You mean, a shooting range?" Linda's thoughts were putting things together and it made her nauseous.

Yeah, I guess that's what it's called. He only said something about it a time or two. That's why I didn't remember, but yeah he was shooting guns inside of a building. Is this important? It was almost two years ago?"

"It might be." Linda was trying to stay calm. "Do you remember if it was far away or did he ever say?"

"You know, I can't think of the name but I see the sign all the time when I drive down Roswell Road. It's right here in Sandy Springs."

Linda was having trouble breathing.

"Is the place called Glover Guns?"

"That's it! Now I remember, because it has two big 'Gs' on the sign. What's going on? Is there something wrong?"

"No, nothing like that," Linda said trying to sound nonchalant. "Just doing important paperwork. Look, thanks again. I have to get this to my boss. Good night."

"Okay. Good night."

It all made sense now. Mark was the killer. At the courthouse, that last file she read had Mark's name in it. His fiancée, Jen, had been killed when the perpetrators in a high-speed chase hit her car head-on. The defendants in the case had each taken 10 years in a plea negotiation. Linda was going to tell the others after reading the file, but after thinking about it, she concluded it couldn't be him. She thought back to the times of all the murders and remembered that she and Mark had been furniture shopping the day Jared and Mrs. Stanley were killed. After learning that Jared had been going to Glover Guns, she also remembered that the day they shopped for furniture, he had called insisting they go shopping. Almost giving her no choice. He was giving himself an alibi.

Linda had to call Brennan right away. She felt like she had betrayed him. He deserved to know about Mark's case. They all did. Hopefully, they would understand her reasoning. She dialed Brennan's cell.

"Linda, what's up? Tell me we got something on this Paul Grier character."

"Actually, no. I called my agents off."

"What? Why?"

"Brennan, I'm pretty sure I know who the killer is now."

"Well, great. Who is it?"

"My boyfriend."

"What?!"

Linda gave Brennan the run down and told him about her seeing his name in the case files at the courthouse.

"Look, Linda. Don't beat yourself up about sitting on it. You had good reason to find it hard to believe. I forgive you and your guys will, too. Let's go bring him in."

Linda talked to her team and they understood. Next, she called her boss and it was hard to come away with still supervising the mission because of the conflict of emotions. She assured him nothing would get in the way of her objective.

Everyone was to meet at Sandy Springs and be ready for an immediate invasion of the Glover residence as well as Glover Guns. Linda walked into her make-shift office to her agents, Jenkins, Brennan, and even Maria Flemez clapping. She couldn't help but smile. She sat behind her desk as the clapping died and Brennan came over.

"When was the last time you talked to this guy?"

"Now that you mention it, it's been awhile. I normally hear from him daily."

"Do you think he knows that we know?"

"I don't see how."

"Well, Maria did some research on the case while we were getting warrants and getting everybody together. Here, I'll let her tell you." He called Maria over.

"What's up?"

"Why don't you tell Linda what you found?"

"Okay." She turned and reached into the chair she had been sitting in and grabbed a manila folder. "Alright. Mark Glover's fiancée, Jennifer Parsons, was accidently killed by Damien Roach, who was driving, and his passenger, John Lichty, on May 19, 2007. Both young men were convicted of simple robbery and involuntary manslaughter on December 12, 2008 and sentenced to 10 years in prison. Of course, we know that it was a plea negotiation. Both men were shipped to Jackson, GA for diagnostics on February 6, 2009. From there, they parted ways with Damien Roach going to Hancock State Prison in Sparta, GA and Mr. Lichty going to Wheeler State Prison, which is a private prison in Alamo, GA. Both men were stabbed to death within six months of arriving. While Hancock is known for that kind of violence, it was their first murder in 10 years. As for Wheeler, they had never had a murder; this was their first. In both killings, there were no weapons found and no witnesses whatsoever, which from what I hear isn't uncommon in prisons."

"He had them killed," said Linda.

"Sure looks that way," Brennan said, nodding his head.

"So, he killed the two defendants in his fiancée's death. Then he kills two random people in front of the grocery stores. I can at least see the motivation in the first two, but why the man and the woman out shopping?" Nobody answered Linda for a moment. Everybody looked to be deep in thought.

"The only thing that makes sense, if they truly aren't connected in some way we haven't figured out yet, is for attention." Brennan let that sink in as he got his thoughts together. "Now, if we believe that to be true and I know it's hard to do being a decent, caring human, then the I-285 shootings have to also be some sort of attention grabber. Just random violence. This one is easier to fathom because there is just no way to have known where his targets were gonna be at that exact moment. I think it would be impossible, too many variables."

"Definitely," Maria said.

"Okay. I'm with you so far," from Linda.

"So he wants everybody watching. He wanted everybody to pay attention to his next act. And his next act was murdering three people. Four, if you count Jared Miller, but I think that was just to keep him from talking. Remember, he knew we were on to him. I think it's safe to say he orchestrated Miller making it out of the house. Back to the three. All three were the wives of the men he obviously believed to be responsible of what, letting Roach and Lichty off too easy?"

"After the note with the testicles and reading the case file, I think it's safe to say he wanted there to be a trial," Linda said.

"Yeah, he wanted to see justice done," Maria agreed.

"Listen, you guys," Linda started, looking down at her hands that were in her lap. "I know my relationship with Mark may alter my perception, but Mark is a very principled guy. He is almost compulsive about things being done right. If I had to guess, I would say it's more than just the death of his fiancée. Maybe that's what opened his eyes to his new mission or twisted crusade, but I would think big with Mark. He most definitely has some moralizing lesson to be seen. I'd bet my badge on it."

"I agree with you," said Brennan, "and so does the

evidence. We could definitely see some distorted logic behind placing the blame on Stanley and Kemp because of Stanley being the prosecutor and Kemp being the judge in the case. Both held direct responsibility over the outcome. But Elcombe was just an administrator in this. He had no real involvement. That points to Mark making a more general point with these killings."

"Sometimes it's hard to understand the motive of someone who's psychotic," Maria said.

"More important right now than motive," Linda said as she got up and paced the room, "is what we can charge him with. I mean what do we have on him?"

"Well, I think we've established he has motive. Then we have the deaths of the two inmates…"

"We have theory," Linda said, interrupting Brennan. "We don't have anything linking him to a crime. Sure, we can go lock him up and try to bluff him, but I think everybody would agree that he is smarter than that. I, as well as my superiors, want him off the streets as much as anyone, but if we arrest him on bogus shit, he'll lawyer up and be back out in 48 hours. I think there is only one thing we can do."

"What's that? Kill him?" Brennan said jokingly.

"No. We act as if we don't have any idea it's him and follow him."

"Yeah?" asked Brennan. "And how are you gonna carry on your relationship with him? Just enjoy the company of a cold-blooded killer? I'm not letting you do that. Sorry."

"I'll just be busy with work all the time."

"And you don't think he'll notice something's amiss?"

"There's only one way to find out."

"Okay. So what do we do now?" asked Brennan.

"I call him."

CHAPTER 61

Mark just finished selling his house and taking a bigger loss than he thought he would. He now had exactly 30 days to leave his home, though in fact, he had already left. He had sold his business and all its merchandise yesterday. The buyer had been after Mark's shop for years and almost went into shock when Mark called and offered to sell him the store.

"Why sell to me now?" asked the elderly Italian entrepreneur.

"I've fulfilled that part of my destiny. Now, it's time to fulfill another part," Mark had replied enigmatically.

Between all the things he was having to part with, the Chevelle was the hardest to come to terms with. He ended up giving the car, free and clear, to a 16-year old kid who had stopped by the gun store on numerous occasions to admire the car as he walked home from school. Mark would really miss the car.

He sat in his air conditioned Lexus in the Bank of America parking lot where he had finalized the sale of his home. He thought of what lie ahead. It was still to be a journey. This plan had been in motion for over three years and it was near its end, but there was still work to do.

After Jen was killed, he was filled with grief and anguish. The pointless, avoidable death of his soul mate sent him into countless, sleepless nights of searching for new meaning. At first he felt that watching justice be done would help him move on in his grief, make it tolerable at least. But justice didn't come. Instead, he watched and realized that the district attorney's office was more worried about how to excel their careers over seeing justice done. The DA and the ADAs were more like baby politicians than civil servants.

After witnessing the pure negligence of their duty to uphold justice and watching them slap the wrist of those responsible for taking the life of a living, breathing angel, he vowed to Jen and all the other loved ones of the fallen like himself, that he would give this incompetent, selfish system reason for change.

While killing Roach and Lichty had been more on a personal level, they were the foundation of his goal. It had been unbelievably easy to have both of them killed in prison. Georgia's prison system was full of gangs. You had the Gangsta Disciples (GDs), the Good Fellas (GFs), the Bloods, the Crips, the Mexicans -13, and the Muslims (which while being a religion, they carried themselves as an organization). Mark learned all about the inner workings of the prison system through blogs and befriending prisoners on Facebook using a phony account. After months of talking to one high-level gang member and building trust, Mark put a hit out on Roach and it had only cost him $2,500. After Roach was killed he used the same guy to call his associates at the prison where Litchty was housed and after paying $2,500 more, he too was stabbed to death. Easy as pie. Mark's hands were clean and it was impossible to trace.

About a year after their deaths, Mark was in the middle of putting together a plan of attack when in walked Jared Miller. Literally. He walked into the gun store one day and wanted, like everybody else, to shoot some guns – but

Jared was different. It's hard to explain, but as Mark worked with Jared and taught him tricks of his trade, he could see a certain deep-seated anger in Jared. Jared loved the destruction. That's all he talked about at first, more firepower, and more damage. And as he spoke, you could almost feel a sadistic aura emanate from him. They talked more and more and Mark soon discovered that he could use Jared. He persuaded Jared to start shooting rifles and made him believe that his practice would pay off as they moved forward with their plan to take out certain government officials around the country. Though, Mark would never allow Jared to shoot anything. He just wanted him away from his gun store so later he couldn't be linked to him, if he needed that safety.

Mark had been uncertain about allowing Jared to play any part at all. But he needed some confusion and misdirection, at first, as he worked on the finishing touches of his mission. He had been very careful when it came to anything connecting himself to Jared, always watching him. Jared had actually done very well until he became impulsive and tried to do something of his own.

Now, Jared was just part of the message. The message was simple. Stop economizing justice. Require compassion in those that hold a position to seek retribution for citizens in society, not political ambitions.

Years ago, when the defendants in his wife's senseless killing were taking a plea deal, Mark wrote Georgia's governor and asked for him to step in on a major injustice. First, he received no response. Then, Mark wrote again asking him to please be of service to his tax-paying, Georgia voter. Mark received a letter back that was as close to boilerplate as you could get stating that he couldn't get personally involved, blah, blah, blah. Mark wrote again insisting that the governor's campaign had been full of a no-nonsense justice system that would crack down on violent offenders. The governor needed to intervene on his fiancée's behalf because she was now dead due to unconscious, violent criminals. He again received a letter back from the governor stating that he had, in fact, looked into the matter personally and, while he is sorry for Mark's loss, it looked to be that justice had been served. The governor even went on to say that, though it may be hard, let the grieving process run its course. Mark had been furious. Run its course?! It was obvious that the governor had never grieved. Well, he would. See, while the governor is not a district attorney's boss, he does have the power and authority to pressure certain issues in the DA's office. Things like being harder on sentencing in negotiated pleas. Like bringing more violent criminals to trial. And if he didn't mean what he said about being harder on violent criminals in his campaign message, he soon would. He would personally get Mark's message.

Mark pulled out of the bank's parking lot and drove south toward the city limits of Atlanta. He was leaving, but he wasn't going too far. He rented a small house in the Buckhead section of the city using one of his many false identities. The hotels would be watched too closely plus the house he rented was also very close to the home of a certain politician that mark was fond of.

Mark's iPhone started ringing. He had the phone's locating GPS function turned off, but Mark knew that the authorities could triangulate his position if it was transmitting a signal, which it was doing just ringing. He didn't need to look at the caller ID to know it was Linda. He had been expecting her call.

"Hello?"

"Hey, Mark. What are you doing?"

"Ahh. I had been wondering how you were gonna play it."

"Play what?"

"It's okay, Linda. I know you and your cohorts are trying to put together a case against me." There was silence on the line for a few seconds. "You still there, Agent

Hunt?"

"Why are you doing this?"

"Going for the confession already?" Mark said with a chuckle.

"Mark, how could you do such evil things? I was falling in love with you."

"You know, Linda, I've gone over this in my head a thousand times and the truth I've found is that I'm incapable of loving again. Not after losing Jen the way I did. I'll never open myself up to that again."

"So what… you were acting the whole time with me? You just wanted some kind of inside track on the investigation?"

"No. Our relationship was just bad timing. I like you a lot, Linda. But I've made some promises that must be kept and I won't let even my heart interfere."

"We're going to bring you down. You know that, don't you?"

"I am absolutely frightened by your competence. I'm sure you have boxes full of evidence against me. Would you like me to come down to the police station with my lawyer so you can charge me with a crime?"

Silence.

"I didn't think so. Face it, Linda. You have nothing. You're grasping at straws and not even this conversation, that you're recording, will help you. Don't worry though. There's more to come. Just sit back and enjoy the show."

"Mark, listen! We know what happened in your fiancée's case. We understand the message you're trying to get across. We, too, see the injustice, but there's a better way to get about getting the message heard. No one else needs to get hurt, Mark."

"What? Was that directly out of the negotiator's handbook? You listen! I've done my research and people have been trying to correct this type of injustice for decades. No, Linda. I think you're wrong. I'm on the right track here. I'm trying to set up a meeting with the big man himself, so for right now just think of me as job security. Talk to ya later."

CHAPTER 62

"Agent Hunt," Fletcher motioned, "this is Special Agent Watkins. He, until this came up, was heading up the behavioral science unit. As per the director himself, Special Agent Watkins will be supervising the 'Justice Case' from here on out."

"Justice Case?" Linda asked.

"After reading your detailed reports, I felt the name fitting. While Mr. Glover's means are completely distorted, he certainly seeks justice." My name is Bradley, by the way," Watkins said extending his hand.

"Well, I'm glad you've read my reports, but that doesn't give you a thorough perspective of this case," she said giving his hand a firm shake.

"Well, I expect you both have a lot to talk about. I don't know the ins and outs of this case entirely. But I do know that when you can't find evidence of something that did, in fact, take place, you most likely haven't looked hard enough or are looking in the wrong place," Fletcher said.

"I certainly…" Linda started, only to be cut off by Fletcher.

"Regardless, I want this man brought in on murder charges and I want those charges backed up by exhaustive evidence. We can't have this guy running around killing people's wives, no matter how noble his message is supposed to be. Find him and bring me some evidence. You're both dismissed."

They left Jeffery Fletcher's office and went into a break room which held coffee makers and several deluxe vending machines. As Linda looked at a selection of sandwiches, she fumed inside. Watkins poured himself a cup of coffee and started to speak.

"Listen, Agent Hunt. I want you to know that I totally agree with your findings. I think you've done a commendable job considering your obstacles and your subject."

"You do, huh?" Linda didn't know what this guy's game was, but she wasn't letting her guard down.

"I'm absolutely serious. I also want you to know that this is going to be a joint command. You were right that I only know what I've read, so I'll be looking to you to help us move forward."

"Well, you sound sincere, Special Agent…"

"It's Bradley, when we're not in the field. Is it okay that I call you Linda? Out of the field, of course?"

"Linda is fine." Was this guy for real? She'd yet to meet an agent willing to share any kind of command. Especially, with a woman. He seemed sincere, but she wasn't exactly batting well when it came to trusting the right men lately. He was 5'10", maybe 5'11", less than 200 pounds, and looked to be in pretty good shape. His suit didn't look to be your average Fed, off-the-rack, either. It fit him perfectly. His gray hair was evenly dispersed among his natural black hair, completing the distinguished salt and pepper look. The gray hair was definitely pre-mature because his slightly tan face was that of a man of no more than his late thirties. His eyes were deep, emerald green and his frequent smile brought small dimples to his clean-shaved cheeks.

"As I was saying, Bradley, I appreciate your

compliments and I'm glad you share my conclusions, but honestly, I could use some help. The guy has completely disappeared from the face of the earth and even if we knew his whereabouts, we couldn't charge him with jaywalking."

"Jaywalking is not a federal offense."

"I was…"

"I'm just kidding, Linda."

"Oh."

"I find it helps to keep things light. I hope that's alright."

"No, it's fine. I'm just a little tense right now. I was intimately involved with this guy, as you already know, and it has taken a toll on me."

"Well, you can talk to me about it. I am, after all, a psychologist."

"No, that's…"

"Another bad joke. Sorry. Listen Linda, I actually do need to speak to you about yours and his relationship. It will help with my profiling and could help us later on with decisions in the case."

"Well, there's no time like now. You want to talk in my office?" Linda asked grabbing the sandwich from the vending machine.

"It's actually my office now. They moved your stuff down to the office next to the mop closet."

"What?!"

"I'm sorry. I'm joking again. It's just that you're so serious. I couldn't resist. Yes, your office is fine."

CHAPTER 63

It was late. She looked at her watch and saw it was after 10:00 p.m. She had officially been off work since six, but something in Jennifer Parson's case was nagging her. Maria was a crime scene investigator, but she was technically a lab technician. She really had no business scrutinizing Mark Glover's fiancée's file. But, she wanted to help Brennan badly after watching him rack his brain all day trying to find something. After she read the entire file, something annoyed her. There was something she was not seeing. Something that would point her in the right direction. A clue as to what Glover was up to. There were several inquiries from Mark to the district attorney's office during the length of the case, but they seemed to be what any grieving significant-other might write. She went back to Steven Stanley's notes and read over them again. It seemed Mr. Glover was writing to more than just the DA. Someone from the governor's office had also inquired about the case. There it was. This was what was nagging her. Stanley's notes read, "It seems as though Mr. Glover has been trying to police this case by going to the governor on several occasions to the point of harassment." Harassment? She continued reading, but there was no other mention of it. Maria needed to talk to Stanley. His number wasn't in Ms. Parson's file, of course, but it was most definitely in his late wife's case file here at the department.

It took her only a minute using the computer before she found Steven Stanley's cell phone number. It was now close to 11:00 p.m., but Maria took a chance and called.

"Hello?" a man answered, surprisingly awake sounding.

"Mr. Stanley?"

"Speaking. May I ask who's calling?"

"Mr. Stanley, my name is Maria Flemez. I'm an investigator with the Sandy Springs Police Department."

"It's a little late, don't you think Ms. Flemez?"

"It is and I apologize for that sir, but other lives may be at risk and I think you may be able to help."

"It's fine, how can I help?"

"I want to see if you remember a case, the victim's name was Jennifer Parsons and there were two defendants; a Roach and a Lichty. They were…"

"I remember the case. Only because I dated a girl in high school with the last name Lichty. Yep, we pled that case out to a 20 do 10 if I remember correctly."

"That's correct. I know it's been several years but, if you can remember, the governor's office had been involved and I was wondering if you could help me understand why."

"It's been a long time, but I remember. It was a multi-faceted case. Two different indictments. The defendants were cousins and had armed robbed an International House of Pancakes in Atlanta that took police on a 20 minute chase up Georgia 400. The chase ended when the cousins exited 400 at Mansel Road and slammed into Ms. Parson's small sports car, crushing and killing her instantly. It was a very tragic case and, you have to believe me when I say, I wanted to prosecute those boys."

"I'm not judging your actions, Mr. Stanley."

"Of course. Initially, we had Mr. Glover contacting us

every couple weeks. Which is not too uncommon where a loved one is killed. About two weeks after we completed the plea negotiation, I received a letter from the governor stating that his office had been receiving complaints about the district attorney's office not showing justified judgment on which cases to try and which cases to plea. Something along those lines. We get complaints from local politicians all the time, you know. I just passed it up the ladder to my boss."

"Which, at the time, was Jeremy Elcombe, correct?"

"Yes. I didn't expect him to do anything you understand. I was just doing my job by passing the info along. After all, it was essentially Elcombe's decision to plea out the Parson case anyway."

"Okay. Then what?"

"Well, normally I wouldn't have anything else to do with the case once I negotiated a plea deal, unless it was appealed or was up for a sentence modification. Then, maybe a week later, I remember getting a call from the governor himself."

"I take it that doesn't happen often."

"How about never. Only time I ever spoke with the man."

"Do you remember what he said exactly?"

"I sure do and it was a strange request. He wanted to know what would need to be done to reverse the earlier negotiated pleas in the Parsons case. I remember thinking at the time that the guy was crazy, but after talking to him a little more I realized he wasn't crazy… he was scared. Not, oh my God scared, but I could tell he was trying to fix something or cover his ass."

"So what did you tell him?"

"I told him the truth. Beyond the defendants themselves putting forth a motion to withdraw their plea on feasible grounds and seeking due process, there was nothing that could be done to reverse the matter."

"Did he ever put in a call to your boss, Mr. Elcombe?"

"He never said anything to me about it if he did."

"Okay, thanks. I appreciate your time."

"No problem. I hope I could help."

Maria hung up the phone and sat there thinking. Was this Glover guy finished or would he kill again? Who was the next target? Was the governor involved somehow? She picked the phone back up. She had to call Brennan.

CHAPTER 64

For some reason, Bradley Watkins and Thomas Brennan did not get along. You could tell right from their first handshake. Was it because they were both alpha males? Both good looking? Both cops? Linda thought they were two of the nicest guys she'd ever met. She believed she understood Brennan's motive after thinking about it. She thought she and him had gotten closer during the case as colleagues and that maybe he didn't like the idea of this other 'suit and tie' coming in and taking over her investigation. Or maybe she was flattering herself and they were rivals in a chess club. Who knew?

It was just the three of them and they sat in Linda's temporary office at the Sandy Springs PD. She was behind her desk while Bradley and Brennan sat opposite her in comfortable office chairs. Brennan had just finished explaining what Maria had dug up.

"Well, I don't see why that necessarily makes the governor a target. I mean, I've read everything on the Roach and Lichty case and if you remember, this Glover wrote letters to a couple other people as well," Bradley said.

"Yeah, but not to the point of harassment," Brennan

countered.

"You know, that would make sense though," Linda said, looking thoughtful.

"What would?" Bradley and Brennan said almost simultaneously, and then looked at each other as if the question was preposterous.

"Would you guys stop?" Now both men looked as if they were being scolded by the teacher and feigned innocence. "It would make sense that he'd target the governor. I didn't put it together before because I didn't know the governor's involvement was what it was."

"I still don't see…" started Bradley.

"At the end of my last phone call… Brennan could you get the disc?" He hurried out of his chair. "At the end of mine and Mark's last phone conversation, he said something about having a talk with the big guy and assured me he wasn't through."

Brennan came back in with a recording device that worked with CD-R's instead of tapes. They were all quiet while the disc started.

"Hello?"

"Hey, Mark. What are you doing?"

"Ahh. I had been wondering how you were gonna play it."

Linda interrupted, "Can we fast-forward a little?"

Brennan held down the search button for a second, then the audio came back in.

"Mark, listen! We know what happened in your fiancée's case. We understand the message you're trying to get across. We, too, see the injustice, but there's a better way to get about getting the message heard. No one else needs to get hurt, Mark."

The three of them sat in rapt attention as the disc continued.

"What? Was that directly out of the negotiator's handbook? You listen! I've done my research and people have been trying to correct this type of injustice for decades. No, Linda. I think you're wrong. I'm on the right track here. I'm trying to set up a meeting with the big man himself, so for right now just think of me as job security. Talk to ya later."

They sat in silence for a few seconds.

"Okay. I see your point now. I think it's far from a direct threat on any one person though. I mean 'the big man' could be a number of people," Bradley reasoned.

Brennan looked as if he swallowed a bug. Linda had to step in.

"You're right. But we have the harassment to corroborate and…" Linda shuffled some papers around on her desk, "and we have this." She handed the papers to Bradley and Brennan leaned over to look.

"What is this?" Bradley asked.

"This is the last position of Mark Glover's cell phone signal before he hung up with me."

Can someone help me out here? I live in D.C."

"That," said Brennan, "is Buckhead."

"What is a Buckhead?"

"Buckhead is the most affluent part of Atlanta.

"Okay."

"It's also where the home of a certain major political 'big man' is," Brennan finished, smiling.

"Okay, Okay. We will check out the governor," Bradley said. "But don't you two know how much security the governor has? Especially once we tell him about this nut? It'll be next to impossible to get near him."

Linda already knew what Bradley was going to say and handed him a folder.

"What's this?

"That is what makes it possible for Mark to get near him."

He opened the folder and first saw a picture of Mark Glover lying on the ground behind a huge rifle. He read the caption below: Mark Glover wins the national marksman long-shot title for the third year in a row. He flipped through the pages and saw more of the same type of stuff.

"Okay. I'm sold. Let's come up with a plan."

CHAPTER 65

Paces Ferry Road was only about ten miles long. It ran from I-75 to Piedmont Road in Buckhead. Nine miles of it was actually West Paces Ferry Road and one mile was East Paces Ferry. The nine miles stretched west of Peachtree Road and the one, east of Peachtree Road. Paces Ferry was some of the priciest real estate in the state of Georgia. West Paces held mostly residential property and the East held, almost exclusively, commercial property. This commercial area was known in the 80s, 90s, and even early 2000s as the heart of Buckhead. And in that heart of Buckhead there were two roads that ran through it that were considered 'The Strip'. You had Buckhead Avenue and East Paces Ferry Road. On any given Friday or Saturday night, these roads were impassable. Young people walked through the streets like packs of hyena. The atmosphere was animated and full of activity. Neon signs littered the street front; windows of the collage of night clubs that, while intoxicated, looked endless.

The other side of Paces Ferry was its polar opposite. Other than an exclusive country club and an ultra-modernly designed Buckhead public library, West Paces was the home of extremely private, extravagant mansions and palaces. The lavishness of some of these properties was grossly exaggerated to the point of ridiculousness. Five and ten acre lots with patterns cut into their lawns had fountains big enough to hold water polo matches.

When Mark moved to Atlanta almost 20 years ago, he didn't know about this part of Buckhead. He used to call West Paces 'The Wonder Street'. He would drive down the street purposefully slow to look at the huge homes and wonder who lived in each one. He would take in each home's different style of architecture and landscaping. Best of all, he would often get to see many different exotic and classic cars. Once, years later, he won a shooting contest and part of the prize was a tour of an old gangster's house by the name of Al Capone. His home had somehow become a museum and said museum had donated tour certificates to one of the shooting event's sponsors. Curious about the history of not only his new hometown, but Al Capone as well, he took the tour.

The place was a gigantic, multi-level, Spanish, Tudor home. It was surrounded by a 12-foot stucco wall with Spanish tile atop which matched the home and several guest houses. The wall was said to have been added later by the gangster so that his wife could sunbathe in the nude.

The house was impressive with all types of hidden passages and walls that turned on an axis. Like in the movies, allowing you to enter the next room without using a door. What Mark had also found intriguing was the huge Georgian mansion that sat next door to Al Capone's with a tall, wrought iron and red brick fence. The person who lived there was also famous, but he was supposedly on the other side of the law from Al Capone. It was the home of Georgia's governor.

Mark was back at the Capone house, though he wasn't a tourist. He sported thick, plastic-framed glasses and a fake goatee and wore gray coveralls with Roy's Roses embroidered on the back. The company was real as was the delivery of flowers to the museum. It seemed the place had fresh flowers delivered to them every day. The real delivery man would still be alive, but he chose to attract attention to them as Mark took the van into custody. Now he had a neat hole in the back of his head and lay in the floor of the house Mark had rented. I guess all those movie theaters were right. Silence was golden.

Mark had parked the florist's van on the far side of the house which had access to a rarely used driveway leading to a side street. From his earlier visit to the home, he knew a secret stairwell and passageway that would allow him to slip out of the house from the third floor without anyone seeing him. He ran into some good luck while planning this little mission. While he sat in a car with binoculars viewing the governor's mansion some days past, he noticed that the governor liked to smoke cigars. Apparently his wife did not because she could be seen walking around opening the French doors in several rooms. Through these doors would now come one of the most aerodynamically sound bullet ever made. Mark should know. He made it. The 1 5/8" slug would leave the third floor of Al Capone's wife's old powder room window at over the speed of sound and make it some 200 yards before entering the governor's mansion. The slug was actually two parts. The back end that absorbed the explosion of gun powder was titanium, while the nose of the slug was made of 99.9% pure gold. Pure gold is very soft and at over 700 miles an hour, it would deform and spread as soon as it touched anything tougher than paper. Yes, Mark made this one special just for this occasion. It would enter the human body through a hole no bigger than a dime, but it would leave the body through a hole the size of a dinner plate.

Mark checked the stairs again and seeing the door at the bottom still closed, he went back to the powder room where his rifle stood ready. He leaned to the eyepiece of the scope, put his hand on the grip and used his other to uncap the scope. Immediately, he was looking into the governor's home through a pair of open French doors and down a hallway where someone was sitting in a leather recliner. He inched the crosshairs a little to the left and put his finger through the trigger guard. Fish in a barrel. He took a deep breath, inhaling through his nose.

CHAPTER 66

Have you ever been slumberously lethargic to the point of absurdity? He stumbled out of the bedroom and into the bathroom with his head feeling as if it were insulated with dryer lint. Brennan propped one hand against the wall and pulled down the front of his boxers with the other. He kept his eyes lazily shut during the entire urination process. His chin was resting against his chest. As his head hung slack, he opened his eyes and shook himself. Brennan was about to pull his boxers back up when his eyes shot wide with surprise. "That's not my penis," he said aloud. He didn't recognize his own penis. Yep, it was going to be one of those days.

His exhaustion stemmed from the previous day's planning. Watkins, Hunt, and himself had planned, called, and organized until 4:00 a.m. It was now 7:30 a.m. and he had 30 minutes to meet up with everyone at the station. Can anyone say sleep deprivation? He jumped in the shower, took care of his other hygiene needs, and was out the door, wearing only jeans and a polo.

He had been staying at Maria's pretty much non-stop here lately. Truth be told, he was already in love with her. He wouldn't tell her yet because – well, because he was scared. Not scared of commitment per se, but scared that her commitment might falter. Everything about her was perfect. He couldn't come up with a reason they could go wrong. But it had started out the same way with Samantha, hadn't it? Weren't they perfect for each other at the start? Or was he just love-drunk and blind to faults and incompatibility. He didn't know. All he knew was that he was happy to have her in his life. He didn't want to do anything to disrupt that.

He walked into the conference room, which now acted as the FBI's command center, and was greeted with a 'bee hive' of activity. Both Linda and Agent Watkins were talking animatedly on the phones. Lucas and the giant Agent Ogles had a huge map rolled out over a table and were studying it intently. A couple secretaries who worked in the station ran in and out of the room bringing paper and taking others out. Brennan slid into a chair next to Watkins just as he was getting off the phone.

"Am I the only one here with an energy deficiency?" Brennan said yawning.

"Nope. You're just the only one who hasn't had at least five cups of coffee," Watkins chirped, yawning also. Linda put down her phone.

"Okay. Did everything go smoothly on your end, Bradley," Linda asked.

"Yes, Ma'am. We now have authority to start World War III and wreak havoc on the unsuspecting community of Buckhead."

"Alright. The governor has agreed to stay indoors until we can do our thing – though he's not happy about it."

"Why should he not be happy," quipped Brennan, "It's not like we're trying to save his life or anything."

Everyone smiled.

"I feel good about this," Linda said.

"I'll save my feelings for later," said Bradley. "Right now, let's look at this map and plot our crash course through Buckhead."

Everyone surrounded the map on the large table including Lucas and Ogles. Bradley, using his hands, went over the plan that everyone already had memorized.

"We will start here on the east side of the governor's abode and circle our way around it in a spiral pattern until there is an absolute certainty that a shot cannot be taken from that position. We will check every pool house, guest house, tree house, and dog house. If he's out there, I want to find him. If he has something set up, I want to find that, too. If he so much as has a duffle bag out there, I want to find it." Bradley looked at the eyes of everyone in the room. "There is going to be a lot of pissed off, rich and influential people during this. Don't let it affect you. We have backing all the way from the top. Let's get this bastard." Everybody did a little hooting, hollering and fist bumping.

Twenty minutes later, three blacked-out Suburbans were racing toward Buckhead. The property next door and to the east of the governor's mansion was minutely less lavish than its neighbors. It was still impressive with its dogwood-lined driveway and privacy wall, but it lacked in amenities what the other homes were profusive in. No one was home except the caretaker and her husband, two Italian immigrants, who were really nervous and spoke no English. They searched the entire property inside and out. Nothing. No bad sniper guys.

They were on their fourth property around lunch time and everyone looked drained. Lucas ran down the street to Steak and Shake and picked up burgers and fries for everyone. Sitting across the street and catty-corner to the governor's mansion, they inhaled their lunch out in front of the property where the Suburbans sat.

Linda and Brennan sat on a lowered tailgate while Special Agent Bradley Watkins stood. Motioning directly across West Paces Linda asked, "Whose house is that? I like the peach color."

"That is the home of the notorious gangster, Mr. Al

Capone," Brennan said between bites. "At least it used to be. Now, it's some type of museum."

"Great," said Watkins, "they'll just be thrilled about us rummaging through their stuff."

"Well, they will have to get used to my favorite motto," she said.

"What's that?" asked Watkins.

"It is, what it is."

After finishing their lunch, they made their way over to Capone's place. Everybody came through the front foyer and started to split up when a comically short man shot into the room. The little man had an absurdly long mustache that curled up at the ends and looked to have wax on its tips. Along with the mustache was a matching, gray 'soul patch' that looked dirty and unruly. The top of his head was a shiny bald plate except for a few white wisps of hair. He looked to be in his early sixties and had a ruddy complexion. You could tell he either had no teeth or a severe under bite by the way he held his mouth.

"May I help you?" came a soft, British accented voice with a lisp.

Linda walked over to the man with her badge extended and the man actually took a step back as if she smelled bad or something.

"Agent Hunt, FBI. We have permission to search these premises in connection with an investigation in progress. If you…"

"You'll do no such thing," the man said almost in a whisper as he picked invisible lint off his sleeve.

Linda took out one of her cards and tried to hand it to the man. She had to lean over. He literally couldn't have been much taller than four feet.

"Feel free to call your local authorities," she said pushing the card an inch from his face. Instead of taking it he turned on his heels and strode out of the room. Linda looked at Watkins.

"That went well I think. Alright everybody let's do it."

Everybody moved through the large palace like ants. This being the fourth residence they'd searched, they had a good system in place. Linda was searching the kitchen looking into closets and pantries, when she opened a highly polished oak door that looked no different from the other pantry doors. Though upon opening this one, it had a stairwell behind it.

CHAPTER 67

He was looking down the hallway at a slight angle seeing more of the right side of the hall than the left. The room in which someone sat was at the end of the hall and on that right side. The doorway opened to the hallway, of course, and from looking down that polished, walnut-floored hallway from his viewpoint, the angle was very extreme looking into the room through his scope. The space between the left side door trim and the right from this angle, which was almost sideways, was that of maybe two inches. Because of the scope, he could see clearly but because of the space the bullet had to enter the room, it would make a clear shot very difficult. He would really have to control his breathing and concentrate.

She was what you would call a handsome woman. She wore her hair short and curly with a lot of makeup on her face that showed off her wide jaw and strong chin. He couldn't see her body very well but he knew, from seeing pictures while doing his research on the couple, that she was big-boned, or whatever they were calling fat people today.

He had the crosshairs lined up in the center of the allotted space between the door's frame and right above the governor's wife's right ear. This would be tough. He took in a slow, long, even breath and slowly squeezed the trigger as he just as slow and evenly exhaled. He heard the door at the bottom of the stairs open just as the gun fired. With no time to look at his shot, he jumped up, leaving the rifle, and ran to the doorway to look down the stairs. He came to the doorway taking a small automatic pistol from his coveralls. He peeked through and saw a woman step in and look up the stairs. Even though he was barely visible to the side of the opening, her eyes found his and they locked together, neither one moving for a moment. It was Linda. She had somehow found him.

Linda broke the spell first reaching for her gun and radio as he shut the door. She couldn't believe it. It was Mark. He had a goatee and glasses, but she was sure it was him. She ran up the stairs, gun in one hand while she yelled into the radio.

"Suspect on the second floor, backside. All units, suspect is in the house. Secure all exits."

She grabbed the door knob and swung the door inward staying to the side for protection. Hearing no gunshots, she entered the room in a crouched position, gun extended in front of her. The room was empty. There was an open window with a big rifle propped in front of it on a bi-pod. She ran to the window and looked out. As she did, Brennan and Ogles came into the room with their guns drawn. Linda was back on her radio.

"Suspect went out the window on the east side of the house. Secure a perimeter around the house."

From the window, she looked onto the tile roof of the lower level and a part of a driveway. Linda holstered her weapon and swung a leg out the window. "You guys get down there and make sure he doesn't get off this property."

* * *

Mark jumped into the van, started the engine, and, careful not to peel out, sped out of the driveway and onto the side street. He came up to West Paces Ferry and took a left toward Buckhead, coming dangerously close to clipping a red Porsche as he passed the front entrance of the Capone house. He saw people scattering and running to several Suburbans. He gave the van some more gas, but there was slower traffic in front of him. If he stayed behind these two slower cars, he was sure to get caught. He checked the other direction of traffic and after a black truck passed him on his left going the opposite direction, he swerved into the oncoming lane across a double yellow line and floored it. The van wasn't made for acceleration, but it slowly made its way up and passed the two cars on the right. He swung the van back onto the right side of the road and looked into his rearview. He couldn't be sure but he thought he saw blue lights. He had the van up to 70 MPH which was insane on West Paces. Mark hadn't planned for this. The house he was renting was only another two miles down, but if he stayed in this slow moving traffic, it would be over with. He was thinking this and he almost had to come to a complete stop. "Screw this," he said aloud and turned off the main road. He didn't know if this side road would lead him to the road the house was on, but he had no other choice.

* * *

Linda had jumped from the roof of the first story onto some lush green grass and rolled to a stop when they told her on the radio that Mark had just driven away in a florist's van on the west side of the house. How the hell did he get over there so fast? She thought it impossible as she came out of the roll from hitting the ground, she ran for all she was worth toward the waiting Suburbans. The SUV she ran to had Big Mike at the wheel and Brennan leaning over the backseats with the backdoor open telling her to come on. She hopped in and Big Mike wasted no time flooring it. Another Suburban was right behind them, both with their hidden lights flashing. Cars pulled to the side as they ran up on them from behind.

"Can anyone see the van?" Linda said out of breath.

"Not yet. He got a pretty good jump on us," said Big Mike.

Linda's phone vibrated, it was Watkins.

"Yeah."

"Atlanta PD is setting up a road block about two miles down."

"Where are you," she asked.

"Right behind you."

They continued down West Paces Ferry Road at break neck speeds and they quickly came to the intersection of Northside Drive where three Atlanta Police cruisers sat with their lights flashing, blocking the intersection. They all looked at each other.

"Fuck, he must have turned off!"

* * *

Mark made it to the house and ran inside grabbing a few things, then looked around making sure he had what he needed. No time. He ran outside and got into this black Jaguar XK8 and floored it. He made his way to Northside Drive using side streets and five minutes later, he had the sleek car at 65 MPH with the cruise control engaged. You almost had me Linda, almost.

CHAPTER 68

They found the house easily because of the van parked out front. There had only been five side streets he could have turned off on, so they and the Atlanta Police canvased the area hitting pay dirt in only twenty minutes. Of course, Mark was gone but they were hoping he left something behind.

"Bingo!" Lucas screamed.

"Bingo, what?" Linda asked as he walked toward her with a sport coat in one hand and what looked like a checkbook in the other. Brennan, Ogles, and Watkins all came into the room to see what the commotion was about. The checkbook turned out to be a passport with the name Terry Griffin in it. The name might have been Terry Griffin but it was a photo of Mark Glover with a mustache. Linda flipped through the pages looking at the stamps.

"Looks like our boy wants to be a Canadian," Watkins said trying to count all the different stamps.

"Yeah, it does," said Linda, "and look. They're all from the Ambassador Bridge. Thirteen times in the past two years.

"Why the Ambassador Bridge?" asked Watkins.

"He probably flew into Detroit and then drove over the bridge into Windsor, Ontario," said Brennan. "Pops and I went up there when I was younger."

"I'll tell you why, you guys," Linda started. "It's because he's driving."

"What?"

"He's driving up to Canada from Atlanta."

"Why would anybody do that, especially when they're rich like Glover?" asked Ogles.

"Mark is afraid to fly. He told me on one of our first dates. He said he had been his whole life. He even gets air sick. He can't fly without being medicated and he is going to have to be alert while he is on the run."

"Well I'd bet dollars to doughnuts that's where he's headed," said Watkins. "He just shot a governor's wife. Sure it only grazed her, but the guy's got to know that he will be on America's Most Wanted before the week's up."

"Damn it, we came really close to catching him," Linda said, sitting on a stool that was the only furniture in the room. "I'd say if he had a place to stay up there or a friend up there, that he'd be on his way."

Another Atlanta Police officer came in then and explained that a neighbor saw the same guy that pulled up in the van take off in a swooping, black sports car. The officer handed Watkins his notes from talking to neighbors.

Everybody went back to searching the house, but besides an air mattress and some cosmetics, the house was bare. Brennan was in the bathroom off the master bedroom where the air mat was when he saw something laying to the right of the toilet. He picked it up. Whatever it was it was just a piece of it. You could see it was ripped at an angle. He read what he could and as he finished, he heard Watkins call everybody into the kitchen. "I was just in a conference call with the SAC and the director. I've relayed every piece of information we have so far and they feel the same way we do. We're going to Canada. We're actually going straight from here to Hartsfield International where an agency jet is waiting. Authorities up top have been informed and our Detroit office is already in motion setting things up. Congratulations, everyone. I think we're finally going to get this sucker." Watkins waited on everyone to get there before beginning.

"What about Brennan. He's been on this since the beginning. He brings a lot to the table," Linda said.

"I can appreciate that," Watkins said, looking back and forth between Linda and Brennan, "And I think you're a very competent investigator, but this case is Federal and moving into another state possibly into another country. I don't have the authority to federally deputize every local I want to come along and I can't be held responsible. I'm sorry. I really am." He held his hand out to Brennan. "I hope you understand."

"I understand. I appreciate y'all having me along this far," Brennan said shaking Watkins' hand.

"Okay, people. We're out of here in 15 minutes. APD will take over the scene," Watkins shouted walking away.

"I'm sorry, Brennan. This sucks." Linda said looking nonplussed. "I know you have a lot invested in this."

"It's gonna be okay, because you're gonna go up there and nail this cocksucker."

She smiled. "You know it. I'll be calling you to fill you in on how it goes down. It's been a pleasure working with you, Brennan."

"Likewise, Agent Hunt"

With that, she turned and walked away. He really wanted to tell her. Wanted to explain what he found, but it would only muck up his plans. Linda was right. He did have a lot invested in this case. This Mark Glover had gotten to him on a level where most couldn't. It was personal and he was going to finish what he started.

CHAPTER 69

So he had shot her, but she wasn't dead, obviously, because the governor's wife was still in the hospital. Of course, as always, the news station he was listening to didn't have any further info at this time. He also heard about the massive man hunt that was taking place. The FBI and seven other police jurisdictions were involved as they scoured the Atlanta Metro area. They even went so far as to say that they believed that he, Mark Glover, was still in the North Atlanta area.

What a crock. First of all, why would they give out that information to be broadcasted? It wouldn't help them telling the public this. They did it for one reason and one reason only. For him to hear it and think they were still looking for him in Atlanta – which they were not. Did they not think that he knew he left one of his passports behind? Did they think that he didn't know they would be hiding behind the scenes at the bridge and tunnel going into Canada? They'd have several different depictions of him circulating to every authority close to the border. Did they really think he was that dense?

Yes, leaving the passport behind was a huge oversight, but his expeditiousness had been necessary. He had already stopped outside of Chattanooga Tennessee and swapped his Jaguar, which had been in Terry Griffin's name, to a two-year old, silver Chevy Tahoe that was in his new Canadian Citizen's name, Mr. Carmine Galassi. The Tahoe was purchased in Detroit, but had Ontario plates on it which was registered to one of the many of Mr. Gallasi's homes.

He felt much safer now. Invisible in fact, now that he was out of the black Jaguar. He loved the super charged 370 horsepower coupe, but he couldn't take the chance that someone saw him drive away in it leaving Buckhead. Who knew? Maybe he would come back for it.

The running away had not been planned. He had guidelines for the escape formed, but this was premature. Linda Hunt was not supposed to find him at the museum. How she knew he was there was unfathomable. Uncanny, when you thought about it.

Mark had made this trip from Atlanta to Canada what felt like a 100 times. The driving soothed him. Driving back and forth on the monotonous, gray interstates was where Mark did some of his best thinking.

Before Jenny was taken from him, he had always thought himself to have normal dreams and aspirations. He wanted a nice home and a sweet, beautiful wife. He always wanted to raise a family and provide for them. To be financially secure later in life so he and his family would have no worries. To grow old with his wife and spend their days watching the sunset together. Pretty much what everybody hoped for, he guessed.

Well, all those dreams had died with Jenny. Now, his aspirations were different and he wasn't finished. Nope, not by a long shot. The authorities may have thwarted him in completing his mission momentarily, but his business with the justice system would not cease until there were steps being made toward repairing the methods of finding equity. He would be gone for a while, but only until he made more plans. This injustice was felt nationwide, so he had numerous options of places for his message to be heard. The only thing people listened to these days was fear, fear of dying. And people are gonna die... lots of them.

CHAPTER 70

Maria had wanted to meet Brennan at his place before he left for the airport. He had explained to her on the phone what his plans were and he was pretty sure she was coming to try to keep him from going.

He was only bringing with him a few things. He didn't want to have to check his gun, but he had no choice. At least he wouldn't have to check any bags and wait for them. Maria walked in.

"Babe, don't you think you should give this a little more thought before you just take off like this?" she said, with her face scrunched up from concern.

"Maria, I have a shot at stopping this madman once and for all. I'm going."

"Can't you just pass the info along to Linda and let the FBI handle it? Brennan, this is way outside of your jurisdiction and you'll have no backup."

"If I get into a situation where I need backup, I'll call in the locals. But part of the reason I'm racing up there is so I get there first and I can surprise him."

"Get where first? You told me some on the phone but please help me see why you're doing this."

"Look Maria, I could be wrong, but I don't think he's

going to cross the Ambassador Bridge. I found this on the bathroom floor." He handed her the small piece of ripped paper.

"What is this? Fort Huron? What's that, an army base?"

"It's Port Huron." The piece of paper was torn taking the letter 'P' off. "It's about two hours north of Detroit and while Port Huron also has a bridge crossing over St. Clare River, I don't think that's why he had this slip of paper."

"It looks like the bottom of an invoice or something," she said.

"It is. I think it's a receipt. Look at the rest of the print that the rip runs through."

"I think," Brennan continued as they both looked closely at the small piece of paper's printing, "that the first line is a name and the second line that ends with 'RINA' is Marina. I think this is a receipt from a marina at Port Huron. I think our murderous Mr. Glover has himself a boat." He looked at her with a mischievous grin. "I'm gonna narrow the Marinas down on the way up there." Maria put her arms around his waist and looked into his eyes.

"Be careful. I know I won't be able to talk you out of this, so please, just be careful." He kissed her then, deep and hard, and when their lips broke apart Brennan looked at her and smiled.

"I love you, Maria. I know it's fast, but I do. I love you." Maria smiled from ear to ear as tears started to well up in her eyes.

"I love you, too," she said and they hugged with a passionate force.

They came out of their embrace and Brennan still had the piece of receipt in his hand. Looking at her and shaking the small piece of paper in his hand he said, "I'm gonna nail this guy." Maria just shook her head.

"I know you are, baby. Just hurry back to me, okay?"

CHAPTER 71

Their flight on the government Gulfstream 3 from Atlanta into Detroit Michigan took just under two hours. Special Agent Watkins talked on the phone most of the flight while Linda and her guys went over the 'what ifs'.

"He could go through the tunnel," Ogles was saying.

"I know he could," Linda said sounding exasperated. "Look, you guys. He very well might try to come through the tunnel or across the bridge for that matter. Agent Watkins and the brass seem to think that it's a foregone conclusion. That he'll try to go through the tunnel or over the bridge with a disguise and a different passport. All we have to do is be vigilant in our efforts to thoroughly check everyone and we will get him."

"But," said Lucas.

"But," Linda continued, "there are just too many other possibilities for me. I mean, Mark knows by now that he left his fake passport behind. Granted, he may not know exactly where he lost it. But regardless, I think he will be extra cautious. And if I were being really cautious, I would just cross the border somewhere else."

"Have you told Watkins about your concerns?" Ogles asked, stretching his 6'7" frame noisily.

"Until I was blue in the face. He's convinced that since there was no deviation in his entrance/exit 13 times in a row through this particular crossing, that he either stays really close or something Glover feels is really important is close by. And you know what? That could be, but I don't think it's as likely as they do."

Watkins, just getting off the phone, walked toward them at the rear of the luxurious cabin. The jet was definitely confiscated from some drug lord or some big financial scam artist. No way the FBI went to the trouble of carbon fiber armrests.

"Alright people," Watkins started. "Everybody should be up to speed when we touch down. The SAC up here in Detroit is Special Agent Upshaw and he and a couple of his guys, along with the help of the U.S. Marshals, will be taking the tunnel. I saved the best for us. We will be taking the bridge and we will also get a couple guys from the marshal's office. What we're going to do is exchange our suits for border officer uniforms and take posts throughout the entrance process. Linda, he obviously will recognize you, so I want you hidden somewhere with a pair of binoculars giving info to the one's that work the passport checking booths."

The pilot came on the intercom then and told them to fasten their seatbelts, that they were starting their descent. After landing, everyone was escorted to the Ambassador Bridge via what looked to be the same black Suburbans they used in Buckhead.

Linda had never been to Canada or even Detroit for that matter. As they started up the entrance of the bridge, she could see the water of the Detroit River and beyond the river was the city of Windsor. Linda couldn't even enjoy the view, inside she was in turmoil. She had the nagging sensation that this was all for nothing. That somehow, Mark was going to get away. While she wanted nothing better than to catch the man responsible for all these senseless killings, she also wanted to look Mark in his eyes and ask him why. Not why he killed those innocent people. She knew his warped reason for why on that. Not even why he ruined the lives of so many of their family members, but selfishly, why had he chose her? Why did he start a relationship with her? Why did he make an impression of wanting to be with her when his mission in life was obviously different? There was no denying it. She had feelings for him. Not the murderous bastard that killed all those people, but the sweet, gentle, and passionate Mark that she fell in love with.

CHAPTER 72

If Mark Glover drove directly from Atlanta to Port Huron it would have taken him 12 hours; and that's if he averaged 80 MPH. Mark left the rented house around 2:00 p.m. So, the earliest he could make it to Port Huron would be 2:00 a.m. Brennan would be there waiting for him.

Brennan had just got into his rental car outside of the Detroit airport. The time was 8:02 p.m. The first flight out of Atlanta had been 5:35 p.m. But it was cool, he had plenty of time, he thought, as he pointed the car north and set the cruise control to 80 MPH. He would be in Port Huron in an hour and 18 minutes, so the car's GPS told him.

He had been online during his flight and found the only marina in Port Huron ending with "EN'S" was Green's Marina. He then called so named marina and talked to Mr. Green himself. Brennan had asked the raspy voice if he owned the place and the old timer said, "If I don't, they sure owe me some money for keeping my name on the sign for the last 30 years." Good to see they used sarcasm this far north. He then told the man he was on his way up to see an old friend that had a boat docked with him and wanted to make sure he was still around.

Brennan gave him the Griffin name that Glover used on the fake passport and was told that he'd never docked a boat for a Griffin. He asked him to check his wife's maiden name, Glover, and again got a negative.

Brennan was a little discouraged but he was determined that he was right. He pulled into Green's Marina at exactly 9:30 p.m. He was hoping that there were some people out at their boats so he could run Mark's description by them or at least a security guard who might have seen him in passing.

The parking lot was gravel and well lit with a big blue sign with white letters, that said, 'Welcome to Green's Marina'. There were 10 to 15 cars in the gravel lot. Most were late-model luxuries that weren't made in this country. Brennan's sexy, white Ford Fusion rental car definitely blended. Brennan walked out of the lot and onto a wooden walkway that was about six-feet wide with sturdy, sanded handrails. The walkway was slightly down hill and had skinny pieces of wood with traction tape every three feet or so that stuck up maybe an inch. Nailed horizontally across the walkway, this was smart. Not a chance to slip. He walked another 50 feet and could see a long, wide, double-aisle, floating dock on the dark water. There were sail boats, speed boats, house boats, and all different sizes of motor yachts at dock here. The area was well-lit along the walkways and looked well-maintained. He was startled when a deep, raspy voice spoke to him from maybe 20 feet further down the walkway.

"Help you son?" If it wasn't Mr. Green himself, again.

"Hey, how ya doing? I'm Tom Brennan. I spoke to you on the phone a few hours ago." He walked toward the older gentleman and held out his hand and the man shook it with a grip like a vice.

"Nice to meet you, fella. Now, what kind of boat you got?" He asked with a southern drawl, maybe Texas thought Brennan. He was well over six-feet and black with a full beard that was entirely gray. He wore Dickies overalls over a dirty, white t-shirt and had on knee-high rubber boots. The guy was a dead ringer for Morgan Freeman.

"Boat?" Brennan said, confused.

"Yeah, you know. Thing that floats on the water. Sometimes they got an engine, sometimes they don't."

"I'm sorry, I'm not here about a boat. I …"

"Gotta be here about something to do with a boat. See, this here is a marina and I done told you that no Griffin or Glover has, or ever had, a boat here. So I figure, you must want to store your boat here, since that's the only thing I do around here."

"Look. When we talked before, I was less than honest with you."

"You mean you made up some story to pump sweet ol' Mr. Green for information? Darn, and I thought you might never find your friend who mysteriously has two last names, I …"

"Okay, okay, already."

"Now, what can I really do for you, son?"

Brennan told him a short version of the investigation and showed the man his ID and badge. He pulled out the piece of paper with the four depictions of what Mark might look like. "This is the guy I'm looking for." The old man took the paper and studied it for a good minute.

"I can tell you a coupla things here."

Brennan's eyes were wide with suspense. "Uh, huh," he managed.

"I've never seen this man before."

Brennan's whole body slumped when Mr. Green said this. He just spent over a thousand dollars and traveled a thousand miles to find out he was wrong. Damn it. He had felt so sure about this. Now he would have to go back to Maria with his tail between his legs looking like an incompetent detective.

"Hold on now, son. Don't go looking like you lost your lucky nickel. I said I could tell you a coupla things. That means more than one. Darn, don't they make you detectives take basic literature classes 'fore they just give you those badges?"

He took the old man's banter in stride though still looking doubtful and told Mr. Green to continue.

"You see, most all my customers have been here for years and have contracts with me for years to come." The old man paused then for so long that Brennan began to think he had finished or perhaps dozed off. He was about to say something when Mr. Green picked back up. "I've had one new customer in the last three years and the only reason I took him on was because of a death of another." Another long pause. Jesus, this was like pulling teeth. Brennan looked at his watch: 10:05 p.m. He wished the old geezer would hurry.

"I know you're sitting there wishing my old ass would just hurry up and spit it out, but I'm still pondering giving you information about a customer."

"Look Mr. Green, I promise you…"

"The only reason I think it possible that it may be Mr. Galassi is the fact that I've never seen him except from afar and he is in fact a white man."

"You said, Mr. Galassi?"

"Galassi. G-A-L-A-S-S-I. First name, Carmine. You need me to spell that for you too?" Actually he did but he wouldn't give the old geezer the satisfaction, "I think I can handle it, grandpa."

"Touché. The reason I've never seen him is because he did everything online. Didn't want to, but I had to modernize to this new e-commerce trend. Anyhow, he has a 42 footer on the west dock, next to last slip and I can tell you – he's not here and never is as far as I can tell."

This info fit Glover like a new pair of underwear. This was his guy, he could feel it.

"I appreciate all this info, Mr. Green. Sincerely, you've helped out a lot."

"I know you're gonna go off loafing around my docks so let me be clear. I told you what I did because I thought it the right thing to do and for the fact that this Galassi fella never felt right to me anyway. Now, if this goes to shit somehow or another, I don't know you and never spoke to you." The old man stuck his gnarled hand out and Brennan shook it. With that, the old man turned and walked away with what Brennan thought could have been a smile.

Brennan smiled and waved to a couple of folks who were out and about on their boats or on the dock as he made his way to Mr. Galassi's slip. When he got there, he marveled at the beauty of the new yacht. The entire boat was a shiny, gloss white with limo tinting on the surrounding glass. He stepped onto the polyurethaned, bleached, oak floors at the stern of the boat and noticed the boat's name stenciled in black: 'Jenny'. Jennifer Parsons was Mark Glover's fiancée who was killed. Brennan's adrenaline shot up as the odds of this being the killer's boat increased dramatically. It was hard, but he still had to keep in mind that all this could just be coincidental – though Brennan had never believed in coincidences.

The sliding glass doors to the main cabin were locked. After making sure no one was aboard, he took out a Swiss Army knife and went to work on the simple lock being careful not to leave any marks on it. He was able to disengage it in less than two minutes. Looking around and seeing no one, he pulled out his gun and went inside the boat. Leaving the lights off, he looked around using his Maglite. It looked like nothing had ever been touched. Everything looked perfectly in place and brand new. He rummaged through every nook and cranny finding nothing but a locked safe. He took his phone out and called Maria to give her an update. She answered on the second ring.

"Is everything okay?"

Brennan sat just inside the back tinted sliding glass doors looking down the dock. "I'm fine. I'm pretty sure I've found our guy's boat and if I'm right," Brennan looked at his watch: 11:30 p.m., "he should be arriving in the next three or four hours."

"Baby, I don't like this. You should get some kind of back-up."

"It'll be fine. I've got my gun and I've got the element of surprise on my side. As soon as I've got him cuffed to something immovable, I promise I'll call in the cavalry."

"Why not just call in the cavalry now. Bre…"

"It's too complicated Maria and there's not enough time. Trust me, I got this. I'm gonna take this guy down. I'll give you an update if anything happens. I got to go, babe. I love you."

"I love you, too. Please be careful, Brennan."

"Talk to you in a little while. Bye."

CHAPTER 73

Linda sat in a toll booth-like structure with a fan and a pair of binoculars. The blinds on the windows of the booth were down, but only partially closed. The booth that she sat in was not in use like the booth that sat 20 feet to the right of her. The steel arms that usually blocked a car from moving past the booth until allowed through were in the up position. This allowed traffic to pass through to the two border patrol booths that were in operation. The two active booths were about 50 yards in front of her with their traffic lanes running right past Linda.

'Big Mike' Ogles was at the booth to Linda's right and Lucas in the one to her left. Looking through her binoculars, she radioed to Watkins and her guys that she had a great view. They figured that the earliest Mark could make it there was around midnight. It was more likely that he would wait until the morning rush, when more than 100,000 people would cross between 7:00 a.m. and 10:00 a.m.

There was a knock at the booth's door. She jumped, startled. It was the U.S. Marshal with the sandwich she asked for. God, she was jumpy.

"Thanks," she said and closed the door back. She was

about to bite into her sandwich when her iPhone started vibrating. She looked at the caller ID and it was a number she didn't recognize. She sat her sandwich down and licked her lips.

This could very well be Mark. It probably was. She took a deep breath and answered.

"Hello?"

"Linda? This is Maria Flemez from Sandy Springs."

Linda finally let the deep breath out. "Oh, hi. Um… What's up?"

"Listen, Linda. I don't know if I should be doing this, but I'm worried about Brennan."

"Doing what? What's wrong with Brennan?"

"Brennan is still trying to get Mark Glover."

"Well, I wouldn't worry too much, Maria. We're pretty sure he's on his way to Canada. That's why we all came up here."

"Brennan's up there too."

"What?!" Linda yelled so loud she almost dropped her phone.

"That's what I mean. I'm the only one that knows." Maria then told Linda about his departure and brought her up to speed.

"That selfish bastard."

"Don't be mad at him, Linda. He was about to show y'all the receipt when that other agent told him to suck eggs. Please, Linda. Go help him. I have a bad feeling about him trying to take this guy down by himself."

"Don't worry, Maria. I'm on my way. I'll call you when I'm closer."

"Thank you so much Linda."

Holy Shit! While she was sitting here in this box with this rinky-dink fan, Brennan was lying in wait where Mark was really headed. Linda was mad. Not mad at Brennan, but mad at herself. Her instincts had told her Mark wouldn't cross here and she had been right. Her actions, instead, got stuck in the bureaucracy of listening to her 'appointed' superior. She was a little jealous of Brennan, really. He had taken it upon himself to follow his instincts and investigative skills to do what he thought. Everybody else be damned. He was going to find a killer.

Linda thought about how she would do this. It was 11:00 p.m. So, that meant if Port Huron was almost two hours north and she left now, she would still be an hour ahead of Mark's earliest possibility of arrival. Linda left the booth and, trying to dodge Watkins, found the U.S. Marshal whom brought the sandwich to her. He was standing by all the government vehicles and she didn't want anyone seeing her take off.

"Hey! You want to do me a big favor?"

"Sure, whatcha got?"

"I need to use the little girl's room and I was wondering if you would watch my post for me in case my boss came to check in. That way I would have my bases covered."

"Sure thing. Go ahead. Take your time. Glover's not expected for at least two hours."

"I won't be long," she said as she went toward where she knew the restrooms to be. She watched him until he went inside the booth. Then, causing no attention to herself, she walked to one of the black Suburbans and slipped behind the wheel. Ten minutes later, she had the big SUV doing 85 MPH toward Port Huron.

She used the internet on her phone to get the exact location of Mr. Green's Marina. She was about to call Brennan and let him know he was getting some company when the SUV made a loud noise from the front of the truck and it jerked hard to the right. She thought she was going to lose control, but somehow was able to wrestle the beast to a stop. What the hell happened? Did she hit something? She hadn't seen anything in the road. She pulled over on the shoulder and got out. She knew immediately by the tilt of the SUV that she had blown the front right tire, but when she saw the tire itself she was shocked at the damage. It looked like someone shot her front tire out with a bazooka. She looked at her phone and saw that it was 11:30 p.m. Damn! She threw her phone on the front passenger seat through the open window and went to the back of the Suburban to check out the spare situation. She could change a tire. She wasn't some prissy girl. She'd changed a couple in her time, but on nothing as big as a Suburban. The tools for changing the tire were in a cubby compartment in the tailgate, but the spare was actually screwed to the underside of the truck in the back. It seemed to be stuck. She tried using the lug wrench as leverage on the large wing nut that held the wheel secure to the frame, but it was slow progress. She had to stop three times to rest. When she finally got it off and wheeled it around front, she checked the time on her phone. Damn. A whole hour had gone by. It was 12:35 a.m. She hated it, but she was going to have to risk calling Ogles and tell him the situation and hope he could somehow leave and pick her up. She was only 20 or 30 minutes from the bridge. It would probably take her another hour to jack up the huge truck, take the bad wheel off and, then, put the spare on. Just then her 'low battery' icon started going crazy on her phone. Damn! She didn't have a charger with her. She quickly dialed Ogle's cell phone and after 10 rings got voice mail. "Come on. Pick up. Pick up," Linda said aloud. She hung up and hit send again, redialing Big Mike and then the phone died completely. "Damn it!" she shouted at the broke down Suburban.

It was almost 1:00 a.m. and here she was stuck in the dark, trying to change a tire on a wheel that weighted as much as she did in the middle of nowhere. There was next to no traffic on the highway, but she decided to try to flag the next car down and, if they refused to give her a ride, she would forcefully commandeer the vehicle. After all, she was FBI and she had a big gun.

She got a flare out of the emergency kit in the truck and lit it. She then made her way to the middle of the highway and prayed for a car to come. It wasn't long before one came along. Linda waved the flare over her head like a crazy woman until the car came to a stop in front of her. She walked to the driver's door and pulled out her badge.

"My name is Linda Hunt. I'm an agent with the FBI and my government vehicle has broken down."

The car was a lime-colored Toyota Prius and the guy driving looked like the character, 'Waldo', who became popular for the 'Where's Waldo' books. He was about 30, skinny, and clean shaven with wire-framed glasses. In other words, he looked like a stereo-typical nerd.

Linda continued, "I'm gonna need you to drive me to Port Huron."

"Wow. A real FBI agent. Can I see your badge again?" Oh boy. His voice sounded as if it was coming through his nostrils. Something like an 'Urkle' from Brooklyn. She showed him the badge.

"Well, you sure are in luck, Agent Hunt, because Port Huron is exactly where I'm going. Get in. It's unlocked." She got in.

"The name is Evan," he said, offering his hand. "Evan McMitten." She shook the hand. The name fit, she thought.

"Yep. Like I said, it's your lucky day. I just happened to get called in to an emergency D and D game in Port Huron."

"D and D?" she asked, looking at the speedometer which read 40 MPH.

"Dungeons and Dragons. It's a role-playing game that is really 'kick ass'. I'm a master DM, which stands for Dungeon Master. Cool huh?"

"Very cool. Look, is there any way you could speed up? I'm really in a hurry and it's a matter of life and death."

"Oh, gosh! Why didn't you say so?" He pushed the accelerator and she watched the speedometer slowly climb to 62 MPH.

"Why did you stop at 62 MPH? You can go faster. It's okay. I'm a cop."

"I wish I could, but you see, my dad put an electronically limiting governor on my car and I'm afraid that's as fast as she goes."

Oh my god! She looked at the clock on the dash and saw it was after 1:30 a.m. God, she thought, please let me get there in time.

CHAPTER 74

He was so tired. He had been up for over 24 hours and on the road for close to 13. Between stopping to switch cars in Chattanooga and stopping a total of three times for gas and refreshments, Mark thought he made pretty good time. He had the luxury Denali version of the Tahoe up over 80 MPH outside of cities, which was most of the time, up I-75.

Port Huron was a small city of around 40,000 that sat on Lake Huron and the Saint Clair River. Mark had only been there once before and that was when he sailed his yacht in and moored it at the marina. An open slip at a marina was a rare thing to find, but Mark had lucked up while searching for availability on the internet. He pulled into the gravel lot of Green's Marina and put the Chevrolet in park. Releasing a big sigh, he got out of the truck and grabbed his bag. He walked out of the lot and onto the wood-planked walkway and at the "Y" where the walkway split into the east and west docks, he saw an old black man in overalls and rubber boots. The old man tipped his hat to him and Mark returned the gesture with a smile and a nod. He had seen the old man the last time he was here. He probably helped maintain the docks and such.

Mark walked down the west dock admiring the works of art moored at his right and left. Like automobiles, Mark had come to appreciate boats as expressions of artwork. He had shopped around for months before finding the 42-foot Hatteras motor yacht. It was the definition of style and luxury and at three quarters of a million dollars it should be. As he was thinking about the boat, she came into view. The yacht took your breath away, which was why Mark thought naming the vessel 'Jenny', after his fallen bride, to be appropriate.

He stepped onto her stern and unlocked the sliding glass doors. He flipped on the overhead lights as he set his bag down on a leather-stitched stool that went to the small bar to his right.

"How ya doing, Mark?"

Startled, Mark jumped as he looked up and saw the detective from Sandy Springs pointing a gun at him.

"What's wrong? Cat got your tongue?" Brennan taunted.

"How did you find me?"

"Well, Mark, I called my good friends at the psychic network and they told me all about your big boat here."

"What are you doing way up here anyway? You're way out of your jurisdiction as I'm sure you're aware. I could just walk out of here and you wouldn't have any authority over me."

"Of course, you're right, Mr. Glover. You could just walk out of here – and I could just shoot you in both of your legs."

"You can't just shoot me, it would be against the law."

"That's cute coming from you. I think I might get a pass on shooting murderous scum like you, though. In fact, I'm having some trouble not shooting you in your face as we speak. So please, feel free to try and run for it."

Mark's eyes were smoldering.

"Now, turn around and put your hands on your head."

Mark did as he was told. Brennan approached him slowly from behind with his gun still trained on Mark's back. When he was close enough, he reached out with his left hand and grabbed Mark's left arm and brought it up behind him so he could cuff him. Brennan put his gun in his waistband. While holding Mark's left arm with his own left, he reached for Mark's right when he was suddenly pushed backwards with tremendous force. Brennan went flailing to the ground, striking the back of his head on the tile kitchen floor. As he fought for dizziness, he reached for his gun only to find it missing from his waistband.

CHAPTER 75

When Linda saw the exit sign for Port Huron, she almost got out of Evan McMitten's car and ran. She had never been more annoyed or exasperated in her life. The 'Waldo' look-a-like had told Linda his life story along the way and listening to it was equivalent to getting your fingernails pulled back with pliers, or at least comparative to getting whipped with barbed wire.

She did get a break when she used his phone to get exact directions to Green's Marina. She wanted to call Brennan, but she didn't know his number by heart and her phone was still useless. At one point in her nightmar-ish ride, she actually thought about holding the phone up to her ear and pretending to talk to someone just to make Evan shut up.

When she saw the marina's sign, she looked at the clock again. 2:56 a.m. Depending on his stops and rate of speed, Mark could be here already. She thanked Mr. McMitten for the ride and literally ran through the gravel lot. At the entrance to the walkway there was a person leaning against the railing. She slowed to a walk and cautiously put her hand on her gun. Coming closer, she saw that the person was an old man with a gray beard.

"Excuse me sir, are you an employee of the marina?"

"You could say that," the man said with a southern drawl.

"I'm…"

"Let me guess," interrupted the man. "You're with some police agency and you're looking for a murderer who has escaped from Atlanta."

"How did you…"

"And you're also looking for your partner who's also up here looking for this murderer."

She just looked at the ancient guy in front of her with confusion all over her face.

""Don't go having crazy thoughts on me now," the man said. He told her about Brennan coming and explained the situation that the man he knew as Mr. Galassi had come in later.

"In fact, he just walked to his boat not 10 minutes ago."

She got the location of Mr. Galassi's boat from him and took off at a run. She slowed half-way down the west dock as to not let her footsteps be heard. She took the 40 caliber, Glock 22 from her holster and tip-toed the last 20 yards toward the yacht named 'Jenny'. The glass was heavily tinted, but she could see that some light was on. She duck walked the last few steps and peeked over the back lip of the yacht. She could see the outline of someone standing up about five feet inside the cabin. She wanted to creep her way onto the back of the boat, but she didn't know if her stepping on the boat would cause the boat to slightly move or not. Did big boats like this rock when someone stepped on? Linda didn't know. She had no experience with boats. She peeked over the back again and saw the shadow moving away from the doors and toward the front of the boat. Brennan could be hurt or dying. She had to do something. She took a chance and as quickly and as lightly as she could, she stepped over the wall of the stern and moved to the side of the sliding glass door, out of sight of anyone who might be looking out. She could make out voices now and one of them was definitely Mark's. There were drapes on the inside of the glass door and they were pulled to either side to allow passage through the doorway. With the curtain blocking some of the view from inside, Linda put her ear to the glass.

"I know you think I'm a monster," Mark was saying, "but you just fail to realize what dramatic measures have to be taken for there to be such an outcry for action from the public, that the government will actually make changes. Surely, even as a detective, you believe in my noble mission."

"I don't disagree with your mission or even with your anger, but breaking the law and murdering innocent people is absolutely wrong." It was Brennan! He was alive and he didn't sound to be badly injured.

"Tomato, tomahto. The people are martyrs. Just collateral damage in a war on justice."

"You're crazy."

"Not a nice way to talk to someone who has a gun pointed at your head."

Linda had to do something. She was weighing her options and snuck a peak around the curtain only to see Mark walking toward her. Had he seen her? She scrambled around the side of the cabin and squatted between the gunwale and cabin wall with her gun at the ready. She heard the sliding glass door open and for a moment, there was silence. Then she heard Brennan scream for help. She almost risked a look when she heard the door shut, instantly muting Brennan's scream and then a heavy thud. Silence. Seconds later the door opened again suddenly Mark came into view and Linda held her breath. He was facing away from her and looking at the other boats and down the walkway. If anyone had heard Brennan's scream, they weren't very curious.

Mark stepped off the boat with a gun in his hand and Linda thought that, now, she would have a chance to go check on Brennan. But Mark was only untying the moor lines. He was trying to leave. Linda got as low as she could in her little hiding spot. Mark got back on the boat, but instead of going back into the cabin, she heard him go above her somewhere. Not knowing how long Mark would be away, Linda hurried around the cabin and quietly opened the glass door. Immediately, she saw Brennan slumped on the floor with a handcuff around his right wrist securing him to a hand rail. She lifted his head by his chin and saw blood running down the side of his face from a scalp wound. She checked his pulse. Finding one, she tried to shake him awake. Then she heard the boat's engine start. With some masking of noise now, she said his name.

"Brennan. Brennan, wake up," she said shaking him furiously.

His eyes opened and looked at her with unfocused eyes. "…inda?"

"Sshh. He's still outside. We have to get these cuffs off you." She went to the key pouch hooked on her belt when she heard footsteps. She clambered around the counter and into the small kitchen. Linda was trembling. She held her gun in both hands ready for anything. The glass door opened.

"Ah, you're awake. And who were we talking to down here? I could have sworn I heard you saying something."

"Yeah, just your average talk show host," Brennan said, wiping blood from the side of his face.

"Such a funny guy. We'll see how funny you are when I throw your dead body over the side with an anchor tied to your leg." Mark squatted down next to Brennan. "It's too bad. You could have lived if you had stayed in your jurisdiction. I had no reason to end your life."

"I can't let you do that Mark," Linda said from the kitchen and stood up with her gun out in front of her. Hearing Linda, Mark immediately grabbed Brennan and put the gun to the detective's head.

"Boy, you guys never run out of surprises. I should have known 'super cop' here would have called for backup. From a woman, no less."

"He didn't call me."

"Oh, yeah? Then, how did you come to find my whereabouts, pray tell."

"That's not important, Mark. What's important is that you put that gun down. Nobody else has to get hurt."

Mark had pulled Brennan into a sitting position and was using him as a shield while having his gun pressed against the side of Brennan's head.

"Linda, Linda, Linda. Such an amazing woman. Your competence continues to shine through. You know, it would be easy to fall in love with a woman like you."

"You only used me," Linda said, her voice shaking.

"Is that what you think? If you'll remember, you walked into my store. Honestly, I don't know what I was doing. You had me in a kind of trance. You even had me questioning my convictions to follow through on this whole thing. I didn't use you, Linda. Mislead you, maybe, but I had no ulterior motives with us."

"Put the gun down and put your hands on your head. This is your last warning." Linda's voice was still trembling as she spoke through clenched teeth.

"Shoot him, Linda!" yelled Brennan.

"Yes, yes. Shoot me. I don't think so. See, Agent Hunt here, unlike you, follows procedure. Now, let me tell you what's gonna happen here. I'm gonna stand Mr. Sandy Springs here up and uncuff him. If he so much as flinches the wrong way, you'll have your chance to shoot me, because I will blow his brains all over this beautiful cabin."

"Put the gun down, Mark, please."

"Aww. I want to sweetie, but you first. No? Okay. On your feet 'super cop'." He pulled Brennan to his feet and handed him the handcuff key. "Uncuff yourself. We're going up top and Ms. Hunt here is going to get locked in the cabin. Linda, I want you to pay attention here. If I hear you try to leave the cabin of this yacht, I promise you I will kill this policeman. Do we all understand each other? He dug the gun in Brennan's head to make a point. Brennan uncuffed his arm and rubbed his wrist.

"See you in a little while Linda," Mark said and they started taking small steps backwards.

Linda didn't know what to do. All her training and never had she been in a situation like this.

"Don't move, Mark." But the threat sounded empty, even to her.

Brennan was not about to go out bad. Learning from his mistakes, he got Linda's attention with his eyes and her facial expression wasn't encouraging. Damn, will Linda shoot? Is she too emotionally entwined to take a shot on Mark? He would have to take his chances. He wasn't about to end up as fish food. Again signaling Linda with eyes as they neared the door, he made his move. Using every pound of body weight that he had, he slammed his head and back into Mark as he pushed with his legs. The back of his head hit Mark hard in the chin as they both fell backwards. They partially hit the glass doors and partially hit the floor. Mark still held the pistol. Brennan went for the gun, but instantly he heard a shot. Another shot followed and he felt hot pain in his chest.

Linda didn't know what to expect when Brennan started wiggling his eyebrows, but he didn't give her time to think. Brennan had exploded backwards and landed on top of Mark. Somehow, Mark kept a hold on the gun and when they hit the ground Brennan went for it. Seeing the barrel coming toward him, Linda squeezed the trigger, shooting mark in the center of his forehead. Half a second later Mark's weapon went off shooting Brennan high in the chest. She fired again and the second bullet hit him again in the forehead almost using the same hole as the first. She ran to Brennan's side and looked at the gun shot. It wasn't fatal. It went in just under the right collar bone and exited above his shoulder blade.

"You're going to make it. Just hold on. Where's your phone? And why didn't you call for backup once you were here?"

"My battery's dead," he said through a grimace of pain and let out a painful chuckle.

"I done called the folks down here." It was the old man with the overalls. At the sliding glass door.

"Thanks," Linda said as the man turned and walked away.

"Oh, that's Mr. Green."

EPILOGUE

Cocktail Cove, formally American Pie, is a sports bar/restaurant that sits on Roswell Road half a mile north of I-285. It has a huge deck that stretches all the way to the sidewalk that borders Roswell Road. Recently, after a lawsuit, the place started putting up tarps on the sides of the big deck to keep drivers from seeing what was going on. It seemed that every Thursday night during their bikini contest, there were several accidents directly in front of the place. Lawsuits swore that it had something to do with the half-naked woman prancing around on the deck not 10 feet from two lanes of traffic. Nah, couldn't be.

"Brennan got out of his taxi, being careful not to bang his shoulder in the process. It was still unbelievingly sore from the gunshot having come out of his cast only a couple weeks ago. He made his way inside and told the barely legal, ¾ naked hostess that he wished to sit on the deck. As he walked toward the deck entrance, there was a bikini-clad girl standing on a chair with a huge cooler in front of her filled with beer and ice. As he walked by, he read the sign that was taped to the front of the cooler: Beer Tub Girl. Nah, couldn't be.

He got seated and ordered a beer. It was pleasantly

warm outside and there wasn't a cloud. The outdoor speakers were playing a Marley classic at low volume and there was a slight breeze in the air.

He looked toward the doorway and saw two impossibly, beautiful women walk out onto the deck. One was tall with long, sexy legs and the other was a curvy, petite, Hispanic brunette – who was absolutely stunning. They walked directly to his table and the brunette said;

"Hey, baby."

"Hey, yourself." The epitome of smooth.

"Sorry, we're late," she said as they both sat at his table.

"It's cool. I just got here myself."

Maria and Linda ordered drinks when the waitress approached and laid down menus.

"Some place, huh?" he said.

"Yep. Can you believe I worked here when I was in college?"

"What? You never told me that. The engagement is off!"

"Oh, shut up," Maria said, shoving him playfully as he started laughing.

"You two are perfect for each other," Linda said. "I can't believe you've only been together for four months. It seems like you've been a couple forever. While I, on the other hand, am stuck dating Special Agent Watkins."

"Oh, come off it, Linda," Maria said taking a long pull from her drink. "He's a nice guy and you know you like him."

"Hmm, I guess. He's alright."

"You're having sex aren't you?" Maria asked.

"A lady never tells. So Brennan, have you thought about the bureau's offer of training at Quantico?"

"Yeah and I'm just not sure yet. Maria and I both agree I should wait until I'm fully healed and have been back to work before we decide."

"Well, I think you should do it. It wouldn't take away from your life like it has mine. Being a consultant, you would sort of be a by-the-job contractor. It's like having the coolest job with no smothering career. I think you'd be great. So give it some thought, you guys."

"Enough about us," Maria said. "What about you? You called us here to celebrate, so what the hell are we celebrating?"

"Okay, okay. Here we go." All eyes were on Linda. "Effective January 1st, I will be the new Special Agent in Charge of the Atlanta office."

Maria went crazy with cheers, while Brennan sat with his mouth open and eyes wide.

"You've got to be kidding me. That's great," he said. "It's about time I had a friend in the upper echelon of law enforcement. Now I can say cool things like, 'let me see if I can pull some strings' and 'I'll talk to my people and see what I can do'."

They laughed heartily as the waitress came over smiling.

"Hi, I'm Nicole. I'll be your server. Have y'all decided on an appetizer?"

Here we go again. Did this woman really think they were confused? That maybe she was a mechanic or an astronaut? Brennan decided to let it go and they opted to share the 'Noah's Nachos'.

"I want to purpose a toast," Maria said. "Let us drink to caught criminals, healthy careers, and great friends. Cheers!"

* * *

The End

ABOUT THE AUTHOR

J.C. Tannelli was born in Atlanta, Georgia. He and his father moved around a lot when he was young but never left the Atlanta metro area. Tannelli graduated from high school in a North Atlanta suburb and studied marketing at Georgia State University. Currently residing in North Atlanta, he and his beautiful wife continue to learn as they raise their two adorable daughters. The Tannellis have two hilarious dogs that they rescued recently and tagged "Trix" and "Bob". Tannelli spends his time writing, reading, and enjoying his family -- though he's been found on one of Atlanta's many golf courses shooting over 90. If he wasn't writing books Tannelli says, "I'd be driving race cars. It's okay to dream, right?"